DEAD GIRLS DON'T BLOG

The Murder Blog Mysteries #1

PAMELA FROST DENNIS

~ To Mike ~
You always believe in me,
even when I don't.

~ *A Big Thank You to* ~

My Beta Readers:

Mike Dennis, Holly Dennis, Jeri Petersen,
June and Irvin Kiger

Elaine Boles

Dr. Dorothy Dink
You continue to inspire me.

~

And to all those friends who always
asked me how my book was going.
Writing is a lonely business
and your support meant a lot to me.

PROLOGUE

Saturday
May 4, 1996

12:05 a.m.

Lindsay woke to muffled rock music. She turned her head, gasping at the sharp pain that exploded into an excruciating headache. She scrunched her eyes, willing it away, but the pain throbbed in agonizing waves.

She reached out for her bedside Tinker Bell lamp, squinting to prepare for bright light, but instead her arm flailed into a void where the lamp should have been.

Lindsay sat up slowly, each fraction of elevation slamming her first-ever migraine. As she held still waiting for the roaring pain to back off, she noticed her top was bunched down around her waist and her bra was popped up over her small breasts. She adjusted it, vaguely wondering why that hurt.

Across the dim room, a lava lamp pulsed an orange glow. *Where did that come from? Why is my dresser over there? Where am I?*

She started to get up and found her legs tangled in the sheets. Reaching to pull the bedding away, Lindsay's fingers touched something warm. She slid her hand further and felt something rough and bristly. *Someone's in my bed?* She jerked her hand away, yanking the sheets off and scrambling to her feet. The sudden move drained the blood from her head and the room exploded into blinding white light before she crumpled to the floor.

———

Lindsay opened her eyes. She lay sprawled on her side facing a dark shadow that focused into a body shape. She shimmied back toward the bed frame and pushed herself to a sitting position, the pain threatening to split her head open. Her stomach lurched. She clamped a hand over her mouth, pressing her lips tight.

While Lindsay waited for the nausea to subside, her eyes darted around the room, desperately trying to understand what was happening, but her muddled mind would not cooperate.

Maybe this is a bad dream. She reached out and poked the body. It felt solid. Real.

On hands and knees, she crept around the body to the door and opened it, peering into a dark hallway. *No Doubt* blasted downstairs, the loud bass notes drilling into her skull. Raucous voices attempting to be heard over the din drifted up from below. She ducked back as a pair of legs walked down the hall. A light flicked on illuminating the battered green walls of the hall before a door shut.

The tiled bathroom echoed the gush of a man urinating, and Lindsay's bladder responded with sudden need. The toilet flushed, the bathroom door opened, and the legs passed the room again.

Once the hall was clear, Lindsay attempted again to stand, but nausea forced her back down, and she crawled to the bathroom.

Inside, she closed the door and groped in the dark for the light switch. She squeezed her eyes shut, waiting until she could tolerate the bright, amber glare, then slit her eyes open. When she could see, she hauled herself up to the pedestal sink, held her long, silky blond hair out of the way, and sipped cool water from the faucet.

Her stomach clenched and roiled, spewing up hot vomit, splattering the sink, the floor, and her pink jelly shoes. She clung to the sink until the wrenching heaves went dry, then rinsed her mouth and face.

The nausea eased and she raised her head, jolted by her grotesque image in the cracked mirror. One eye was swollen and blood leaked from a gash in her eyebrow. She touched the cut, wondering what had happened as her fear mounted.

The pressure in her bladder became too much and Lindsay lurched to the toilet, knocked the seat down, pulled her short skirt up, and was bewildered to find her panties gone. Gingerly, she lowered herself onto the toilet seat, clutching the edges. As urine trickled out, the searing burn startled her, rendering her breathless and releasing a flow of tears. She gently dabbed herself dry and was alarmed to see blood on the tissue. Then she saw dried blood on her thighs. *Did my period start?*

Lindsay finished and tugged her skirt as far down as it would go. Cracking the door open and seeing no one, she ventured into the hallway, using the walls for support as she made her way to the other end. Stopping short of the stairway, she peered around the corner and saw a crowd of people blocking the bottom. Frantic, she glanced around for another way out and saw none.

Gripping the wood banister with both hands, Lindsay overstepped the first tread and lost her balance, thumping down the stairs on her rear-end and slamming into a fat, bearded guy lounging against the wall on the bottom step.

He laughed at her. "Hey, party girl. Havin' a rough night?"

Holding her skirt down, Lindsay scuttled back up a few steps and used the rail to pull herself to her feet. Across the packed, rowdy room, she saw her escape. The open front door. Ignoring the snickering man, she tried to ease around his hefty bulk in the tight space but swayed against him and clutched his shoulder for support.

"Whoa. You're totally shit-faced." He reached to steady her and then offered his water pipe. "Want a hit?"

The pungent odor gagged her and she slapped it away, knocking the glass pipe out of his hand to shatter on the wood floor.

"You bitch." He grabbed her wrist, twisting it hard. "Get outta here!"

"Let go of me!" Lindsay wriggled out of his clammy grasp and shoved her way through the crush to the door. Outside she tumbled down the porch steps and landed hard on the flagstone path, skinning her hands, knees, and chin, her teeth sinking deep into her lower lip. She lay there weeping, hurt, confused, and scared.

Long minutes passed as people coming and going stepped over her prone body. The brisk night air revived her and finally she stood and limped to the sidewalk, where she leaned against a parked car.

Lindsay pressed her fingers into her temples, willing the pain to stop and her head to clear but accomplishing neither. With no idea where to go but needing to get away from where she was, she began walking.

CHAPTER ONE

THURSDAY, APRIL 4

NOW

"Daisy! Get back here." My papergirl was supposed to retrieve the morning newspaper at the end of the front walk but had opted instead to chase a squirrel into the next yard, leaving me no choice but to leave the shelter of my vine-covered porch to chase after her. When I caught up, she had the scoundrel treed and was waiting for all the hugs and atta-girls she knew I'd bestow upon her.

"Bad. Bad, naughty girl." I wagged my finger at her. I'd rarely scolded my near-perfect yellow Labrador since rescuing her from the pound four months before, and her smile drooped along with her head and tail.

"Thanks, Daisy," said a masculine voice nearby. "I really needed another squirrel in my yard."

I looked across the yard and saw a tall, hunky guy standing by a silver BMW sports coupe convertible and he was drop-dead gorgeous. Tan, perfectly mussed honey-blond hair, dazzling white teeth, male-model two-day stubble. Nordic looking, like a Viking.

He waved. "Hey, Cookie. We finally meet."

Cookie? That's kind of creepy, I thought.

"I'm Josh."

I waved back weakly. "Hi."

"Nice slippers."

He was referring to my fuzzy bear claws, a Christmas gift from Grandma Ruby back in my college days.

"Thanks." I ran my fingers through my auburn bedhead mess, fluffing it back behind my shoulders, trying to act like I always ran around the neighborhood in my pajamas. "I'm Katy, and you already know who this is."

"Hi Daisy."

My dog was grinning from ear to ear and her tail was wagging so hard I thought her butt would fall off.

"Nice finally meeting you two." He backed out of his driveway and zoomed away with a screech of rubber.

What a show-off. So not impressed, I thought, curling my lip with disdain.

Daisy nudged me. She was ready to go home with Josh's paper in her mouth. To her dismay, I left his paper on his porch. She made amends by pouncing on the newspaper at the end of our front walk and proudly trotting it into the house.

I curled up with Daisy on the comfy, overstuffed chair by the living room French doors to read the paper, but my mind wouldn't focus on the top stories of the day. Instead, I found myself obsessing over my humiliating meet-up with Josh-the-creepy-Viking. I tossed the paper on the floor, revealing my flannel clad, Oreo print legs.

"Cookie." Oh. Now I felt really stupid.

My cell phone rang on the table next to me. It was Grandma Ruby. If I didn't answer, she'd worry, so I put on my happy voice. "Hi, Grandma!"

"What's wrong?" No fooling her. "You never call me Grandma." Everyone calls her Ruby, even her kids.

"Nothin'," I said in a woebegone tone, and then thought, *Snap out of it, Katy. So you got caught in your pj's in front of your neighbor who has the nerve to be a delectable hunk of man-candy. Get over it already.*

"I take it you've seen the paper. Sooner or later it was bound to happen, you know."

Ruby is seventy-four, and for the past couple of years her friends have been dropping like flies. Every morning she checks the obits before reading the front page. If anyone she was even remotely acquainted with has passed, she calls and shares with me. I guess that makes me her grief counselor, but I draw the line at attending funerals.

"Who died?" Silence on her end. This had to be bad.

"Ruby. Who died?"

"It's Chad."

My official ex-husband as of one month ago. This time last year, I had been nursing him through a horrific cancer battle. The chemo-diet had shed the extra pounds he'd accumulated during the course of our seven-year marriage, so once he was back on his feet, he got a trainer, started working on his long lost abs, and the next thing I knew, Chad was moving out and in with his twenty-two-year-old trainer. And now he was dead.

For seven months, I'd been paralyzed with bitter resentment, and in that instant my anger flew out the window like it was nothing. Who knew death could feel so liberating? "So what happened?"

"The two-timin' weasel married that bimbo, that's what happened. It's in the wedding announcements and I assumed you'd already seen it."

My five-second euphoria was officially over and I felt a tantrum rearing its ugly head, but I kept my cool for Ruby's sake. She'd loved the weasel almost as much as I had. "Wow, that was fast."

"They're expecting. In August."

I furiously counted forward on my fingers. May, June, July,

7

PAMELA FROST DENNIS

August. Jeez, that didn't take long. He'd told me he wasn't ready for babies. "I gotta go, Ruby," I said, choking on a lump of rage.

"I'm so sorry, kiddo. I know it hurts. You know I love you."

We hung up, and I immediately opened the paper to the local section. There it was—a photo of a beaming Chad and *her*, the bitch who had stolen my husband and my life.

At one in the afternoon, I was still slumped in my chair in my pajamas when someone knocked on the front door.

"Sweetie. It's Mommy." She peered at me through the window near the door.

I should have closed the damned shutters before going into seclusion.

"We're worried about you. Have you eaten anything?"

Then Ruby hollered, "That jackass ain't worth it, honey. You got your whole life ahead of you."

"Everything okay here, ladies?" called Josh-the-creepy-Viking as he climbed the wooden porch steps.

Oh, crap. It just keeps getting better and better.

"My daughter's had some bad news," said Mom, "and she's not answering her phone."

That was because I'd been too busy diabolically plotting elaborate revenge scenarios involving buses and Chad's rear-end to take calls. Now the three of them were looking at me through the shutter slats and Daisy was barking furiously at them, which is her job as head security guard, but they took it to mean she was telling them I was in dire jeopardy.

"Honey, I can see you in there. Please open the door," said Mom. "I just need to make sure you're all right. And stop biting your nails. I thought you were trying to grow them out."

"I'm fine! And my nails are fine too!" I hollered from my chair, wishing I could hide behind it, so I could bite my damned nails in peace. "Just under the weather, that's all. Don't want you to catch it." I coughed a few times for effect.

8

"We have to get in there," said Ruby. "I'm psychic, and there's no telling what she might do."

Ruby has possessed incredible psychic powers ever since she electrocuted herself years ago while hanging outdoor Christmas lights in a drippy fog, so you'd think she'd know I hadn't done anything desperate. The strongest medication I keep in the house is ibuprofen. She is the one with the medical marijuana card. But I had been swilling chamomile tea for hours and desperately needed to pee.

I heard the sash window in my bedroom scrape open, which set off the security alarm and put Daisy into howling mode. I bolted to the keypad by the front door to punch in the code, but totally blanked on the numbers—my birth year. Duh.

I was too busy shouting, "Shit! Shit! Shit!" and pounding the keypad into submission to notice the Viking had joined me.

"Hey, Cookie," he said, scaring the bejeebers out of me.

I screamed, jumping about a foot off the floor as he opened the door to my mother and Ruby, plus several nosy neighbors rubbernecking at the foot of the porch steps.

And then I lost my tea.

———

After a couple of days of hiding out to avoid embarrassing run-ins with the Viking or those other neighbors I don't know and probably never will now that I am the neighborhood incontinent crazy lady, I decided to clean my house and get on with my pathetic life.

I gathered the newspapers for recycling, and was once again subjected to Chad's happy and very much alive face. I resolved to be magnanimous and wish him well. Wasn't I the grown-up one? Well, anyway I tried, but it wasn't working for me. So I wished the baby well. That worked. Then another familiar face on the opposite page, attached to a short piece, caught my attention.

CHILD-KILLER UP FOR PAROLE

Phillip Hobart raped and murdered local girl Lindsay Moore in 1996.

In the late hours of May 3, 1996, Lindsay Moore, a promising fifteen-year-old sophomore at Santa Lucia High School was brutally gang-raped by three college students at a fraternity house party. A police investigation was underway when several days later Lindsay was reported missing by her mother, Belinda Moore.

Weeks later, Phil Hobart led police to Lindsay's body. She had been kidnapped and murdered by Hobart and two other boys, Jake Werner and Erik Mason, all involved in the frat house gang-rape. Hobart was nineteen at the time and was sentenced to fifteen years to life, and will soon be eligible for parole. The parole hearing date has tentatively been set for July 13. Hobart is incarcerated at Folsom State Prison in Sacramento County.

I sat on the leather ottoman by the sofa, gazing at Lindsay's photo while the sad, distant memory refreshed. How could someone who had committed such heinous crimes ever be up for parole, let alone this soon? Surely they wouldn't let this happen.

Lindsay had been a cute, popular cheerleader—friendly to everyone, including geeky me. If you're a kid and a friend your age dies, it's hard to wrap your head around it—your first realization that you are a mere mortal. It was something I had not forgotten.

I cut out the article and put it in the desk drawer. It didn't feel right throwing Lindsay's story into the recycling.

CHAPTER TWO

SATURDAY

April 6

I was online paying bills when my BFF Samantha texted, *Lunch?* I replied, *Pizza?* Ten minutes later her horn honked outside.

Sam was arguing with her stepdaughter, Chelsea, through the Bluetooth speakers as I folded my 5'9" frame into her Ford Escape.

"The answer is no. Not maybe. No."

Chelsea's pleading voice whined, "But——"

Shaking her head, Samantha rolled her sky-blue eyes at me. "No buts. Just watch your little brother, do your homework, and I'll be home in a couple of hours."

"But——"

She pressed the End icon on the navigation screen before Chelsea could whine some more. "God, Katy. I'm way too young to have a teenager." She peered into the rearview mirror and fluffed her blond pixie cut. "Why did I marry a man eight years older than me with a kid?" She pointed to an infinitesimal frown line. "Look! I need Botox. Already. At thirty-one. She's aging me before my time."

"You married Spencer because he was the sweetest guy on the planet and you absolutely adored Chelsea."

"She was nine at the time. I didn't realize she wouldn't stay nine. Now she wants a tattoo but needs a parent's permission to get one. I'm afraid her space-case mother might agree. The kid's only fifteen, for criminy sakes."

"Do you have to go to work later?" I asked to change the subject. She is a maternity nurse and after the birth of her son four years ago, she has taken to wearing scrubs all the time. I know it is because she still has a leftover muffin-top from the pregnancy, but I don't get it. She used to be so stylish. Today's ensemble was a blue bunny print. "No, why?"

"No reason."

We were on 101 heading south to our favorite restaurant, Klondike Pizza, in the charming old town area of Cala Grande. The owners had migrated from Alaska, so hence the name and rustic decor: bear skins, moose antlers, snowshoes… and peanut shells on the floor. A short line was at the register when we walked in, so we got a menu and debated our choices, then ordered what we always ordered. We fetched our sodas and a basket of peanuts and sat at our favorite table under the wood stairs.

Neatnik Sam was rooting around in the basket for a triple peanut. "Got an interesting call from your mom yesterday."

I grabbed a handful of nuts and smashed them to smithereens on the blue gingham tablecloth, causing Sam to wince. "What did she want?"

Sam delicately cracked a peanut into two perfect halves. "She asked if I knew any nice guys I could introduce you to." She poured the three peanuts into her mouth.

"So not ready." I concentrated on sifting through my peanut shell mess for a nut. "Please say you said no."

"Uh, I may have mentioned that Spencer knows a guy you

might like. He has most of his teeth and is gainfully employed in the food service industry."

"Really?" I smashed another handful of peanuts just to annoy her. "Nice going. Now I'll never hear the end of it." I sipped my root beer, thinking real beer would have been a better choice. "So, what happened to his teeth and where exactly is he gainfully employed?"

Samantha swiped my mess off the table with a paper napkin. "Are you interested, Katy?"

"Hardly."

"He lost his front teeth in a nursing home brawl where Spencer's grandpa lives. He works in the kitchen." She tried to keep a straight face as she cracked another peanut. "The residents were protesting the bland food and in the ensuing food fight, he got belted in the chops with a portable oxygen tank."

I nodded, holding a poker face. "Sounds painful. How did the protest turn out?"

"They now have salt and pepper on the dining room tables and Tuesday is taco night.'

A perky teenaged girl, June according to her name tag, set our pizzas on the table and asked if we wanted anything else.

"No, we're good," I said. "Oh, wait. Would you bring me an Alaskan Amber?"

"I need to check your I.D."

"I'm thirty-one."

"Sorry, it's the law. Anyone who looks under thirty has to have valid I.D."

I rummaged through my purse and extracted my driver's license. "Here ya go." I smirked at Samantha, knowing this was making her fume over her aging frown lines. Hee-hee.

June scrutinized it and glanced at me. "Wow. I sure hope I look as good as you when I'm old." She handed back my I.D. and scurried off to get my beer.

Sam propped her elbows on the table, resting her chin on her hands. "Wow."

"Oh, be quiet. She meant it as a compliment. And you don't need Botox. Yet." I slid a slice of hot veggie pizza onto my plate and forked off a section. "This was a good idea." I chewed in blissful contentment. "I can't wait until I'm gainfully employed so we can do this more often."

"I will never understand why you took the house and let Chad keep the business," Samantha said. "You put your heart and soul into The Bookcase Bistro. At least you'd still have a steady income."

"I've told you I wanted a clean break from everything having to do with him, and no way did I want to run the business by myself. I got great joy when I sold that ostentatious monstrosity of a house that he had to have for a humongous profit. So it's not like I'm broke. I just need something to do. You know, something that gets me up in the morning. I'm sick of feeling sorry for myself." I smacked the table. "Oh! Did I tell you I finally cleaned out that dirty old garden shed in my backyard and set it up as an office? I've got my drafting table out there and all my art supplies."

June set down my beer and asked Sam if she wanted one.

"I wish. But I have to take my little boy to gymnastics, not to mention I'm driving."

I watched the girl walk away, then turned back to Sam. "The bookstore years were great, but that was Chad's dream, not mine and I've always missed being a graphic artist." I held my glass aloft and offered a hardy, "Here's to new beginnings," and took a refreshing swig.

"That's great about the shed," said Sam. "Where'd you put your gardening stuff?"

"Everything's been in the garage since I moved in. I kept meaning to move it all to the shed, but this is a much better use of the space." My pizza was now cool enough to pick up, so I chomped a bite and spoke with a full mouth. "Yup, Chad can have the business and all the headaches associated with trying to keep a bookstore afloat these days. With the mood I've been in, I might've gone postal on some of those customers and wound up in jail. Especially that irritating woman who always returned books because she didn't like the endings." I shook my head, relieved I would never deal with her again. Yup, right decision. "Speaking of jail, did you see the story in the paper about Lindsay Moore?"

"No. Why would there be a story about her after all these years?"

I told her about Phil Hobart's upcoming parole hearing. "I'm wondering if there's something I can do to make sure this guy doesn't get out."

"I would think Lindsay's mother will be at the parole hearing to speak up for her daughter. I know if I was her and he got parole, I'd be waiting outside the prison gates the day he was released and get a little justice of my own."

"You're probably right. This is her business, not mine." I sipped my beer. "It's not like I knew her that well in high school, anyway."

"Cheerleaders and band geeks—not really the same crowd."

"She was a really nice girl though, and what happened to her was so awful," I said. "It hurt everyone in our school. God! I get so sick of monsters like him getting paroled. It just doesn't make any sense."

"But getting caught up in something you can't do a darn thing about isn't going to be good for you right now." Sam was in mother-mode and patted my hand. "I've got an idea for you. Ever thought of writing a blog?"

"Why would I do that? I don't even like Facebook. Especially when people write about their oh-so personal problems for everyone to see. The other day, one of my friends posted, 'I think my boyfriend gave me herpes 'cause I'm really itchy.' Eew. So not my business."

"Yeah, I saw that because you *shared* it, thank you very much."

"I meant to hit the *like* button, but, oops. Too funny."

"Anyway, a blog would be like a diary or a journal."

"Then why don't I just get a diary or a journal?"

"You can, but by having it on the Internet, you'll never lose it and you can set it up so it's totally private. No one'll ever see it but you, and you can access it from wherever you are and add entries. Even on your phone."

She paused, waiting for me to say something, but I remained silent, listening to the white noise in my head.

"Chelsea can help you set it up. She set up mine. It could be very cathartic for you. Write about everything you've been going through this past year. Get it all out there. Purge your anger issues before you make yourself sick."

"Let me think about it." I tapped my chin. "Mmmm. Sounds like work to me. No thanks." I decided to button her up by changing the subject. "Know anybody who needs a new logo?"

"Mmmm. Sounds like work to me."

Guess I'd annoyed her. Now I felt bad. "Okay. You may have a valid point about my anger issues. I'll *think* about doing a blog."

CHAPTER THREE

MONDAY
April 8

Graphic Design Work

Freelance graphic designer with years of experience. Logo designs, cartooning, advertising layouts, business cards, design concepts, etc. I will take your idea and make it a reality. No job too small. My rates are reasonable, my hours are flexible, and I'll give you a fast turn-around.

I posted the ad on Craigslist, then Daisy and I hopped in the car for a run to the bank to transfer some money from my savings to checking. I could have done it online, but Daisy wouldn't have gotten her doggy treat at the drive-thru window.

I drive an orange 1976 Volvo DL wagon that I grew up riding in. At eight years old, I discovered a box of Mom's old *Betty and Veronica* comic books while snooping around in the garage. I thought Veronica was so glamorous. I wanted to dress like her, wear my hair like her, have boobs like her, and change my name to Veronica. Mom said no to the first two and the boobs never happened, but she agreed to a compromise and we named the Volvo "Veronica."

Veronica became mine on my seventeenth birthday, even though it killed Mom to part with her. I appreciate not having a car payment, but power windows sure would be nice. Especially at the drive-thru when Daisy wants to stick her head out the back window to say "hi," and I have to twist into a pretzel to roll down her window.

After I completed my banking, I decided to run over to my stepdad's appliance repair shop to talk to him about Phil Hobart's parole hearing. Pop had been a cop until he was forced into early retirement after pursuing an unhappy, gun-toting housewife who was chasing her philandering husband down the street. She had tripped over a tree root and Pop had caught a bullet in his knee.

After Pop's retirement, he had driven Mom bonkers. He was bored but clueless as to what to do with the next stage of his life, and poor Mom had borne the cranky brunt of it. When the escrow office next door to her beauty shop had become vacant, she had suggested he take the space and open an appliance repair shop. Ever since I can remember, Pop has rattled on about how people hadn't thrown things away when he was a kid: "You bought a toaster once, and you kept it forever. If it broke, you fixed it. My grandmother had the same Toastmaster she got for a wedding present in 1932 until the day she died in 1978."

Pop's Fix-It Shop is a quaint throwback to a simpler time—or more simply put, a symptom of having watched *The Andy Griffith Show* in his youth. An ongoing chess game sits on a table under the window, and there is a vintage appliance museum on shelves lining an entire wall featuring Great Grandma's gleaming old Toastmaster. Under the shelves is a working mahogany Magnavox Astro Sonic Stereo Console, circa 1969, that Pop inherited from his folks, along with all of their old records, when they moved to a condo in Palm Desert.

The little bell over the door jingled as Daisy and I entered. Cool jazz filled the room, so I stepped to the stereo to check the current selection playing. It was the soundtrack to a 60's movie called *Walk on the Wild Side*—music by Elmer Bernstein.

"Hey, Pop. What'cha doing?"

He was perched on a stool behind the counter, hunched over a commercial espresso maker. "Darn thing won't steam." He switched the machine on and it wheezed as though suffering an asthma attack.

"That can't be good," I said.

He turned it off and continued tinkering. "What brings you here on this beautiful spring day? Shouldn't you be outside playing?"

"Did you see the story in the paper about Phil Hobart's parole hearing? You know, the guy who kidnapped and murdered Lindsay Moore back when I was in high school?"

"Of course I remember who Phil Hobart is, and yes, I read it." He set down a tiny screwdriver and pushed his "cheaters" down his nose, giving me his full attention. "So why are we talking about this?"

"It's just not right that her death has so little value that fifteen years covers the debt."

"Nothing can cover that debt, Katy. Should have been life with no possible parole. Better yet, should have been death for what those boys did to that little girl."

I shuddered. I don't believe in the death penalty. So barbaric. A dark, cold dungeon works for me, or even better, a lifetime sentence of *Jerry Springer* reruns 24/7. The crime rate would plummet.

"There must be something I can do to help stop this guy's parole," I said.

"Like what?"

"I don't know. Protest? Picket the prison? But before I do

anything, I want to be absolutely sure he's guilty. That there's no possibility that he was wrongly accused. You know, bad DNA, that sort of thing."

"Katy, he confessed. He and his friends raped her, kidnapped her, and murdered her. He doesn't deserve freedom. Come over for dinner tonight and I'll tell you what wasn't in the paper."

Pop was relaxing on the patio when I arrived, nursing a Firestone Pale Ale while grilling chicken breasts and a vegetable kabob for me. I went to the kitchen and pulled a bottle of Chablis out of the fridge and poured a hefty glassful before flopping on the chaise lounge next to him.

"Where's Mom?"

"Working on a wedding. This may be the last wedding she ever does. Too much drama. The bride can't decide if she wants her hair up or down. She's so upset about it that she's broken out in a rash."

"Sounds like the problem isn't really about her hair but maybe second thoughts about the wedding."

"That's very astute of you." Pop got up and slopped more BBQ sauce on the chicken. "These days the marriage is usually kaput before the wedding bills have been paid off." He saw my puckered brow. "Katydid, I'm sorry. That was thoughtless."

"I'm fine."

"No, you're not."

I sipped my Chablis. "I will be. Far worse things happen in life than getting divorced from a rat. Like what happened to Lindsay."

He took a long pull on his beer. "I don't know what you can do to stop Hobart's parole, Katy, but it's unlikely he'll get out on his first go-round anyway."

"I'm confused. He's serving fifteen years to life and this is his first parole hearing. But the crime happened in 1996, so it's been more than fifteen years. Why didn't he have a parole hearing sooner? Bad conduct or something?"

"It took over a year for the case to go to trial, plus it had to be moved to another county to get a fair trial. Then several postponements on final sentencing. These things drag on and on. It's not like the TV shows, honey."

Pop pulled the chicken and my kabob off the grill, set them on a platter, and we went into the kitchen. "Your mother said to go ahead and eat if she isn't home in time. You get the salad in the fridge, while I get the rolls out of the oven. Oh, and grab me another beer, will ya?"

I did as told and was about to top off my wine when he said, "Are you walking home?"

No, I wasn't walking. I put the bottle back.

A few bites into the meal, I said, "Why did they kidnap and murder Lindsay *after* she'd already made a statement? The police had their descriptions, so what was the point?"

"They were morons, Katy. None of them had a criminal record and Lindsay had no idea who they were or what they looked like."

———————   ·

Pop and I finished dinner, and while he caught the basketball scores on TV, I scavenged in the refrigerator hoping to score something "dessertie" and came up empty-handed, as usual. Pop keeps a slim figure, but is pre-diabetic, so Mom diligently keeps the house sweet-free. But I know she has a chocolate stash somewhere in their house and one of these days, I'm going to find it.

"Did Mom tell you your sister's coming home for a while?" he called from the next room.

"No. When?"

Pop returned to the kitchen. "Sometime in June or July, when her lease is up."

"Why's Emily coming home?" I love her, but I love her more from afar.

"So she can concentrate on her *writing*." Pop finger-quoted.

"Please tell me it's not rap."

Emily is my half-sister, nine years my junior. Two years ago she dropped out of college in her sophomore year to come home and become a rapper, LayZeeE. A gritty, street-wise, middle-class, suburban rapper, rapping about growing up in the 'hood. We're talkin' quarter acre lots on tree-lined streets with a strict homeowners association pushing you around and not allowing you to paint your house pink kind of 'hood. The mean streets of Santa Lucia.

The high point of LayZeeE's career was an "open mic afternoon" in the bistro at the senior community where Grandma Ruby lives. Yes, it really happened and I have the video proving it. Since then, she's been living in San Diego with friends and working at Bed, Bath & Beyond.

"She's writing a murder mystery," said Pop. "She called it a paranormal-fantasy with ghosts, alternate universes, fairies, were-wolves, zombies, shapers or shafters—"

"Shapeshifter?"

"That's it. What the hell is that?"

"It's a human who morphs into other things, like a werewolf."

"And how would you know this?"

"I read the *Sookie Stackhouse* series that the TV show *True Blood* is based on. Speaking of writing, I'm thinking about starting a blog." I was interrupted by the squeaky rumble of the garage door opening. "Mom's home."

"Pour your mother a glass of wine while I dish up a plate. I'm sure she's frazzled. You'll find an open red in the pantry."

"No more weddings!" Mom hollered as she came through the door. "I've had a day and a half, let me tell you." She threw her purse and tote bag onto the rattan settee in the kitchen, then ripped off her sweater and tossed it onto the pile. "I am boiling."

"Here, Mom." I gave her a glass of Justification—a delicious local blend of cabernet and merlot and pecked her cheek.

"Thank you, honey." She took a slow deep sip. "Ooo. The good stuff. What's the occasion?"

"We love you, and it was already open."

"I love you, too. But if I ever sign up for another wedding, promise me you'll get my head examined."

"Hungry?" asked Pop, as he pulled out a chair for her at the ancient harvest table in the nook.

"I'm starved." She glanced at the plate waiting for her. "Looks yummy. I've got a huge headache, probably because I'm so hungry." She ignored the chair, opened the patio glass door and fanned herself with it. "Is it hot in here, or is it just me?"

"Having another power-surge?" I asked warily, suppressing a wince. You never knew what might set her off.

"Come here and feel my back."

"You gotta do it, Katy," said Pop. "It's amazing."

I tentatively stepped close and she grabbed my hand, jamming it under her shirt into hot sweat streaming down the small of her back. "Eew. Gross." I jerked my wet hand away and wiped it on my pants.

She laughed at my disgusted expression and Pop tossed her a dish towel to mop up. "Will you throw this in the laundry room?" She dangled the towel at me.

I took it by the edge. I thought PMS was bad. So not looking forward to the peri-menopausal years.

Mom sat at the table and ate a bite of the grilled chicken slathered with Pop's apricot-chili-cilantro sauce and half-closed her eyes in appreciation. "I might live after all."

"What's the bridal hair verdict? Does she want it up or down?" I asked as I sat next to her.

"Neither. I got the call on my way home. The wedding's off and they're eloping."

"And they lived happily ever after." Pop started clearing the table.

"Pop, sit down. I'll do the dishes."

"Stay put and talk to your mom. You know I can't sit for very long with this bum knee. You were about to tell me about starting a blog before Marybeth got home."

Mom arched an eyebrow and smirked. "You're going to write a blog? You've always said blogs are stupid."

"True, but Samantha says it might be cathartic to write about my pent-up feelings about my divorce from that jerk whose name we won't mention. Like a diary."

"You already have a diary. It's still in your bedroom on the closet shelf, behind the—" She stopped, looking guilty as all get-out.

"You read my diary? Mother, how could you? Those were my private sacred thoughts."

Mom held her glass up again, and Pop emptied the bottle into it. It was only a few drops, but it gave her time to compose an answer. "The truth is you were fourteen and becoming very weird."

True.

"And I was worried."

"We both were worried," said Pop.

"It's a difficult age to be or to be the parents of—"

"Amen to that," Pop agreed.

"And your safety and well-being overruled your right to privacy."

I could have recited the next inevitable line having heard it about a gazillion times through my younger years, but I let Mom hold the spotlight.

Her lips twitched, trying to suppress a laugh. "And you will never understand until you have kids of your own."

"Hallelujah!" shouted Pop, waving his arms like a holy-roller.

"Besides, you only made three entries, so it's not like we read a bunch of deep dark secrets."

"Something about hating school, hating boys, hating your hair," said Pop. "Pretty heavy stuff."

"You forgot the lima beans, Kurt. She hated those, too."

I crossed my arms and morphed into a fourteen-year-old. "It was personal and you had no right. I'm going to start a blog, a *private* blog, and you can't stop me. And you won't be able to read it, so ha."

"All right, dear." Mom patted the top of my head.

I still hate lima beans.

CHAPTER FOUR

1996
Friday, May 3

10:05 p.m.

Belinda Moore tried to focus on the show *20/20*, but her attention kept flicking to the clock next to the television. Her fifteen-year-old daughter, Lindsay, had gone to the movies with her best friend, Jenny and Jenny's older cousin, Mallory. The cousin drove, inaugurating a new phase in her teenaged daughter's growing independence that Belinda was not ready for. After the movie, the girls planned to eat at the pizza place next to the theatre.

10:15 p.m.

"If you think this is hard, Belinda," she said aloud, running her fingers through her short, dirty-blond hair, "wait until she's driving. Then you'll really have something to worry about."

10:20 p.m.

Belinda called Jenny's house and her father answered.

"Hi, Bill. It's Belinda Moore. Are the kids there?"

"No. I called Jenny's beeper a few minutes ago. I'm sure they're on their way. Not to worry."

"Yeah, right. Kinda goes with the territory, huh?"

He laughed. "I guess we're finally getting a taste of what we put our parents through. Payback's a bitch, ain't it?"

"I'll say! You'll call me?"

"As soon as I hear. And they better have a damn good excuse."

10:45 p.m.

Beside herself with worry, Belinda cradled the phone in her lap, willing the damned thing to ring. No longer able to wait for Bill's call, she phoned him again.

"I don't know what to tell you," Bill's tone was no longer jovial. "This is so unlike Jenny. I shouldn't have let Mallory drive them. I'll call you the minute I hear anything."

11:30 p.m.

The phone rang, and Belinda, rigid with dread and terrified to answer, snatched it up before the second ring. Bill told her that Jenny and Mallory had just walked in the door.

"Thank God." Belinda sagged back into the sofa with relief, then a flood of anger washed through her. "Let me speak to Lindsay."

"She's not with them. I haven't had a chance to talk to them yet, but I assumed they'd dropped her off at home."

Dread replaced Belinda's anger again. "I need to talk to Jenny."

"Hold on," Bill put his hand over the phone, but she still heard him yell. "Jenny! Where the hell is Lindsay? Get in here and talk to her mother."

Jenny took the receiver and spoke in a thin, tremulous voice. "Hello?"

Belinda loved Jenny but not so much right now. "Where's Lindsay?"

"I dunno." The girl's speech slurred. "Isn't she home?"

"Oh, for God's sake. If she were home, why would I be asking you? Where is she?"

"We went to a party and——"

"What party? You were supposed to be going to the movies and dinner."

Jenny took on the belligerent tone usually reserved for one's own mother. "We did, but we ran into some kids and they invited us to a party. When we left the party, we couldn't find Lindsay, so we thought she'd already gone home."

Belinda wanted to reach through the phone and shake Jenny until her teeth fell out. "How? How would she have gotten home?"

"I dunno." Jenny was sobbing. "Maybe walked or called you?"

Bill took the phone back. "They both smell like a 60's rock concert, so I've a pretty good guess what was going on." He turned from the receiver and said, "Were you smoking pot?"

"No. No way."

"Yeah, right. Of course, I'm just a stupid dad, so what the hell do I know? Do not walk away from me, young lady. I want to look at your eyes." A pause. "You're stoned. You must really think I'm a complete idiot, huh?"

Belinda couldn't listen to any more and screamed into the phone. "Where was this party?"

"Where was the party?" he asked the girls.

Belinda heard hysterics in the background but nothing coherent. Bill came back on. "I can't get a straight answer out of either of them. I think this is more than a little pot! It's a miracle Mallory didn't crash the car and kill them both! Lindsay was safer not being with them."

Except they're home and I don't know where Lindsay is.

———

Belinda Moore's minivan bounced on the curb as she jerked the wheel sharply into the emergency room parking area. She'd broken the sound barrier getting there and was thankful she hadn't been stopped for reckless driving while under the influence of parental panic.

Her daughter had been found sitting on a train station bench and taken to the hospital, and Belinda's brain was stirring up the worst possible scenarios.

Oh God, what if she was dying? Or already dead? She turned off the ignition, grabbed her purse, and ran to the automatic doors. "Open!" she screamed at the slow moving glass doors.

A wall sign pointed to the reception desk down the hall and she sprinted the distance. She slapped the counter for attention. "I'm looking for my daughter. She was brought in by the police."

A hefty, middle-aged woman wearing a purple pantsuit and a "been there, done that" expression on her face stepped to the counter. "Name?"

"Belinda Moore. No, that's me. Lindsay Moore. She's my daughter."

The clerk sat at her desk and typed Lindsay's name into the computer. "Yes, she's here in cubicle four."

Belinda stepped to the entry door beyond the desk and placed her hand on the door handle and the clerk stopped her.

"We need to do some paperwork, first. Do you have insurance?"

"Yes—but I need to see my daughter first."

The door was locked. She turned to the clerk, tears streaming down her pleading face. "I have to know if she's okay."

The jaded woman softened. "Of course. We can do this later."

The door lock buzzed and Belinda pushed through. A nurse approached her. "Where's cubicle four?" asked Belinda.

The nurse pointed at two police officers standing in front of the curtained area. Belinda's heart thudded with dread, making it hard to breathe as she approached them. "I'm looking for Lindsay Moore."

"I'm Officer Gabe Miller and this is my partner, Officer Dan Martinez. We found Lindsay sitting at the train station. Are you her mother?"

"Yes." *Please let her be okay. Please.*

"She's been asking for you," said Miller. "I have to warn you; she's pretty banged up."

Apprehension and relief surged simultaneously through Belinda, nearly buckling her knees. Martinez took her arm to steady her and drew back the curtain, revealing a nurse blocking Belinda's view of her daughter.

"Lindsay? Your mother's here," Martinez said.

The nurse turned and stepped aside.

"Momma!"

Lindsay had not called her "Momma" since she was six or seven and the word wrenched Belinda's heart as she rushed to the bed and pulled her daughter into her arms, barely registering her daughter's ravaged face. "Baby, what happened?"

"Oh, Mo-mommy. I was so scared."

"Shhh. Shhh." She wrapped her arms around her daughter and felt spasmodic shivers rolling through Lindsay's slim body. "It's okay. You're safe now." Belinda gently pulled away, fighting to maintain a passive expression as she surveyed her girl's face. A sob deep inside her threatened to erupt as she tenderly touched Lindsay's swollen eye and wiped away her tears. "Who did this to you?"

"I don't know." She burrowed into her mother's soft chest. "I just want to go home."

"We will, honey." Belinda slid her hand under Lindsay's green hospital gown and stroked her slender back. She rested her chin on her daughter's blond head, wrinkling her nose as she caught the unmistakable aroma of cigarettes and pot in Lindsay's hair.

The attending nurse said, "I need to finish Lindsay's preliminary exam and draw some blood. Would you like to take care of the paperwork while I do this?"

Belinda rose from the bed and moved out of the way.

"Momma, please don't go."

"Not going anywhere, I promise." She stepped to the foot of the bed and spoke in a cheery voice. "Just getting out of the way."

The nurse shone an ophthalmoscope into Lindsay's eyes. "Lindsay, have you had any alcohol or drugs tonight?"

Belinda became indignant. "She's only fifteen, for God's sakes." As soon as she said it, she realized how stupid she sounded. A mother in total denial. "Sorry. I didn't mean to snap at you."

"I understand. I asked because her pupils are dilated. Lindsay, I know how hard this must be for you, but you need to answer my questions truthfully so we can help you." She glanced at Belinda for backup.

"Honey, please answer her. I won't be mad. Did you drink or take drugs?" She choked on the words and felt like she was betraying Lindsay by asking. She knew how her daughter felt about drugs and alcohol. A drunk driver had killed Lindsay's father. And yet her child reeked of marijuana.

"No," said Lindsay. "I mean, I don't think so."

Belinda's back stiffened. "What do you mean, *you don't think so?*"

"I don't know, Mom. But something really bad happened." She began to cry again. "I feel so weird."

The nurse pulled down the sheet to check Lindsay's feet, and Belinda saw dried blood smears on her daughter's thighs.

———

In the early hours of that bleak Saturday morning, Lindsay was subjected to a grueling head-to-toe forensic examination. Even in her foggy state of mind, the inspection of her naked body was an intensely discomforting violation that no young girl was ever prepared for. Blood, urine, and other body secretion samples were collected. Her mouth, vagina, and anal area were swabbed. Fingernails were scraped and the findings placed in a small paper envelope. Then her nails were clipped off and saved in another envelope. Her body was photographed, all injuries documented, and each item of clothing was bagged individually. Lindsay's hair was combed and hairs were plucked from different sections of her head—the same procedure was followed for her pale pubic hair. Those samples, along with other fibers and hairs collected from her body, were placed in separate envelopes.

During the long exam, Angela Yaeger, a statuesque, thirty-nine-year-old African-American police detective, waited in the ER lobby to interview her. After Lindsay was returned to her cubicle, the motherly detective entered the curtained alcove and gazed at the pitiful little girl huddled in the bed, holding her mother's hand for dear life.

"Hello, Lindsay. I'm Detective Angela Yaeger." She displayed her badge.

"Hello," said Lindsay with a timid half-smile.

Belinda stood up. "Detective Yaeger, I'm her mother, Belinda Moore."

Angela extended her hand and they shook. "I hope I'm not intruding, but I have to ask Lindsay some questions about what happened. I know it's been a long night, but we must do this now while everything's still fresh."

"Mom? Am I in trouble?" Lindsay asked.

"Oh no, sweetheart. The detective just wants to know what happened. That's all."

Yaeger dragged a steel chair to the bedside and sat. "That's right. We need to get to the bottom of what happened to you tonight. Why you're injured and confused. Maybe we can figure it out together. Deal?"

Lindsay nodded. "Deal."

The detective extracted a notebook and pen from her large handbag. "Let's start at the beginning. Tell me where you were going."

Lindsay released a slow shuddery sigh. "We were going to the movies."

"Who's we?"

Belinda sat on the narrow bed again and took her daughter's hand. "She went with her best friend, Jenny Farrell, and Jenny's older cousin, Mallory."

"Last name?"

Belinda looked at Lindsay for the answer.

"Farrell, too."

"What were you going to see?" asked Yaeger.

"*James and the Giant Peach.*"

"Oh, that's a great movie. I went with my daughter and we loved it. Did you like it?"

"Yeah. It was pretty good. It was the only movie my mom would allow me to see."

"Because practically every other movie was rated R," said Belinda.

"What happened after the movie?"

Lindsay broke eye contact and picked at a loose snag in the thin, woven blanket covering her. "Um. We were going to go have dinner at the pizza place next to the theatre."

"PizzaShmizza?"

"Yeah." Lindsay hesitated and then continued, barely above a whisper. "While we were waiting for a table, there were some older boys in line that Mallory started talking to. Anyways, they invited us to a party."

Belinda inhaled sharply but remained silent.

"Mrs. Moore? Would it be easier for you if you waited outside?"

"No. I want my momma here," Lindsay cried out.

"Do we have to do this now?" Belinda felt as though she were trapped in the middle of a *Law and Order* episode and desperately wanted to turn it off. "I'm sorry. I do understand why you have to do this."

"It's all right. I know this is upsetting." She gave Belinda a reassuring smile and then turned back to Lindsay. "Take your time."

"Mallory wanted to go, but me and Jenny said we should have pizza like we planned." She stopped, peeping at her mother's stoic expression. "Mallory told us they were college boys and she'd gone to college parties before and it'd be fun." She took a breath. "I said, no way. You'd kill me, for sure." She glanced at her mother for reassurance.

Belinda wanted to scream but forced a smile and said, "You're right about that."

"Go on," said Angela.

"Mallory said we'd be home in time so our parents would never know. We still said no, and then she got all mad that she was hanging out with babies. She's almost eighteen. Then Jenny said okay and that really surprised me. I guess she didn't want Mallory to think we were babies."

Belinda stood abruptly. "Oh, for God's sake. You *are* babies."

Lindsay's voice rose to a whiny pitch. "I didn't know what to do, but Mallory promised we would be home by ten, so I had to say yes. What else could I do?"

"You could have called me and I would have come and got you, and we wouldn't be in the hospital now."

"I'm so sorry, Mom. I know it was wrong. I didn't think." Then her eyes widened. "Is Jenny okay?"

"Yes," she answered tightly, feeling her anger flare at Lindsay's best friend for abandoning her daughter. "When you missed curfew, I called her house and spoke to her. She said she looked for you and when she couldn't find you, she thought you'd gone home."

"That's dumb. I never would've left without her." A tear dribbled down her cheek. "That's not what a best friend would do."

"You're right about that." Belinda took Lindsay's hand and squeezed it. "She's lucky to have you for a friend."

Yaeger cleared her throat. "Okay. You agreed to go and then what?"

"We walked with the boys to the house where the party was."

"Do you know the address?"

"No."

"How about the street?"

"I didn't really pay attention. Me and Jenny were super nervous about going to the party and Mallory was walking ahead of us with the boys, so we just followed." Lindsay looked at her mom. "I really didn't want to go."

"I believe you," said Belinda.

"Can you tell me what the house looked like?"

"Umm. It was a big house." She paused to think. "There was a weird-looking sign on the front."

The doctor who had attended Lindsay earlier, entered and asked if he could speak to Belinda and the detective in his office.

Belinda was reluctant to leave her daughter. She stood and pulled the thin blanket up around Lindsay's chest. "Are you warm enough?"

"Yes. Please don't be gone long."

Doctor Stewart led them down the hall to his office where they sat opposite him at his desk. The certificates on his wall assured Belinda of his training, and the photos told her he was a family man. He removed his glasses and rubbed his eyes. "There is no easy way to tell you this, Mrs. Moore."

"Belinda. Please call me Belinda," she said to stall the bad news she knew was coming.

He nodded. "Belinda. Our examination confirmed what we suspected. Lindsay has been raped. I am so sorry."

An icy chill seeped through her as she tried to grasp what the doctor had said.

Yaeger reached over and took her hand. "Are you all right?"

Belinda's voice was barely audible. "I think I knew it when I saw the blood on her legs. But I don't understand why she doesn't seem to know what happened."

Dr. Stewart put on his glasses and picked up a paper on his desk. "Her urine sample showed she ingested Rohypnol, which would explain her amnesia and disorientation."

"What's that?"

"Have you heard of roofies?"

"The date-rape drug?" She gasped and closed her eyes. It was too much to process. Her little girl had been defenseless.

Dr. Stewart cleared his throat. "I'm afraid there's more. I've looked at the samples we took, and it looks like she was raped more than once. The samples showed sperm from three different males."

Belinda choked out a strangled, keening moan. "It's my fault. All my fault."

Yaeger leaned forward in her chair, looking at Dr. Stewart intently. "Are you sure?" It was a reflex question. She knew he wouldn't have given Belinda such devastating news if it weren't true.

He slumped back in his chair. "We'll know more when we get all her lab results back. But yes, I'm sure."

Belinda stared down at her lap. Dr. Stewart set a box of tissues near her. Blinded by tears, she reached for it and knocked it to the floor. Yaeger retrieved the box, pulled several tissues out and placed them in Belinda's lap.

"We'll want to set her up for counseling as soon as possible," said the doctor.

"But she doesn't even know it happened," said Belinda. "Oh God, how will I tell her?"

———

Lindsay was dozing when Belinda and Detective Yaeger returned to the curtained alcove. Yaeger stood at the foot of the bed while Belinda sat on the edge and took a moment to look at her daughter before waking her to destroy her innocent world. The doctor had assured her that the facial injuries had not caused any permanent damage, but she wondered about Lindsay's young spirit. Would she ever be the same again? Was this the abrupt end of her childhood?

"I really hate to disturb her," Yaeger whispered. "But..."

"I know." Belinda touched her daughter's shoulder. "Baby? You need to wake up."

Lindsay opened her good eye. "Can we go home now?"

"Not yet. The doctors want to observe you for a while." She removed a stray hair stuck in the corner of Lindsay's swollen eye. "Do you think you can answer some more questions?"

Lindsay peered down the bed at the detective and nodded. "I'll try, but I don't understand why. I know I shouldn't have gone there, but why do I have to keep answering questions?"

Belinda took a deep breath and glanced at Yaeger for support. The detective nodded but knew now there would be no more answers to her questions.

Lindsay caught the exchange and became fretful. "What's wrong?"

Belinda took her daughter's hand and spoke softly. "You were raped, baby."

"What are you talking about?" Lindsay jerked her hand away and sat up straight. No way would she have forgotten something as awful as that. She would have fought and screamed and kicked and bit and hit. No one could have done that to her. No one. "Why would you say that to me?"

Her mother cupped Lindsay's face in her hands, and her sad eyes said it was true.

CHAPTER FIVE

1996
Saturday, May 4

After a light lunch, Dr. Stewart told Lindsay she could go home. "I want you to rest. No phone calls, no computer. Just rest. Otherwise, I'm going to make you stay here and keep me company," he said with a wink.

"Okay. I just want to see my dog, Muttley, and nobody else 'cept Mom, anyways."

"What kind of dog is Muttley?"

"He's a Great Pyrenees. The best dog ever."

"Muttley is a very lucky dog to have a nice girl like you," said Dr. Stewart. "If it's all right with you, I need to steal your mother for a minute to sign some paperwork. Then she can help you get dressed. Okay?"

"Okay."

Dr. Stewart guided Belinda to the nurse's station before speaking. "We've scheduled an 11:00 a.m. appointment tomorrow with your OB/GYN, Dr. Clater."

"But tomorrow is Sunday."

"Given the extreme circumstance, Dr. Clater didn't want to wait until regular office hours on Monday." He looked at her meaningfully.

"Go on," she said, knowing he had more to say.

"Among other things, Dr. Clater will be checking for intrauterine damage."

Belinda suddenly felt stone cold. "What about AIDS?"

He shook his head. "It's highly unlikely in this situation. But we did take blood samples for that and other sexually transmitted diseases. Herpes, gonorrhea..." He saw the panic seize her and stopped. "All very treatable. We already have her on a broad spectrum antibiotic as a precaution."

Belinda forced her next words out. "What about pregnancy?"

"She's been given a postcoital contraceptive. It's highly effective when used within seventy-two hours of unprotected sex. I discussed this with you before we did it, but I can understand if you've forgotten. You've had a lot to take in."

That's putting it mildly. All Belinda wanted to do was take her daughter home and never let her out of her sight again.

He handed her a business card. "We have to make sure she heals properly, both physically and mentally."

Belinda glanced at it.

"Dr. Greenburg is an excellent child psychologist. I can personally recommend her. My son was being bullied at school, and she has made a big difference in his life. Probably saved his life."

"I'll call her." Belinda stuck the card in the side pocket of her purse.

"I already have. You have an appointment on Tuesday at 4:00."

———

Lindsay was resting on the family room sofa, propped against several goosedown pillows with her favorite faded and threadbare quilt tucked around her. Muttley sat on the floor next to her with his giant head nestled on her lap. A taped episode of *Sabrina, The Teenage Witch* was running on the television, but she couldn't concentrate on it. Her mother's words ran in an endless loop through her mind. *You were raped, you were raped, you were raped.* She couldn't fathom how something that disgusting could have happened to her and have no memory of it.

The doorbell rang and Muttley grumbled but wouldn't leave her to answer it. Her mother led Detective Yaeger into the sunny room.

Lindsay paused the show and dully said hello.

"I just made a pot of coffee. Would you like a cup, Detective Yaeger?" said Belinda in a forced chipper tone.

Yaeger dropped her huge brown leather purse on the beige carpet next to an easy chair. "I am so far over my daily caffeine quota already, but yes, I would. I still have a few hours to put in. And please, call me Angela."

Belinda smiled and nodded. "How do you take your coffee, Angela?"

"A little milk and one sweetener, if you have it. I brought the mugshot book with me and I thought Lindsay and I could look at it." Angela set the heavy book on the coffee table and addressed the dog, who was giving her the stink eye. "Aren't you a beautiful dog. What's your name?"

"He's Muttley."

"Pleased to meet you, Muttley." She reached out and when he didn't object, she stroked his soft white fur. "My sister-in-law raises Pyrs. Such wonderful dogs." She turned to Lindsay. "Before we look at the photos, I'd like to ask some more questions. Is that all right with you?"

It wasn't all right, but she knew she had to do it. "Yeah."

The girl's reluctance was obvious to both women, and they

glossed over it with exaggerated cheeriness. As Belinda left the room, she called over her shoulder, "Honey? Can I get you anything while I'm in the kitchen? Juice? Soda?"

"No thanks, Mom."

Angela settled in the easy chair and opened her notebook. "Let's talk about the weird sign you saw on the house. Could it have been Greek letters?"

"Yeah, maybe." She scrunched her face. "Actually, I don't think I know what Greek letters look like."

"That's okay. We'll get back to that later. You said it was a big house. Was it a new house?"

"No. Old."

"Do you remember the color?"

Lindsay gazed at the ceiling in thought. "I think it was light colored. Not dark."

"Gray? White? Tan?"

"I'm not sure. Anyways, it was a big, old house and... and it had a porch. There were lots of people on it and I remember I was really embarrassed to walk by them. We went inside and stood around, and then this one nice guy got us some sodas."

"Who's us?"

"Me and Jenny."

"What about..." She scanned her notes. "Mallory?"

Lindsay shrugged. "I don't know where she was."

"And the boys you came with? What were they doing?"

"I don't know. I wasn't paying attention. I felt really stupid and just wanted to go home."

"Okay. Let's go back to the boy who gave you the sodas. Do you know his name?"

"No."

"What did he look like?"

"I don't remember," she said. "Just a boy."

"How old do you think he was?"

"I dunno. Maybe twenty?"

"Ethnicity?"

Lindsay was stuck. "I'm not sure what you mean."

"Was he white, Hispanic—"

"White."

"Hair color?"

Lindsay shook her head no.

"Was he shorter or taller than you?"

The girl's face brightened. "Taller! Brown hair, I think."

"Heavy, slim?"

"Uhh, kinda medium, I guess."

Angela read her notes. *We got a medium build, average height, maybe brown haired, white male, maybe twenty, who gave the girls a soda in an old light-colored house with a porch. This is going well,* she thought sardonically.

Belinda returned with the coffee and a plate of chocolate chip cookies and set them on the table. She sat next to her daughter. "I made those cookies yesterday." *Before our world came crashing down,* she thought.

Angela sipped her coffee and nibbled a cookie, then continued. "What happened after you got the sodas?"

Lindsay thought a moment. "I remember Jenny and me drinking our sodas and, and, oh yeah, he showed us where the party food was, and then I think she went to the bathroom and..."

Belinda smoothed her daughter's damp bangs back from her face. "And then?"

"Umm... I ate a few chips," she furrowed her brows in concentration. "A different guy gave me another soda. A Dr. Pepper."

"Can you describe him?"

Lindsay slowly shook her head and pursed her lips. "Dark hair, I think. He kept laughing at me. I didn't like him."

"And his ethnicity?" said the detective.

"I dunno." Lindsay huddled down on the sofa and clutched the quilt. "I didn't like him." She leaned against her mother. "Can I have some orange juice?"

Angela took that as her cue to back off and worked on her cookie as Belinda dashed to the kitchen. "These cookies are very good. Sure you don't want one?" She offered the plate to Lindsay, who shook her head.

Belinda returned with the juice and both women waited while Lindsay gave it her undivided attention. She finally drained the glass and gave it to her mother.

Angela picked up the mugshot book and addressed Muttley, who was still stationed at his girl's knees. "May I sit next to Lindsay? We have some important work to do."

Muttley sensed her good intention and adjusted his huge body to accommodate her intrusion.

"If anyone here looks even remotely familiar, say something or point at their picture. Don't stop and second guess at this point. You never know what might jog your memory."

Lindsay hesitantly opened the book and stared at the first page. The men all looked scary, and most were too old to have been at the party. Belinda sat across from them in the easy chair and watched her daughter's face. She was apprehensive about what might happen if Lindsay recognized anyone. Would seeing the faces of her molesters send her over the edge?

"Don't want to remember." Lindsay turned the pages. "I really don't."

"I understand." The detective patted her arm. "This is truly awful, but we need to stop these creeps, right?"

"Yeah." Then Lindsay looked confused. "What do you mean creeps? You meant creep, right?"

Belinda sucked in her breath in horror. She'd planned to wait a few days before adding this knowledge to her little girl's burden. She glanced at Angela, who'd been unaware that Belinda had not told her daughter that three men had raped her. The detective looked sick at her unintentional gaffe. Belinda pleaded with her eyes for Angela to tell Lindsay for her.

Angela set the mugshot book on the coffee table and took Lindsay's hands in her own. "Honey, it was more than one boy who assaulted you."

Lindsay's eyes widened and her lips trembled. "What do you mean?"

"The doctor said three boys… hurt you. They drugged you and that's why you can't remember what happened."

"Momma?" Tears slid down Lindsay's face as her mother moved to her side and gathered her in her arms.

"Shhh, baby." Belinda rocked her back and forth. "They can't hurt you again."

Lindsay cried for a while, not able to fully comprehend the magnitude of her assault. It was strange to be told something this terrible and all you had was a big, blank hole in your memory. "I want to look at the pictures again," she said in a voice suddenly older than her fifteen years.

Belinda placed the book back on her lap. Lindsay swiped at her tears and opened the book again. She scanned the pages, scrutinizing each photo, but she recognized no one.

"I'm sorry," she said as Angela took the mugshot book from her and stood to leave.

"You did your best. What more can I ask? You're a very brave girl."

Belinda followed the frustrated detective out to her car. "I know you don't want to hear this, but I hope to God she never remembers."

Angela opened the car door, tossed in her purse, and turned to her. "I understand how you feel. Believe me, as a mother, I do. But if she doesn't we may never catch these monsters. And no doubt they'll do it again." Angela shook her head in disgust. "Maybe next Friday night I'll be visiting another innocent young girl in the hospital." She paused, looking past Belinda to the houses across the street. "But knowing how Rohypnol works, I think you'll get your wish. It's highly unlikely she'll ever remember what happened." She checked her watch. "I need to go talk to Jenny and Mallory."

Belinda let out an involuntary snort. "Some friends they turned out to be. I wasn't going to mention this because I don't want to get anyone in trouble, but when Lindsay missed her curfew last night, I called Jenny's house and according to her father, both girls were pretty stoned when they got home."

"Well, that figures.

CHAPTER SIX

Daisy snored next to me in our big cozy chair, exhausted after her morning paper retrieval duty, while I sipped my coffee. The paper remained unopened on my lap, as my thoughts kept sliding back to Lindsay. I'd barely known her, but now she was stuck in my head and driving me nuts.

I slipped from under Daisy's head on my lap and went to the kitchen for a second cup. I leaned against the tile counter, sipping and staring blankly out the large picture window that overlooks the backyard, pondering my self-imposed dilemma. Obviously, the first thing to do would be to find Belinda Moore and ask if there was anything I could do to help her. With hope she wouldn't think I was a big buttinsky and with any luck, she'd tell me she didn't need my help.

I retrieved my laptop from the ottoman in the living room and sat at the kitchen table. I logged on and did an internet search and came up with fourteen Belinda Moores in California. Two in Santa Lucia, one in Santa Verena, one in Colinas De Oro, and the rest scattered around the state. I started with the two local Belindas. She'd be in her fifties now, so that ruled out ninety-four-year-old Belinda and left me with fifty-two-year-old Belinda on Church Street, not far from my house.

I clicked on her name, thinking her phone number would come up but was immediately redirected to a site where I could get her number if I paid ninety-five cents. I am not made of money, so I went old-school, pulled out an old phone book, and found her number and full address on Church Street. I wrote it down on a sticky note and picked up my cell to call her. I got three numbers punched in and stopped.

What would I say? *Uhh. You don't know me, but I kind of knew your daughter in high school and I want to help you keep her murderer in prison.* Now there was an icebreaker.

I decided to drive over and knock on the door. Face-to-face, she would see I am a nice, normal, sincere, caring person. Not a psycho. I touched up my makeup, tightened my ponytail, grabbed my purse, and started out the door; then I decided to take Daisy. Nice, normal people have yellow Labs. Right? I tethered her in the backseat and revved up Veronica. On the way, I remembered that Daisy's bag of dog food was almost half empty. That needed my immediate attention and Belinda would have to wait.

Once inside the grocery store, I figured I should stock up on essentials. Mint chip ice cream being the most essential. When I got back in the car, I worried the ice cream would melt. Who knew how long my visit with Belinda would take? Better to play it safe and go home and put it away. Once there, I thought I should make sure the ice cream was okay.

Half a carton later, I reluctantly put the top back on and stowed it in the freezer. I couldn't put off going to Belinda's any longer. It was a warm blue-sky day, so I decided we would stroll over.

813 Church Street was a charming tan and barn-red Craftsman style bungalow with a wide porch and a carefully tended front yard. On the side of the house, a woman was pulling weeds in a vegetable garden. I watched her while I tried to formulate a dialog. She saw me before I was fully-formulated and came out to greet me.

"You look lost," she said, wearing a neighborly smile.

Daisy wagged her tail furiously and the woman asked if she could pet her.

"Sure, she'd love it."

She crouched and was immediately subjected to a face full of Daisy kisses.

"Oh, you're a sweet thing, aren't you?" She looked up at me. "I used to have a Lab. She passed last year and I miss her so much."

"I'm sorry. I don't know what I'd do without my girl." There seemed no point in stalling, so I said, "I'm looking for Belinda Moore and your address was listed in an old phone book. Are you by any chance Belinda?" The attractive brunette looked the right age.

She stood up, brushing her pants now covered in dog hair, the only downside to living with a Labrador. "She used to live here. We bought the house a couple years ago. By the way, I'm Melanie Rogers." She held out a grubby hand to me and then thought better of it. "I'm a little muddy."

"No problem. I'm Katy McKenna and my sidekick here is Daisy."

"Pleased to meet you, Daisy." Melanie scratched my dog behind her ears, which promptly caused her to collapse in rapture. "Were you and Belinda friends?"

Were? I wondered why she used past tense. "No. Actually I was friends with her daughter in high school." That was stretching the truth a tad.

"Oh, yes. So awful." She shook her head. "We didn't live in the area back then, but our realtor told us about it. Really heart-breaking."

"Yes, it was." I paused a moment in respectful silence, then asked, "Do you happen to know where Belinda moved?"

She visibly flinched. "Oh, I'm sorry, but she died."

"She died?" I was dumbfounded. "Was she ill?"

"No. She was hit by a car."

"Was it an accident?"

Melanie shrugged. "I don't know." She crouched to rub Daisy's tummy, probably to avoid eye contact with me. "Tragic accidents happen."

I was completely flummoxed. How could Belinda Moore be dead?

Melanie stood up and gave me a hug. "I feel like I've ruined your day."

"No, I'm okay. Just a little shocked." I chewed on a nail for a moment. "I wasn't holding out too much hope I'd find her at the first house I tried, but—"

"But instead you got me, and bad news." She smiled ruefully. "Hey. You know what? I was about to knock off for a break and make a pot of coffee. Come sit on the porch and have a cup with me."

How could I say no? She led me up the steps to a porch straight out of *Better Homes and Gardens*. Daisy settled on a colorful Indian rug.

"Have a seat and I'll be right back." Melanie went through the front screen door and returned a few minutes later with a tray laden with a French press carafe, cups, all the essential mix-ins, and some tasty looking cookies.

I was a little overwhelmed by her kindness, but I grabbed a cookie anyway. Homemade. "Oh, wow," I mumbled while chewing. "I'm not usually a peanut butter cookie fan, but this is sensational."

"Neither am I, but a few years ago, I watched a bake-off contest on the Food Channel and this recipe won a million dollars, so I had to try it. Now I'm addicted." She poured the coffee and settled back in her chair with a sigh of contentment. "I love this porch. When I first saw it, I knew I wanted this house before we even stepped inside. My stubborn husband insisted we actually see the rest of the house before making an offer." She laughed. "But I just knew. We both love it. The place has a good vibe."

I was on my third cookie and wondering how many more I could eat before it became rude, when she leaned forward. "Can you tell me why you were looking for Belinda Moore?"

I told her everything, even the truth about how well I'd known Lindsay. It felt a little awkward, but I couldn't lie to the gracious lady.

"I know it must seem odd that I'm poking my nose into this, but from the moment I read the story in the paper, something has been compelling me to do something." I shook my head. "I just don't know what."

She paused a moment in thought. "When we bought this house, it was a probate sale. There was no will and no living relatives, so there's no one to speak for Lindsay now. I believe things happen for a reason, and I think you have to follow your gut feelings on this, not only for Lindsay but also for her mother. I'm not exactly sure what karma is, but it seems like this would be it. Your karma."

That flustered me, and I didn't know how to respond.

"So what do you think you'll do?" she asked.

"I had planned to ask Belinda if there was anything I could do to help her keep this guy in prison. You know, like go to the parole hearing with her and speak up..." I trailed off in uncertainty. "Now I don't know what to do."

"What about a petition?"

"You think it would do any good?"

She pushed the cookies closer to me. "Looks like I've corrupted you." She refilled my cup. "Yes, I do. Someone has to speak up for that little girl. Why not a thousand?"

"A thousand signatures? How will I get a thousand?"

"I can help. You get a petition put together and I'll take some to my office and my husband can take some to his."

I got excited. "My friends could help, too. My mother can have one in her hair salon."

"What's the name of her shop?"

"Cut 'n Caboodles."

"You're kidding. You're Marybeth's daughter? She does my hair. What a coincidence." She leaned forward and patted my knee. "Katy, we can definitely get thousands of signatures."

Thousands?

Back at home, I poured a glass of water and took my cell phone and laptop out to the patio. The dog door in the laundry room slapped open and shut, and Daisy joined me for whatever super exciting thing I was doing in the yard. I set the water and computer on the table and picked up a tennis ball and flung it across the overgrown grass. "Fetch."

Daisy tore out after it and caught it on a bounce as I shouted, "Bring it here. Bring Momma the ball." That concluded our game as she laid down to gnaw on it.

I sat down at the teak table and checked phone messages before opening my laptop. There was a text from Samantha's stepdaughter, Chelsea. *Blog?*

Perhaps it wasn't such a bad idea. Maybe not cathartic like Samantha had said, but a daily journal of my action packed life might be fun to read someday when I'm in the old folks' home. I texted *okay*, hit send, and immediately thought, *Oh, crud. Why'd I do that? Now I'm stuck.* I should never act on impulse. There are a lot of expensive and extremely uncomfortable stilettos gathering dust in my closet that could attest to that.

I opened the laptop and went online to search for information about Belinda Moore's death. Since I now felt officially obligated to follow my karma, destiny, fate…whatever, I deemed it necessary to know what had happened to her.

Melanie said they'd bought the house two years ago, but who knew how long it had sat on the market or how long before it even went on the market, what with probate and all. I decided to start my search at three years ago and work my way forward.

I typed in "Belinda Moore's death in Santa Lucia, CA" and got zilch. I tried 2008, 2009, 2010, and 2011. Nada. My next idea panned out. I went to our local newspaper's online obituaries and spent a few minutes being distracted by the area's recent losses, which was silly considering I have Grandma Ruby to do that for me. There she was: Tuesday, August 12, 2009.

Her listing didn't go into details about the actual cause of death, but as I read, I learned that Belinda had been fifty-one and predeceased by her husband, her father, and Lindsay. Her photo revealed a cute, vibrant looking woman. She'd had a degree in horticulture, which explained the beautiful yard now lovingly tended by Melanie. She hadn't remarried.

Since I had the date of Belinda's death, I clicked the newspaper archives and quickly found the news story about her fatal accident.

Police are searching for a person who caused a fatal injury in front of Saint Bartholomew's Church on Mill Street yesterday morning. Traffic Detective Matthew Lockhart said a vehicle described as a light tan or gray, late model, possibly Toyota Camry or Honda Civic traveling north on Mill Street hit local resident, Belinda Moore, who had just attended a church luncheon.

Witnesses said the car "came out of nowhere, traveling extremely fast" and after hitting Ms. Moore, did not stop or slow down, confirmed by the lack of skid marks. Half a block further the car turned onto Oak Street. While there was confusion on exact color and make of the vehicle, most agreed it had California license plates. Drunk driving is suspected. Ms. Moore, a widow, was the mother of Lindsay Moore, the fifteen-year-old Santa Lucia High School sophomore who was raped, kidnapped and murdered in 1996.

The account went into a heartbreaking rehash of Lindsay's story, then ended with: *Police are asking anyone who has information to call the hotline at (805) 555-TIPS.* I checked later issues, but found only a short blurb stating there had been no new leads on the case.

It had to be an accident, probably a drunk driver. It wasn't like Belinda had been a mobster with a contract out on her. She was the mother of a deceased child and a widow who kept a beautiful garden.

Curiosity compelled me to type in Lindsay's father, Jonathan Moore. His photo showed a George-Clooney-handsome man in his late thirties. He'd coached his daughter's soccer team and had loved camping with his family. A wonderful husband and father who truly would have been missed.

Finally I read Lindsay's obituary. Her photo had caught her laughing and hugging a big loveable-looking dog. I tramped across the lawn to Daisy, now lounging on her back in the sunshine, batting at moths. I knelt down to hug her and found myself crying. Her warm doggy smell and kisses comforted me.

I didn't know these people, yet I was mourning their deaths. Lindsay had lost her father when she was only twelve. She so easily could have pulled into herself and become a weird, angst-ridden teen. Like me.

I'd had enough for the day. I had a headache and felt cranky. My stomach grumbled a reminder that I hadn't eaten a proper meal all day, unless half a pint of ice cream and six cookies counted. I figured I'd better eat a nutritious dinner to counteract the earlier transgressions, especially if I was going to finish off the cookies that Melanie had sent home with me.

A few blocks from my house there is a sweet little vegetarian diner called Suzy Q's Café. The organic menu is inventive and delicious. I thought of my favorite dish—a creamy, smoky-flavored mac and cheese covered in a crust of crunchy butter-browned panko—and actually salivated. Decision made, I fed Daisy and walked there.

New Age music filtered through the open windows to the sidewalk seating area, setting a tranquil tone as I shoved my way through the annoying crowd blocking the entrance. There was a forty-five minute wait for a table, so I settled at the colorful broken-tile mosaic bar and ordered a glass of local zinfandel, and the mac and cheese dinner special which included a side of spicy fried kale and a slice of baked quinoa loaf.

I sipped my wine and glanced around the restaurant, recognizing a few of the neighborhood regulars and hoped none of them recognized me as the "crazy incontinent lady". My phone chirped in my purse. It was Chelsea texting that my blog was ready. Yippee.

My organic dinner was as close to orgasmic as I had been in a long time. I toyed with the idea of another glass of wine since I was walking. But a *Frantic Hausfraus* was recorded on the DVR that I was desperate to watch, so I paid my bill and strolled home.

CHAPTER SEVEN

1996
Sunday, May 5

Lindsay clutched at the thin paper gown, trying to maintain her dignity as she scooted her butt to the end of the paper-sheeted examination table, and placed her bare feet in sock-covered metal stirrups while keeping her bent knees tightly clamped together.

Before the pelvic examination, Dr. Clater explained everything that would happen and showed her the instruments she would be using, including a scary looking metal thing called a speculum.

Now the doctor sat on a rolling stool, focusing a glaring spotlight on Lindsay's genitalia. Dr. Clater asked her to spread her legs apart, but she couldn't stop shaking and her knees clenched tighter.

Her mother stood beside her, holding her hand and stroking her forehead. "Focus and breathe, honey."

After Lindsay's father died, Belinda had taught her the Lamaze technique of breathing she had used when delivering Lindsay. Whenever her grief felt as though it would drown her during that gloomy time, her mother said, "Focus and breathe, honey. Focus and breathe."

Belinda reminded her now. "Don't hold your breath. Try to relax and take long, slow breaths. Focus and breathe."

Lindsay held her mother's hand in a bone-crushing grip, and they breathed together.

Dr. Clater gently coaxed Lindsay's knees apart. "Good girl, you're doing great. I'm going to insert the speculum now. It might feel a little cold."

Lindsay was cold to her bones and her teeth chattered a rapid staccato in the warm room.

"You know what? It's a little chilly in here. Let's get you a blanket," said Dr. Clater. She removed one from a drawer and draped it over Lindsay's thin body. "That better?"

Lindsay nodded, pulling it to her chin, and reached again for the security of her mother's hand.

Tuesday Afternoon
May 7, 1996

Belinda knew that a bad therapist could cause a lot of damage to a young, impressionable psyche, but the pleasant woman standing before her quickly dispelled those fears. Plump and seventyish with short-cropped silver hair and wearing a lavender hand-knit cardigan, Belinda thought she was like a nice cup of tea.

Her office was homey, the lighting soft and warm with a hint of apple pie scenting the air. The large, overstuffed chairs held fuzzy throws and cushy pillows.

"It's so nice to meet you both. I know this must be difficult and I will do my best to make it as easy as possible." Dr. Greenburg gestured at the inviting chairs. "Sit wherever you like. Would either of you like something to drink? Water? Soda?"

Lindsay hunched in a chair, hugging a throw pillow against her stomach. "Have you got a Sprite?"

"Will 7UP do?"

"Yes, thank you," she said, barely audible.

Belinda perched ramrod straight on the edge of her chair, looking like she was going to bolt at any moment. "Nothing for me, thank you."

Dr. Greenburg removed a soda from an under-counter refrigerator and poured a glass. She put a plate of oatmeal cookies on the table centered between the chairs and sat down. "I will talk with both of you for a few minutes and then I'd like to have some time alone with you," she said to Lindsay. "Is that all right with you?"

Lindsay avoided eye contact, feverishly nibbling a cookie as though she were biting her fingernails to the quick. "I guess."

To put them at ease, Dr. Greenburg spent a few minutes talking about herself. When she asked Belinda to wait in the outer office, Belinda felt more comfortable leaving Lindsay alone with the compassionate woman.

She waited in the small reception area outside the office, holding open a garden magazine that she couldn't focus on. Ten minutes passed and Dr. Greenburg came out with a tearful Lindsay.

"I think Lindsay's had enough for today. These things take time and I don't want to push her too quickly." She went to the reception desk and checked her appointment book. "Can you come in on Friday about this time?"

Belinda glanced at Lindsay and said, "Yes."

As soon as they left the office, Belinda said, "Focus and breathe, baby. Focus and breathe."

Friday Morning
May 10, 1996

Lindsay decided it was time to go back to school. She wore her favorite pink and purple top with a matching fuzzy, purple cardigan, and her mother had French braided her long, blond hair. She dabbed concealer over the fading bruises around her eye, and if you didn't know, you'd never notice.

On the drive to school, Lindsay sat silent in the front seat, her lips set in a tight, grim line. Belinda tried to relieve her daughter's tension by popping a *No Doubt* cassette into the player and one of Lindsay's favorite songs, "Just a Girl," filled the minivan. In the old life, Lindsay would have sung along, dancing in her seat. Now the music made her squirm, and she turned it off.

Belinda was surprised. "You're turning off your favorite music? What's up?"

"I don't know. I don't think I like them anymore."

That's strange. Why all of a sudden? "Are you sure you're ready to go back? You can wait until Monday if you want."

"I want to get the first day over with, Mom. Then Monday will feel more like normal."

"You're a very wise girl." Belinda stopped the car just past the school entrance next to the flagpole. When Lindsay didn't ride the bus, this was their usual drop-off and pick-up zone, away from the traffic jam in front of the entrance.

Jenny was waiting there, her body language tense. Lindsay stared through the windshield, not budging.

"Sweetie, she's your best friend, and she feels guilty. Look at her. She is absolutely miserable."

"She should be." Lindsay flicked a glance in Jenny's direction. Jenny saw it and smiled tentatively, her fingers twiddling a shy hello.

"If you can forgive her," Belinda said, "you'll feel better, I promise."

Jenny didn't wait and opened the car door. "Lindsay. I am so, so, so sorry." Her gray eyes flooded with tears and her freckled face flushed as she grabbed for Lindsay's hand. "I promise I will never be so stupid again. You were so right. We shouldn't have gone there. Please. You have to forgive me. I will never let you down again, I swear."

Lindsay got out of the car and hugged her best friend. "It's not your fault. I didn't want to go, but instead I wimped out."

"But I left you there. I will never forgive myself."

"I forgive you." Lindsay reached back into the car for her backpack. "Thanks, Mom. You're pretty wise yourself." She cracked a smile and Belinda saw a trace of the old Lindsay emerge.

As Belinda drove away, her heart ached fiercely and she longed for her deceased husband's strong support. *Oh, Jon, I need you so much. Please tell me what to do.*

CHAPTER EIGHT

WEDNESDAY
April 10

I checked my email and found two responses to my Craigslist ad. One was a local upholstery shop that needed a new logo. Acme Upholstery had been in business since the 1960's and felt it was time for an update. *Ya think?* The other wanted to know if I'd be willing to pose nude for his high school photo class assignment. *Yeah, right, you little perv.* I called the first one and arranged a meeting later in the day at their shop.

Before logging off, I checked Facebook to see what exciting things my thirty-four friends were doing. Chelsea had announced that she was helping me start a blog. That got a few "likes" and a "can't wait to read it." That is not happening.

There was a "friend request" from Bert McKenna, my bio-dad, the famous "plastic surgeon to the stars." Mom had put him through medical school by running a beauty shop in their kitchen with little me underfoot, only to be dumped once he was established. I ignored it. If it weren't for my stepdad and Samantha's husband, Spencer, I could be a total man-hater.

My appointment at the Acme upholstery shop wasn't for a couple of hours, so I made my favorite sandwich for lunch. I had seen a variation of it on the *Oprah* show several years ago. Her BFF Gayle had been traveling around the country looking for the best sandwiches in America. She'd swooned when she bit into this one, created by Café Muse in Royal Oak, Michigan.

It is a fancy grilled cheese sandwich. The original calls for havarti, mozzarella, and fontina cheeses, but I make do with just havarti. The other ingredients are fresh basil, sliced tomato, and here is the kicker—honey drizzled over the basil and tomato and a sprinkle of sea salt. I always use a cast iron skillet that has been in the family for over one hundred years and was passed down to me as a wedding gift from Ruby.

While my lunch sizzled, I touched up my makeup and pulled my shoulder-length hair into a ponytail. I read somewhere that ponytails are never out of style. Thank goodness, or I'd never be in style.

The sandwich was so good that I made another half. I am five-nine with a fast metabolism, but Ruby keeps warning me that it won't always be this way. *You just wait. Those damn peri-menopausal years will get ya. Your mother was just like you and look at her now.* Mom is five inches shorter than me and looks terrific, but she has been battling a little pot belly and some back-fat for the last couple years and is always saying, *Where did that come from?* So I guess I am doomed.

––––––

ACME Upholstery is located in an old brick building in a mixed-use area of town. I found a parking spot about a block away and dug through my purse for stray quarters to feed the meter. I'd be adding seventy-five cents to my bill.

I entered the dusty, cavernous shop carrying my large portfolio and was greeted by the scariest cat I've ever seen. It jumped onto the worn laminate counter and leaned towards me, drooling and making menacing gurgling sounds. It had sparse patches of gray fur, random snaggle teeth, a bitten off ear tip, three or four long, screwy whiskers, and was skin and bones. I figured this must be some horrible disease like leprosy that I didn't want to catch, so I backed away.

"Oh, now, don't let Doris frighten you," said an unseen female with a Midwestern twang.

A plump, middle-aged platinum blond wearing designer jeans and a rhinestone studded top entered the area from the back office and came to the counter.

"She's a love, aren't you, sweetie?" She scratched Doris's head, and the cat leaned into her making that weird sound. Maybe it was a purr. "She loves everyone. Go ahead and pet her."

The thought of touching that mangy mess gave me the heebie-jeebies, but I had to be polite, so I tentatively reached out to her and she hissed and bit me.

"Bad, naughty girl." The woman put Doris on the floor behind the counter. "Sorry about that. I've never seen her do that before, but she *is* getting old."

"How old is she?" I rubbed my hand where she'd bit me, or more like gummed me.

"She's twenty-nine, which in human years is about a hundred and thirty-three. She doesn't look so good now, but she's still going strong. Still a great mouser."

I was dumbfounded. Who knew that eating mice was the key to a long, healthy but not so pretty, life? "Wow. I'm impressed. By the way, I'm Katy McKenna." I held out my hand and we shook.

"Nice to meet you, Katy. I'm Wanda. Did you want to get something reupholstered?"

"Actually, I'm here to talk about your logo. We had an appointment?" I placed my portfolio on the counter.

"Oh, right." She laughed. "Don't mind me. I was doing the

books, and sometimes it's hard to switch gears. You're 'Craigslist Katy.' That's what I've been calling you. I've never used Craigslist before, and my son-in-law told me to be careful." She whispered out of the side of her mouth, "Lot of wackos, don't ya know." Then she laughed, "But you look okay." Then she narrowed her eyes. "And yet, you're the first person Doris has ever bit. Mmmm."

"My dad was a cop," I blurted.

"I'm just kiddin' ya." She pointed at my red portfolio. "What'cha got there?"

I opened the case, revealing eighteen by twenty-four inch pages with examples of past projects encased in plastic sleeves. Most of my work is several years old now due to the "Bookcase Bistro" years, but I have to admit, it's still pretty impressive.

Wanda worked her way through the pages, making the appropriate appreciative sounds, ending with, "Wow. You're good. You know, I can't pay much." She snapped her fingers. "Tell you what. You can have one of Doris's kittens."

Kittens? I assumed she was kidding and gave a "yeah-right" laugh, and asked her if she had any idea of the logo style she wanted.

"Oh, my goodness, no. You're the expert, and I'm sure I'll love anything you do."

I inwardly groaned. It makes the job so much easier if I have a clue what the client likes. "All right. I'll work up a few design ideas, and we can meet again in a few days."

"Call first, because I'm in and out all the time." She hoisted up a gargantuan, genuine Prada handbag from under the counter and extracted a calling card from a Louis Vuitton wallet. "If I don't answer here at the shop, here's my cell number. Just try to keep the cost down, okay? The economy is killing us."

I left minus an elderly kitten, although I had to admit the one named Dave was pretty darn cute and still had most of his hair. On my way home, I swung by Samantha's house to see if Chelsea was home. I figured I might as well get the blog debacle over with so she wouldn't drive me crazy about it.

Samantha answered the door dressed in yellow bumblebee-print scrubs and looking like she'd given birth to quadruplets during her ten-hour nursing shift in the hospital maternity ward. "You're just in time for a caffeine fix," she said as I walked in.

"Forget about the coffee. You should go to bed. You look pooped."

"No can do," she said over her shoulder as we walked to the kitchen. "There's a PTA meeting tonight, and Spencer's in New York on a layover."

I sat on a barstool at the granite counter. "Is that man ever home?"

"The airlines have laid off so many pilots, we're lucky he's still working, but I sure could use his help around here. Especially on long days like this."

She poured our coffees and split a warm cinnamon roll between two plates. "I'm off tomorrow, so I'll catch up. Are you here to blog, my dear?"

"Yes." I sighed like a put-upon drama queen.

"Chelsea!" Sam yelled. "Aunt Katy's here."

No response.

"Come on." She picked up my plate and started down the hallway with me in tow. Outside Chelsea's door, she said, "She's probably on the phone."

"I don't hear anything."

"You are *so* 2005." Sam knocked on the door. "Nobody actually *talks* now days. "

"This generation is going to be a bunch of arthritic-fingered inarticulates by the time they're our age. God, I feel old."

"We're not old, but I do think Chelsea's missing out on a lot of fun." Sam lowered her voice to a whisper. "Spencer and I are working out a plan to limit her tech time. You know—texting, tweeting, Instagram, Facebook, whatever. We're going to talk to all her friend's parents and try to get them on board, so we're not the only bad guys."

"Good luck with that."

"Come in!" called Chelsea.

As I opened the door, I whispered, "Hey, maybe we could throw an old-fashioned slumber party for her."

"Good idea!"

Chelsea's room could have been my room as a teenager, except for all the pink. I was more of a purple and green girl. But it was a mess like mine had been, and there were teen heartthrob posters on the walls. I don't get the "Bieber" thing at all, and don't think I would have even as a teenager. I pointed to a new poster since my last visit. "Who's that?"

Chelsea tossed back her pink-streaked, straight blond hair and clutched her hands to her chest. "Oh, my God. That's Robert Pattinson."

I was clueless. "Is he a singer?"

"Aunt Katy, you definitely need to get out more. He's in the *Twilight* movies. He's *Edward*." Just saying his name made Chelsea look like she was going to pass out.

"He's cute if you're into the dead look," I said. "We were crazy about Jason Priestley when we were your age." I inwardly winced at those last few words. Am I really so old that I'm already saying stuff like that? This little visit to Chelsea's room had really accelerated my aging process.

"Who's that?" asked my extremely young friend.

"*Beverly Hills, 90210*," Sam said. "He was soooo cute."

Chelsea stared at us like we'd landed from another planet. Very deflating.

"I guess I'll leave you two alone." Samantha backed out of the room into the hall. "Have fun."

I plopped next to Chelsea on her flouncy daybed under a swag of fuchsia netting. She opened her pink laptop and logged into the site. She had set up a free WordPress blog, decorated with pink flowers and butterflies, which I agreed was absolutely adorable but so not me. After an intense, twenty minute lesson on blogging, she placed the computer on my lap. "Okay, Aunt Katy. It's all set up and ready to go. Time to make your first official entry so I can be sure you know how."

The pressure was on. I took a deep breath and cracked my knuckles. This would have to be good. Meaningful. Life changing. Spiritual. Deep. And above all, impress my young friend. I started typing and suddenly the words flowed like honey.

Hello World!
Wednesday, April 10
Posted by Katy McKenna

I hate Lima beans. Always have, always will.

Chelsea gazed at me like we were kindred spirits. "Wow. Me, too."

———

When I got home, I piled a plate with munchies, poured a glass of wine and settled into my favorite chair to do some blogging. I figured I might as well give it a try since Chelsea had taken the trouble to set it up.

I easily accessed my site, then sat and stared at it. Hmmm. What to write? Already talked about the lima beans, ●and I pretty much like all other beans, except fava beans, but that may be due to the movie, *The Silence of the Lambs*. Come to think of it, I'm not fond of Chianti, either.

Hello World. It's Me Again!
Wednesday • April 10
Posted by Katy McKenna

This is my first official all-by-myself blog entry!

The laptop screen glared at me. Now what? I caught sight of myself in the wall mirror across the room. My hair was half out of its ponytail and was a frazzled mess. Inspiration!

I hate my hair.

Then I sat and waited for the next revelation. And it came.
I hate boys.
I read my two sentences. Then I wrote:
I seriously need to get a life.
I stared at the screen and my mind drifted to Lindsay, and I knew what to write.

———

Daisy was poking her nose into my thigh and whining, "Bedtime."
I'd been blogging for hours and had lost track of time. Once I'd begun writing my thoughts about Lindsay and what my role should be, it made sense to write everything I knew up to that point. My case notes.
Turned out I knew more than I realized, and the more I wrote, the more questions I had. Like, who was Phil Hobart? Yes, he was a murderer, kidnapper, and rapist. But was that it? He'd started life as an innocent baby, so what had happened?

CHAPTER NINE

1996

Phil Hobart had been a scrawny, sickly kid. The damp Portland, Oregon weather where he had lived with his family had aggravated his chronic asthma, so in 1989, his father, Adam, had accepted a job with an accounting firm in Santa Lucia and they had moved to sunny California.

The mild central coast climate had improved the boy's health and he blossomed into a healthy young man. Although aggressive sports like soccer or basketball still triggered an asthma attack, he participated in the ASB, debate, varsity golf, and earned an Eagle Scout badge in his junior year. At 5'11", brunette with hazel eyes, the girls swooned over him, not just for his good looks but because he was a genuinely nice guy. All four years he was in advanced placement classes and honor society, and he graduated in the top twenty of Santa Lucia High School's class of 1994.

Phil was now in his sophomore year at University at Santa Lucia, studying to be a high school history teacher much to the disappointment of his father, who'd wanted him to attend an Ivy League law school and become a hot-shot lawyer. His mother was proud and supportive, telling Phil he had to follow his own dreams not his father's. To pacify his father, he'd joined his father's old fraternity, Alpha Gamma.

Phil lived in the frat house in a large room on the second floor with his two roommates, Jake Werner and Erik Mason. Jake was a farm boy from Wisconsin, studying for a dairy science degree on a full-ride wrestling scholarship, and Erik, a rich kid from Greenwich, Connecticut, was majoring in partying, with a minor in chasing skirts.

Phil's mother, Penny, worked as a police dispatcher for the Santa Lucia Police Department, and his sixteen-year-old sister was a junior at Santa Lucia High School, who spent most of her time holed up in her room writing miserable poetry about how miserable she was.

His folks were members of the local country club, and every Sunday, Phil would meet his father for breakfast and eighteen holes. Phil had a +1 handicap to Adam's 14, so the links were the one place where his dad praised him.

Recently his mother had been talking about getting an RV and in the coming summer, visiting a few national parks. Adam was reluctant, his sister thought it was a miserable idea, and Phil felt he should be working a summer job to save money. But he also knew it would most likely be his last family vacation, so maybe that was more important.

Then Friday night happened and Phil's life changed forever.

Friday
May 3, 1996

Another Friday night mixer was underway at Phil's fraternity house. Although the night was young, most of the one hundred plus crammed into the ground floor of the decrepit old Victorian were already drunk, thanks to several kegs of cheap beer and a refrigerator full of gelatin shots.

The music pounded, and the temperature inside was pushing eighty-five, even with the doors and windows open. Scantily clad, inebriated freshman girls were flashing, some were dancing, and one was puking into the kitchen sink.

Phil wasn't a partier, which didn't mix well with frat life. Since there was no escaping the noise and the chaos, he was lounging in a threadbare chair tucked in a corner of the living room, nursing his umpteenth beer and thinking about his father. Had it been this way back in his day? He'd spoken of the lifelong bonds forged with frat brothers, but he'd failed to mention all the partying, vomit, hangovers, and drunken sex.

He was debating about another beer when three girls entered the room. They looked way too young to be there, so he watched them with curiosity. The tall one looked older than the other two but still too young. She whispered to one of the girls, and then left them standing there looking ill-at-ease. He felt sorry for them, so he got up and went to offer them a soda. Up close, they looked around the same age as his younger sister.

"Aren't you a little young to be at a frat party?" he asked, suddenly feeling like an old man.

The plump redhead with braces and too much mascara said, "My cousin wanted to come and she's driving, so..." She trailed off, shrugging.

"Want something to drink?" he asked.

The nervous-looking skinny one with long, blond hair and startling blue eyes eyeballed his beer and whispered, "Do you have any sodas?"

"Follow me." Phil led them to a garbage can packed with sodas and ice.

He had no intention of babysitting them, so after they got their drinks, he steered them to the food table, got himself another beer, and settled back in his chair. That was the last he saw of them.

An hour later, it was still early and the party was going strong, but he'd consumed more than enough and now his options were to sleep it off in the chair or go to bed. He pried his lethargic body out of the chair and into a standing position. The alcohol slammed him, spinning the room around him, and he wobbled against the chair. He struggled to regain his balance and staggered to the stairs, where he had to climb over the people sprawled on them. In the upstairs bathroom, he ignored a couple swapping spit in the shower, and peed about a gallon of beer into the toilet, then stumbled down the hall towards his bedroom.

Phil stopped at the bedroom doorway and blearily peered into the dim room, lit by a glowing lava lamp.

"Yo, Phil." His roommate, Erik, called from the room. "Get yo' ass in here."

He squinted to focus and saw Erik with his pants puddled around his ankles, straddling a girl lying spread eagle on his bed. The scene didn't register as his eyes continued to roam the room and found his other roommate, Jake, passed out on his bed.

"This girl is so fucking hot, I can't keep up with her," Erik said, as he stood and hauled up his pants and zipped the fly.

Phil entered the room and stared with little comprehension at the writhing girl whose face was buried under a pillow.

"See what I mean, bro? She wants it bad."

Phil turned to cross the room to his bed and Erik grabbed his arm. "Hey. Where do you think you're going? You gotta do me a favor and keep her happy until I can get it up again."

He pulled the confused boy to the bed and forcefully shoved his face down into the girl's wet crotch. Her musky scent instantly aroused Phil, and he was suddenly overcome with the biggest hard-on of his life. Every shred of decency drained from him, leaving him senseless with a blinding need beyond any coherent thought and it demanded immediate release. Like a primal out-of-body experience, he jerked down his pants and thrust himself into her. She groaned louder, squirming under him, driving him wild as he pumped furiously. When he was spent, he collapsed on top of her, euphoric, and within moments he passed out to the distant sounds of Erik laughing and yelling for him to move over.

Phil woke on the floor next to Erik's bed. *Whoa. I must've had one beer too many.*

His head pounded and his body ached, but hydration and a couple of ibuprofens usually cured anything when you were nineteen. He grabbed a towel, some clean underwear from his dresser, and headed for the bathroom down the hall to shower the party off.

Dried, dressed, and refreshed, he went downstairs to get something to eat. He found Jake at the kitchen table, hunched over a smoothie. Phil took a carton of orange juice from the refrigerator and poured a tall glass. "A little too much party last night, Jake?"

His roommate stared into his beverage and didn't respond.

Okay, thought Phil, as he picked up an open bag of taco chips on the counter and sat opposite him. "You sick or something?"

Jake looked awful. His greasy sun-bleached blond hair was matted to his head and his red-rimmed gray eyes sunken and bloodshot. "I'm thinking about moving home."

Phil reached into the bag, grabbed a handful of chips, and stuffed them in his mouth. "Why?" Jake glanced up and Phil saw tears filling his eyes. "Dude, what's going on? Did you get some bad news?"

"Something happened last night." Jake's voice broke. "Something really bad."

Phil was afraid to ask but had to. "Are your parents okay?"

"Nothing like that."

"Heidi break up with you?"

Jake shook his head. "No. But she'll never marry me after this."

He folded his arms on the table and rested his forehead on them. "I think I screwed a dead girl last night."

"No way." Phil reached over and shook Jake's shoulders. "Dude, there aren't any dead girls here. If there were, the place would be crawling with cops. You were drunk and probably just dreamed it."

"No, it was real." Jake rolled his head back and forth on his arms, whimpering, "Oh God, oh God."

Phil ran his fingers through his wet hair, wishing he could leave the room. "Tell me what happened."

Jake raised his head. "I was seriously tanked last night, but I remember there was a girl in our room, and I think I was screwing her, but she wasn't moving or talking so she must have been dead. Maybe alcohol poisoning or something."

He jumped up, knocking his chair over, and ran to the sink to puke. Phil followed and turned on the water and the garbage disposal. The fetid smell gagged him and he held his breath, squirting a heavy dose of lemon scented dish detergent into the disposal. Jake rinsed his mouth under the faucet and then hung his head, staring at the sudsy drain, waiting for the inevitable next onslaught.

As Phil watched his friend's misery, a cold unease seeped through him as lurid snapshots flashed in his head. His silence got Jake's attention and he glanced up from the sink. "Say something," he pleaded.

Phil could not meet his eyes. "I don't think you were dreaming." His voice was flat and unemotional. "I was there, but you were passed out when I came in… I screwed her, too."

Jake dropped his eyes back to the drain, trying to comprehend Phil's words. His mouth flooded with saliva as another vomit tsunami rolled through him, pitching the last of his banana smoothie. He yanked a wad of paper towels from the roll hanging under the cupboard, mopped his sweaty face, and sat back down at the table.

Phil recited what he could recall from the night before. It was fragmented, but coupled with Jake's memory, it became a reality. "So you're saying we *all* screwed some girl?"

Phil nodded, feeling sick. "Yeah. I think so. On Erik's bed."

"That's fucking twisted." Jake slumped in his chair, pressing the paper towels to his mouth. "Is she still there?"

"I don't know." *Everyone knows this stuff happens at frat parties, so she must've wanted it or why would she have been there?* Phil thought it was degrading and had never partaken, but now, thinking about the hazy memory, he felt his penis stiffen. He remembered her pale, smooth legs spread wide and he was filled with an unwelcome, overwhelming desire to do it again. He was ashamed.

"I know I was really drunk," Jake said, "but I can't even remember her face."

"Neither can I. We need to talk to Erik. She was on his bed and..." His memory flashed a clip of Erik shoving his face into the girl's crotch.

"And what?"

"Nothing."

They found Erik in the steamy bathroom, drying off after a shower. "Man, that was some party last night," he said jovially. "Woo! Good times." He wrapped the towel around his slim waist.

Phil leaned against the wall and crossed his arms. Jake stood beside him, his shoulders drooping, and let him take the lead. "What happened last night in our room?"

"What do you mean? We par-teed." Erik squirted hair gel into his hands and ran it through his short, dark hair. "Sweet little piece of ass, huh?"

"It's a little hazy." Phil squinted his eyes, shaking his head. "Did we *all* have sex with her?"

"Yup. I got her hot little buns all buttered up for my two best amigos. Kinda makes us like blood brothers now, huh? The three amigos."

Jake spun around and left the bathroom.

Erik's goofy grin melted under Phil's cold glare and he turned back to the mirror to fuss with his hair. Phil watched a moment, unable to scrape up the words to convey his feelings of disgust, then shook his head and left.

As he walked down the hall, Erik called after him. "What the hell's got your panties in a bunch?" A few minutes later he sauntered into their room, whistling like he didn't have a care in the world. Jake was sitting at his desk and Phil was leaning against the edge of it, as they watched Erik pull on a pair of faded jeans and a t-shirt. "So what's your problem? You both look like someone died."

"Who was she?" Phil said.

"We're still on this? Who cares? Just some freshman hoochie. There's always girls like that at a party. They want to get drunk, and they want to get laid." He lightheartedly punched Phil in the bread basket. "Right?"

Phil shoved Erik away. "Wrong. Do you even realize we all had unprotected sex last night? And not just with the girl, but... with each other."

Jake choked a sob. "Oh God. That's sick."

Erik's smug attitude dropped a notch. "Figures the Eagle Scout would think of that." He flopped on his bed and rested his head on his hands, staring at the ceiling.

"Heidi and I are... Were... We were saving ourselves for marriage," Jake said.

Erik was taken aback. "Are you shitting me?" He turned on his side and propped himself on his elbow. "You're a virgin? No wonder you spend so much time at the gym pumping iron."

Jake smacked his desk, sending a pile of papers fluttering to the floor. "God, what am I going to tell her?"

Erik waved dismissively. "Why tell her? Just because you're not doing anything doesn't mean she's not getting a little action back home on the farm. I mean, come on. This is 1996. Women's lib and all that shit."

Jake catapulted his five-five muscular frame out of his chair and charged Erik, aiming a punch at his face, but Erik saw it coming and rolled away. Jake's fist connected with the pillow instead. Phil pulled him away before he could go at Erik again.

"Let me go." Jake thrashed in Phil's grip. "I'm gonna fucking kill him."

Erik scrambled to sit up and lean against the wall behind his bed, pulling his knees into his chest. Jake had come to USL on a wrestling scholarship, and the normally docile boy could have done major damage to Erik's face. "Chill out, dude. I was just kidding."

Jake returned to his chair and collapsed in it, defeated. "Not funny."

Phil said to Erik, "He could have killed you, you know. But you're not worth going to prison for."

CHAPTER TEN

THURSDAY • APRIL 11

Posted by Katy McKenna

I'm officially blogging!

Last night, I set my alarm clock to go off at 6:30, thinking that would give me plenty of time to have my morning coffee, do my makeup, and dress business casual for my first day of work in my garden-shed-office. My intentions were good, but when the alarm clock started beeping this morning, all good intentions flew out the window.

I finally sat down at my drawing board at 9:45, still in my pajamas, no makeup (I decided that's one of the perks of working out of a home office), and only semi-enthused to work on the Acme job. I had to produce several thumbnail sketches for Wanda to choose from before creating the final product. And I gotta say, "Acme Upholstery" definitely ain't inspiring.

I stared at my sketchpad, waiting for my eureka moment to hit.

As I waited, I noticed it was a little chilly in the office, so I went to the garage and hunted around for the space heater I'd stuck somewhere when I moved in. After reorganizing a few shelves and making a pile of junk to get rid of, I found it and brought it to the office. Soon I was toasty warm and ready to create.

I opened my mind to the cosmos, willing an idea to present itself, and then thought, *Flowers would be nice in here. I'll run outside and pick some from my wild flower patch.* More than a few flowers in the patch are actually weeds, but I say it's only a weed if you don't want it growing there.

After I had a lovely bouquet arranged in a crystal vase that had been a wedding present from my Great Aunt Edith in England—a lucky discovery while rearranging those garage shelves—I got back to work. That's when I noticed the empty bird feeder outside the grimy window. Can't have innocent little birdies starving to death, so I went outside and filled the feeder. The birdbath was empty, so I filled it, and washed the window.

Back to the drawing board. Acme Upholstery. I wondered what "Acme" meant. I went to the house and got my laptop and searched it. *ac me n: the highest point of perfection or achievement.* No pressure there. I would have to come up with something phenomenal to reach the highest point of perfection. As I pondered, I looked out the window and saw several finches enjoying brunch and was relieved that I'd saved their lives.

———

Hours later, I had a few sketches completed. My favorite had a "Frank Lloyd Wright" feel to it. Contemporary while paying homage to tradition and quality craftsmanship. My least favorite was the volcano with the word "acme" exploding out of it. It was a hard call when you had no idea what your client wanted.

During my burst of creativity, I'd skipped lunch. I was starved but not inspired, so I slapped a piece of cheddar on a slice of whole grain and popped it in the toaster oven. I was coaxing the hot cheesy toast out of the oven onto a plate when Ruby called.

"Have you read the paper today?" she asked in a woe-be-gone voice.

Oh crud. Who died now? I wondered, not wanting to ask. I could feel my appetite ebbing. "No."

"They've canceled *All My Family.*" Her voice broke, and I heard muffled sobs. "They're taking it off the air in three months. What..." She hiccupped a sob. "What am I going to do-o-o-o?"

Ruby has been living in a soap opera parallel universe for one hour a day, five days a week, for over forty years. Mom had been thirteen when the show started, and she is an avid follower, too. Thank God I had not allowed myself to be sucked into that vortex. But what could I say that would make this better? *All My Family* was Ruby's extended family. She'd seen them through births, marriages, deaths, divorces, drug addictions, misery, mayhem, and more misery. No matter what Ruby's troubles were, she always knew that soap diva, Monica Lane, had worse problems.

"Think of it this way, Ruby. You've just gained an extra hour of daylight."

Silence. I swore I could hear crickets chirping in the background. I had tried to put a positive spin on it; obviously something more sympathetic would have been a better choice, but it was too late now.

Then dear Ruby dropped the bomb. "Guess what else?"

I did not want to ask. "What?"

"I consulted the tarot cards to find out if there might be a reprieve for my soap, but something else came up instead."

This was not going to be good. I could feel it in my bones, and I did not want to hear it. "Oh, gotta another call coming in, I have to—"

"This is *Frantic Hausfraus'* last season. Ha." She hung up.

"NOOooooo," I howled to the dial tone.

CHAPTER ELEVEN

FRIDAY · APRIL 12

Posted by Katy McKenna

I called Acme Upholstery first thing today, and told Wanda I had some sketches for her to look at; we made an appointment for eleven a.m.

I am beginning to see the light at the end of the unemployment tunnel, so to celebrate I took myself out to breakfast at Suzy Q's. Usually I walk, but I was going straight from the cafe to Acme, so I stowed my portfolio in Veronica's backseat and drove over.

After a scrumptious omelet, I set out for Acme. I probably should have walked there since I wound up parking four blocks away and feeding the darned meter three dollars in quarters. When I entered the shop, I found the place in an uproar.

Dave, the elderly cat who still has hair, had brought a new feline girlfriend home. She was a sweet young thing, and he was strutting around yowling like he was "the man." Wanda was fit to be tied and his mother, Doris, was so annoyed she didn't even try to bite me.

"I can't have any more cats," Wanda said. "They get hair on the newly upholstered furniture, snag the fabric, and sometimes," she dropped to a conspiratorial whisper, "even pee. I tell you, I go through gallons of fabric freshener."

The young feline, a skinny little gray tabby with no collar, looked at me with her big needy eyes and I could almost hear her saying, "Oh please, nice lady, please take me home."

I have never been a cat lover. So I resisted reaching out to her and opened my portfolio to show Wanda the sketches. I spread the drawings out on the counter and as Wanda perused them, curiosity got the better of me. "Uh, Dave, uh, he can't, uh, you know—"

"Make babies? Good Lord, no. He was fixed years ago. But he thinks he can, which will drive me crazy. I suppose I'll have to take his girlfriend to the pound."

Oh no, not the pound. "Won't he settle down after a while?"

"Last time he did this, he carried on so long, he wound up having a heart attack and I had to resuscitate him. I don't think he could survive another one. And I am not paying for another bypass."

I had nothing to say to that, so I pointed at the sketches. "Do you see anything here you like?" As soon as I said that, I felt like smacking myself in the forehead. I should have said, *which one do you like?* I do not want to go back to the drawing board and sweat out more Acme logo creations.

"Well, darlin', they're all nice, but this," she tapped a sketch with her long, magenta, rhinestone studded acrylic, "this is the one." She picked it up and went to a grimy window to admire it. "It's as if you read my mind."

We discussed some business details and then I loaded my portfolio and new kitty into the car and set out for the pet store for cat supplies. Yup, I'm a pushover.

When I brought Tabitha home, Daisy was incredibly cordial to her new sibling. She followed all the proper welcoming protocol. First, she sniffed the young cat thoroughly, while Tabitha purred and twitched her tail. Then she gave the house tour, walking into each room with the cat following obediently. This gave me time to set up the litter box in the laundry room.

After the royal tour, I showed Tabitha the litter box and she climbed in and did her business. I was impressed. Smart girl. I fed them, then took her to the box again and she went again. Genius. Maybe I should change her name to Einstein.

After they settled down together for a nap in a warm sunbeam near the French doors, I decided to go to work. During the grueling commute to the backyard office, I thought, *I have my own little family now.*

Wanda had picked my least favorite Acme creation, the spewing volcano, so I was not enthused about working on it. I could hear her voice in my ear: *It's as if you read my mind.* Rats.

I knocked off at five and called Mom to finagle a dinner invite. "Hey, Momma. Watch'a doin'?"

"I'm sitting on the couch with my swollen feet up because I've been on them all day long, earning a living, and they hurt," she said curtly. "I am also watching today's episode of *All My Family* on the DVR, as if you care."

Ouch. "Oh, yeah. I heard. I'm so sorry."

"Too little, too late. I am well aware of what you said to your grandmother about gaining an extra hour of daylight. Hope you enjoy your last few episodes of *Frantic Hausfraus*. Hold on." I heard a paper rustling. "I did a little research and do you know we have watched 10,413 episodes, counting today, to your measly 146? Can you even begin to imagine how this feels for us? No, you cannot."

I could see my dinner plans would need altering. "Well, for what it's worth, I truly am sorry, Mom. And I'm sorry about what I said. It was thoughtless and coldhearted and I apologize." Then I threw out a pitiful, "I love you."

"Love you, too," she muttered and hung up.

I went to the kitchen and poured a hefty glass of wine. I leaned against the tile counter, reflecting on our conversation and wound up feeling like an ass, which led me to sending them both condolence flowers.

Bedtime came and after my bathroom beauty routine and Daisy's perimeter check, we climbed into bed. She was sawing logs before I even had my pillows fluffed. I read *A Dog's Purpose* on my e-reader until I reached the blurry-eyed stage where my brain supplied nonsensical words of its own, and then I turned off the light and drifted off to dreamland.

Around midnight, Tabitha jumped on the bed, stealthily squeezing her ever-purring body between Daisy and me. That jolted Daisy out of a dream, and she reared up with a yip, trampling me and the cat, who hissed and swung her paws in self-defense. I got scratched on the arm and Daisy took one on the nose, yelping pitifully.

"Out. Both of you. Out!" I shrieked like a banshee, wondering what had possessed me to bring home a cat.

I attended to my minor wound and went looking for Daisy. I found her snuggled with Tabitha on the couch, both fast asleep. They were so cute I took their picture.

CHAPTER TWELVE

1996
Sunday, May 5

Phil was in no mood for his weekly Sunday breakfast and golf game with his father at the country club. Adam's jovial golf buddies always got a kick out of teasing him about his wild fraternity life and up until now, he'd dutifully laughed at their lame toga party jokes, but no way could he laugh at their friendly ribbing now. He called and begged off, saying he had to study for an exam. His mother phoned later and guilted him into coming over for dinner.

Phil usually ate at least three helpings of his mother's pot roast, but depression had killed his appetite and he pushed his food around his plate.

His mother leaned across the table and felt his forehead. "You're a little feverish. Are you coming down with something? Your sister's running a fever. Maybe you both have the same thing."

His father chuckled. "More like recovering from something, would be my guess." He sighed wistfully. "Fraternity life is definitely for the young."

You can have it, thought Phil. "I'm okay, Mom. Just worn out from studying."

"And not eating right," she said. "Speaking of frat houses. This is awful. Late Friday night, dispatch got a call from a worried mother whose daughter had missed curfew."

"You get those kind of calls all the time, Penny," said Adam. "Dumb kids not paying attention to the time."

"This one turned out to be a lot more." Penny pursed her thin lips and tucked her chin-length, coal-black hair behind her ears.

"How so?" asked Adam.

"I tell you, it always makes me grateful that our Phil is such a good boy. Never gives us an ounce of worry." She reached over and ruffled Phil's hair, to his annoyance. "This one was a fifteen-year-old girl who'd gone to the movies and dinner with two friends, supposedly, but when the friends got home close to midnight, way past curfew, neither one of them knew where she was."

"What did you mean by *supposedly?*" Adam asked.

"The kids didn't actually go to dinner after the movie. They went to a frat party instead."

"What the hell are fifteen-year-old girls doing at a frat party?" said Adam. "That's no place for a kid that age."

"I know," said Penny. "The girl, Lindsay Moore's her name, was found in the wee hours of Saturday morning sitting at the train station, dazed and crying, and all banged up."

"All banged up?" asked Adam.

"Black eye. Scrapes and bruises. Looked like she'd taken a bad fall."

Adam looked at Phil. "Train station's not too far from your frat."

"There's a lot of fraternity and sorority houses in that area, Dad."

Penny continued. "I spoke with Angela Yaeger—"

"Who's Angela Yaeger?" Phil cut in, growing uncomfortable with the conversation.

"She's a detective. You've met her before at Christmas parties. Tall, African-American, with gorgeous copper colored hair?"

Phil shrugged.

"Well, you have. Anyway, this afternoon, she told me the officers who found the girl had taken her to the hospital."

"Why?" asked Adam. "Was she hurt that bad?"

Penny whispered, "They suspected she'd been sexually assaulted." She paused to glance over her shoulder. "I just want to make sure your sister hasn't come out of her room, because this girl goes to the high school here and I do not want Christy to hear this." Satisfied the coast was clear, she continued. "Oh, dear God, this is hard." Her voice trembled. "She'd been gang-raped by three different men, according to her lab report. Angela was called in at the crack of dawn to question her."

Fear bubbled in Phil's stomach. Was it possible the girl his mother was talking about had been the same girl who'd been in Erik's bed? No way. Erik had said she was a freshman who wanted to party.

"This sort of thing never happened when we were in college," said Adam, rubbing a hand over his five o'clock shadow. "Did they get the guys?"

"Right now Lindsay doesn't remember anything. Can you imagine having to tell someone they've been raped? Let alone your own child? My heart would break." She sighed deeply, her hand over her ample breast. "Anyway, it turns out she was drugged. Rohypnol. You know, the date rape drug? They found traces in her urine sample."

Adam shook his head sadly. "That little girl is going to need some serious therapy."

Penny turned to Phil. "Honey, I know I can trust you not to

repeat any of this. But if you hear anything, anything at all, let me know immediately and I'll pass it along."

"And you need to be careful, Phil," said his dad. "Parties can get out of hand real fast. If you think anybody in your frat could do anything like this, steer clear of them. Got that?"

"Got it." Phil's heart was pounding so hard, he thought he was going to have cardiac arrest. *Had Erik lied to him? Had he drugged a girl younger than his little sister? That would make it rape and would mean he and Jake had raped her, too. No, no way. Erik's a player, but no way could he have done this.*

"Hopefully," Penny continued, "she'll start remembering things and those lowlifes will be arrested and put away for a long time. The courts are taking this date-rape drug thing very seriously. Just didn't think we had to worry about it here in Santa Lucia." She looked at Phil's full plate. "Oh, sweetheart, I'm sorry. I completely ruined your dinner." She got up and pressed her lips to his forehead. "You do feel warm. I hope you're not getting sick."

Phil had to get out of there. "Maybe I should go home and go to bed."

"You can stay here, you know," said his father.

"Can't. Got an early class. It's easier to go back to the house."

His mother wrapped his leftovers and gave him idiot-proof instructions for reheating. As she droned on and on, it was all he could do not to scream, *Shut up! Let me go!* Finally he escaped and drove home in a daze.

The fraternity house reeked of fried fish and the smell turned his stomach when he entered. He barely acknowledged a few guys watching TV in the lounge as he passed through, going straight up the stairs to his room. He stashed his food in the little fridge that also served as a nightstand.

Jake was lying on his bed reading an animal husbandry book

and did not acknowledge Phil when he entered the room. After a couple of minutes, Phil noticed he wasn't turning the pages.

"We need to talk," he said to Jake, moving to the window overlooking the backyard.

"Really don't want to." Jake kept staring at the book.

In the twilight, Phil could see a gray squirrel lounging on a branch of the old sycamore in the backyard. He wished he were the squirrel. No worries. Just gather nuts and hang out. He turned to Jake and said, "About the girl on Friday night."

Jake exhaled loudly and flipped a page. "I told you I don't want to talk."

"Listen to me, Jake. My mom said a fifteen-year-old girl was gang-raped by three guys at a party on Friday night. The police found her at the train station. That's only two blocks from here."

"So? What's it got to do with us?" Jake spoke slowly, still staring blindly at his book. "I'm not proud of what we did, but we didn't rape a kid." He closed the book over his fingers to mark the page and looked at Phil. "Don't you think if it had been a rape, she would have been fighting it? She just laid there and let us do it. How is that rape?"

Phil stepped to his bed, tossed aside some clothes piled on top, sat down, and told him about the three young-looking girls he'd seen earlier at the mixer. "Mom said it was three high school girls. Two made it home and the third one didn't. She was drugged with roofies and raped by three guys."

Jake shook his head, hanging on tight to denial. "Nope. No way. Erik's a player, but he doesn't need to drug anybody to get sex. He always has a hottie on the line."

"I dunno, Jake. It's too much of a coincidence."

The door opened and Erik walked in, sweaty from a long run. "Hey, guys. What's going on? Got anything to drink?" He checked Phil's refrigerator. "Ooo, what's this I see? Leftovers." He unwrapped the food. "Oh, yeah, your mom's pot roast." He waved the packet. "You don't mind, right?" He took a bite and cold gravy dribbled down his chin. "Mmm. Speaking of leftovers, you guys okay now about what happened the other night?"

Loathing his roommate's flip attitude, Phil asked quietly, "Just how drunk was that girl? I mean, she had to be pretty trashed to want to do it with three guys."

"*Wellll...*" Erik returned the food to the refrigerator and wiped his greasy mouth on his orange t-shirt. "I wouldn't exactly call it drunk, maybe more like a little... drugged." He sank into a yellow beanbag near the window, wearing a guilty grin.

"Was it roofies?" Phil prayed the answer would be no.

"You know what? You two should be grateful." Erik settled his body into the squeaky bag, snickering at Phil. "About time you guys got some action."

Phil jumped off his bed and grabbed the front of Erik's t-shirt, jerking him up. "Tell me!"

"Yeah, okay. It was roofies." Phil shoved him back into the bag. "No need to get so ticked off." Erik had never seen Phil lose his cool and it unnerved him, but he maintained his bravado to cover his growing realization that maybe he'd made a bad choice on Friday night. "I put a roofie in her soda. So what? I was pretty high and I wanted to get laid, but she wasn't having it. Kept saying she needed to go home, but I knew she really wanted it. Why else would she've been here? So no big deal."

Phil turned his back on him, his fears confirmed. "Do you have any idea how much trouble we're in?"

"What trouble? She's gone, and the beauty of that drug is, she won't remember. So we're good."

"Oh, yeah, we're good, all right." Phil sat on the edge of his bed, hanging his head. "We all screwed a girl you drugged." He shook his head with a grim laugh. "But hey, we're good."

"Dude, come on. It was a party, so that makes it consensual. If she didn't want to party, she should've stayed home."

Jake flung his heavy book across the room, snapping its binding against the wall. "You're a fucking idiot, Erik." He stood up, clenching his fists, the veins in his neck throbbing. "She was fifteen!"

Erik remembered Jake coming after him the day before and kept his tone calm. "What would a fifteen-year-old be doing at a frat party?" Doubt crept into Erik's voice. "And how would you know this?"

"Phil's mom. Remember she's a police dispatcher? You tell him, Phil."

"She told me cops found the girl at the train station and took her to the hospital. They know she was raped by three men, and they found Rohypnol in her urine." Phil angrily shoved the pile of clothes on his bed to the floor. "They're calling it a gang-rape."

"Shit, we are so screwed," Jake said, pacing the room and wringing his hands. "Why did she come here? She should have known better. If she remembers what happened, she'll be able to identify us and we'll all go to prison for the rest of our lives. Who's going to believe we weren't part of the drugging? No one."

"Even if she hadn't been drugged, it's still sex with a minor," said Phil. "That's statutory rape, even when the girl wants it. And she didn't want it, did she, Erik?"

CHAPTER THIRTEEN

SATURDAY · APRIL13

Posted by Katy McKenna

I woke around 7:30 and after a shower and a five-minute makeup, I sipped coffee and read the paper on the patio while Tabitha warily explored the yard for the first time. I hope she will be a stay-at-home cat and not a neighborhood gadabout, but there is no way I can keep her housebound and still have a dog door for Daisy.

I was about to commute to the office to work on the Acme project when she leapt into my lap and curled into a pulsating fur ball. I didn't have the heart to dump her on the ground, so I remained on the chaise lounge, telling myself I'd give her five minutes.

Five minutes stretched into thirty as I pondered the "Lindsay petition" idea again. I decided that I should quit procrastinating and just do it. I carried Tabitha into the house and deposited her on the sofa and then sat at my desk in the living room to write a list of places to leave the petition.

Cut 'n Caboodles, Pop's Fix-it Shop, Suzy Q's Cafe, Melanie Rogers' office, her husband's office, the hospital where Samantha works, Klondike Pizza... I tapped the pencil on my chin. *Where else?* The Bookcase Bistro—because Chad owes me. Plus, it might do me good to bury the hatchet. No, not in his back. But it is a small town and I'd rather choose the time and place that we finally face each other, and I'd rather it not happen by chance in Target.

That brought me to Holly and Erica, local friends I've neglected during my divorce and long pity-party. Erica is a stay-at-home mom, working her butt off chasing after toddler twins. She belongs to every mommy group there is in Colinas de Oro, about twenty minutes north up the road, so she could probably muster up a lot of signatures. Holly is a physical therapist in a big clinic here in town, so plenty of signature opportunities there. Who else? Ruby's senior community. Maybe I would get thousands of signatures after all.

I typed up the petition and after proofing it about a hundred times, I printed it out, immediately caught an error, and printed again.

I changed into a more formal outfit than my office attire of baggy, faded sweats. Jeans, T-top, cardigan, and sandals—pretty much my year-round uniform on the temperate California central coast. I refreshed my makeup, tightened my ponytail, and added a floral print scarf and a pair of silver hoops.

Daisy kept a close eye on my mini-makeover, and when I picked up my handbag and walked to the front door, she danced around me, thrilled about whatever super-exciting adventure I had planned for us.

"Sorry, Daisy. Not this time."

I went to a print shop on South Oliva Street first. My legal size petition had room for fifteen signatures below the brief account of the crime and the plea to stop Hobart's parole. I printed one hundred, which would get me fifteen hundred signatures. The girl at the counter asked if she could keep one to print out and gather signatures from her customers. As I walked out, I heard her asking the shop manager to sign it.

Before returning home to work on Acme, I decided to drop off a few petitions at my parents' businesses. The rest would have to wait a couple of days to get distributed. Pop's shop was closed and I found him next door in Mom's beauty shop about to get his usual "Bruce Willis" buzz.

"Hey, guys." I dropped into the empty chair next to Pop and spun around to face them. "What's up?"

"I'm trying to persuade your dad to grow his hair out while he still has some, but he won't listen to me."

He winked at me and went back to annoying Mom. "Too much trouble. Then I'll have to comb it."

Mom always fell for the bait. "Every morning I have to wash, dry, *and* style my hair, plus put makeup on. It's a pain. How would you like it if I stopped doing that?"

"Go ahead."

"Fine then. Maybe I will."

"Don't forget to stop shaving your legs," I said, "and plucking your eyebrows, and covering your gray, and clipping your nose hairs, and bo—"

Now Mom was glaring at me, so I wisely shut up before I gave out all her beauty secrets to her staff; although, the "B" word had definitely gotten their attention, so oops.

Pop smiled sweetly. "I'll still think you're beautiful, Marybeth."

"Give it up, Mom, he's not going to change. But before you turn on the clippers, I have some petitions for you." I handed one to each of them.

Mom set down the clippers and put on her reading glasses. While she read, Pop said, "When you're done, let me use your glasses. I left mine in the shop."

"It's good, honey." She went to the receptionist desk and signed it.

"Can I leave some here for customers to sign?"

"Of course." She waved the petition in the air and announced to the other three stylists and their clients, "Please make sure you read Katy's petition before you leave today. It's important."

Since I'd been exonerated for my thoughtless remark to Ruby about the *All My Family* cancellation, I figured it was safe to swing by her house on my way home and drop off some petitions. She lives in a charming two-bedroom cottage in the independent living section of a posh senior community, "Shady Acres," on the south end of town.

Gramps died years ago and his life insurance policy allows Ruby to live a comfortable life with no financial worries as long as she lives within her means.

Through the years she has supplemented her income as an independent sales consultant for several multi-level marketing companies, and for the most part has done well. The only one that had not been a success was "Rubber-Wear." Clothes and accessories made out of recycled tires. The purses and belts were actually cute, and I still use mine, but the clothing was hot and uncomfortable, and I swore on a hot summer day my "Goodyear" cardigan smelled like burned rubber. It was probably all in my head, but it was a huge relief when she moved on to her next money-making scheme; although, every time that happens she expects me to host another party and invite all my friends. Needless to say, they do not appreciate this.

I parked in the visitor parking area in her cul-de-sac, gathered my petitions, and walked to the front door. When she didn't answer, I peeked in the garage window and saw her car, so I figured she might be in the clubhouse.

At the front desk, I asked Elaine if she'd seen Ruby and she pointed to the bingo room. As I approached the double doors I could hear raucous laughter, but it didn't sound like a bingo game was in progress. I cracked the door and peeped in.

Ruby was standing at the front of the room behind a long, folding table, talking to about thirty women sitting at tables facing her. From a distance, she looked different—oddly different. I was closing the door when she spotted me and motioned me in.

"Look who's here. Katy, my beautiful granddaughter. Come in, dear."

As I reluctantly pushed the door open, the ladies started chanting, "Do Katy! Do Katy!"

I had no idea what they were shouting about until I got into the room and saw their faces. They all had enormous red lips. So did Ruby. It felt like I'd stepped into a scary clown convention. Ruby had a new business.

"E-Z Lip Stencils." The E-Z way to apply lipstick. Are you tired of smearing lipstick all over your face because of shaky hands? Want big, pouty, youthful lips like the celebrities? Do you wish your lipstick would last for days? Try E-Z Lips Stencils and E-Z Lips semi-permanent lip colors. Use it once a week for your perfect E-Z Lips.

"Do Katy! Do Katy!" The ladies were in a frenzy, pounding on the tables, and I was trapped with no gracious way out.

Ruby pulled out a chair for me and I sat facing the women. Year ago I watched the Stephen King miniseries, *It*, with that evil clown, Pennywise, and ever since, I have not been a fan of clowns.

Ruby dove into her sales spiel. "The starter kit includes three lip stencil choices—the "Jolie," the "Griffith," and the "Jagger." She held them up for my perusal. "Which glam lips would you like to try?"

None. "Uh… Are there any other options, like maybe, ummm…" I frantically sifted through my memory bank searching for a celeb who had not blown her lips totally out of proportion. "Like Ellen DeGeneres?"

"Ellen DeGeneres?" She smiled patiently at me. "When I think of glam lips she doesn't come to mind."

"Then I guess I'll take the Jolie."

"Excellent choice." She turned to the group. "How many of you gals used the Jolie?"

Everyone raised her hand, except for one butch looking eighty-something who pumped her fist in the air and yelled, "Jagger, baby. Rock on."

Ruby removed my neutral pink lip color and then opened one of the various bright reds in the kit. The end of the tube had a spongy tip that oozed out color when she squeezed it. She placed the stencil over my lips, and while holding it firmly in place, she daubed the color on. Next, she held a hairdryer to my lips for three minutes before peeling the stencil away. She finished with a high gloss sealer. "Well, ladies? Is she gorgeous? Or is she gorgeous?"

The thunderous applause made me excited to see my new lips. I picked up a hand mirror on the table and flinched. I looked like I was having an anaphylactic reaction.

"You like?" asked Grandma.

No, I did not like; however, I wasn't ruining it for her, even though I hate it when she's in her "sales-pitch-carnival-barker" mode. It's like watching one of those screaming pitchmen on TV selling cleaning products. Did I mention she had on a microphone headset?

"Wow. I absolutely love it. Can I buy a kit?" I gushed. "Give me a kit for Mom, too. It'll make a swell Mother's Day gift." That brought a round of "ahhhhs" and more applause. I stood and continued. "Ladies? If I could have your attention for a minute, I have something I'd like to share with you."

Ruby whispered in my ear, "Katy, what are you doing?"

"This is really important." I puckered my clown lips and kissed her cheek. "Pretty please?"

She pulled off her headset and handed it to me. "You better put this on. Most of them are hard of hearing."

My voice boomed through the room as I told them about Lindsay and the petition to stop Phil Hobart's parole. It killed the festive mood, but I got thirty-two signatures and several women took petitions with them. Luckily, they'd all purchased a kit before I'd arrived, or Ruby would have killed me.

As soon as I was out of the building, I bolted for Veronica and dove into the driver's seat, before anyone could see me. The first thing I did was take a picture of myself on my phone and text it to Samantha. She would die when she saw it, plus it was good payback (to me) for the time I (so embarrassed to admit this) outlined her lips with a red marker when she was asleep. In my defense, I was only fourteen, but she has never let me forget it. Then I turned the rearview mirror towards me and wiped my lips with a tissue. That merely dulled the gloss. I rubbed some more, but the color didn't budge and now white tissue lint was stuck to my lips. Then I remembered the ominous words "semi-permanent," "lasts for days," and "once-a-week," and I freaked.

As I turned into the driveway at home, I thought of the Viking. I didn't see him outside, but I couldn't risk it, so I clicked the garage door opener. When it was halfway up, I saw the pile of junk I'd set there while searching for the space heater, blocking the entrance. Rats.

I turned off the car and checked to see if the coast were clear. No Viking. I opened the door and stepped out, ready to dash for the front door.

"Hi, Cookie."

Oh, crap. Where'd he come from?

"I saw you drive up and I have something for you." He was walking across the lawn carrying Tabitha. "Look who I found on my kitchen counter when I came home. She must have come through my dog door. I hope you weren't worried."

I kept my head down, hand over mouth, not making eye contact. "I didn't know you have a dog." I held out one arm to take Tabitha, still keeping my head down and my mouth covered.

"I don't. The previous owners did. And I didn't know you had a cat until I saw her tag." He bent at the waist and looked up at my face. "You okay?"

I used Tabitha to shield my mouth and spoke through her fur. "I'm fine. Just gotta a toothache, that's all. I'm a little swollen, so kind of embarrassed to be seen."

"Hope you don't need a root canal. Have you tried swishing with warm salt water? Or vodka? Taken anything for the pain?"

"Gonna do that right now."

"Which one?"

"All of it. Really gotta go now." I scuttled to the front door, unlocked it, and slammed it behind me, leaning against it, breathing hard. Then I remembered the alarm and punched in the code before it went off. I wanted to throw Tabitha across the room, but I set her on the couch and collapsed next to her.

I was annoyed with myself for constantly being the village idiot, plus the fact that I hadn't even thanked Josh for bringing my cat home. I berated myself for several minutes, then went into the kitchen and started a pot of coffee.

While it brewed, I went to the bathroom to scrub my mouth. I'm a cosmetic junkie with drawers of everything imaginable, so I wasn't worried about getting the lip color off. I found some heavy-duty makeup remover that I use for waterproof makeup, so it should have worked. It didn't. I scrubbed with soap and a scrubby and the color flaked and cracked but remained on my face. I tried dish detergent, oil, Goo-Gone, S.O.S. pad, and nail polish remover. Nada.

I gave up and heated up a blueberry scone, poured my coffee, and trudged across the backyard to my office to finish the Acme job. Thank goodness my coworkers, Daisy and Tabitha, weren't fazed by my freaky appearance.

CHAPTER FOURTEEN

Posted by Katy McKenna

Quote for the day: *"A foolish man tells a woman to stop talking, but a wise man tells her that her mouth is extremely beautiful when her lips are closed."*

Except if her grandma stenciled her lips with E-Z Lips! So I'm going with:

"A cosmetic is a boon to every woman, but a girl's best friend is still a near-sighted man." – *Yoko Ono*

I need to deliver the Acme job tomorrow, but there is no way I can set foot out of the house with my Bozo lips, not to mention the enflamed, puffy skin around my mouth from all the scrubbing, so I called Ruby. She got me into this mess, so she can deliver the project for me. My call went to her voicemail, and I had to listen to her recorded sales pitch.

"*Hi. You've reached Ruby Armstrong, your E-Z Lips consultant. Leave your name and number after the beep, and tell me when you want to earn oodles of money hosting your own E-Z Lip party.*"

Beep. "Hey. It's me. Your granddaughter. Call me."

Ten minutes later, I was thinking about making my bed when she returned my call. "Hello, dear." She sounded like a worn out three-pack-a-day smoker.

"What's wrong? You sound awful. Have a rough night?" I could picture her sitting in her recliner, wearing the ratty, green chenille robe she only wears when she is sick.

"I just can't party like I used to and I'm paying for it this morning."

I walked out of my bedroom leaving the bed unmade, as usual. "What'd you do?"

"The gals were feeling glam-fabulous after the E-Z Lip party, so we went clubbing."

I had to smother a giggle. Not about clubbing, they do that all the time—the part about feeling glamorous with those silly stenciled lips. "Where'd you go?"

"First we went to Chili's for their happy-hour nachos and margarita special and then hopped over to Benny's for their Saturday night senior deal."

"Which was..." I already knew what it was because she has dragged me there so many times.

"Liver and onions with creamed spinach."

Ruby's favorite dish. One night when I was a junior in high school, she tried to get me to taste it and I blurted, "I can't. I'm a vegetarian." Been one ever since. Well, almost. I eat free-range eggs and occasionally, fish, so I guess that makes me a pescatarian.

She belched a burp a fifth grade boy would have been proud to take credit for and continued. "I had a couple of glasses of chardonnay with dinner, and then for dessert, the bartender bought us a round of tequila shooters. He said it was for the pretty ladies. Isn't that sweet?" Another burp. "Well, one thing led to another, and before ya know it, we'd each bought a round."

"How many of you were there?"

"Six." Ruby burped again. "Woo. Excuse me. Oh, I can taste the liver."

I had just opened the fridge to look for a snack, but that comment did me in, and I slammed the door.

"We'd planned to go to the brew pub downtown and check out the action, but it was already 8:30 by then, so we decided to call it a night."

"You weren't driving, were you?"

"Nooo," she said with pitch-perfect adolescent attitude. "Give me a little credit, will ya? We used the senior dial-a-ride service. The driver was really cute, and I told him all about you and he wants to meet you. His name is Duke."

No way was that going to happen, so I acted like I hadn't heard her. "Ruby, I need a favor."

"What?"

I heard a series of farts in the background, but I took the high road and didn't comment on her toots. "I need you to deliver a job I did for Acme Upholstery. It's due tomorrow, and I can't go because I can't get my lips off."

"I'm surprised. The EZ-Off lotion in the kit should have done the job."

I'd left the kit in the car yesterday while trying to elude the Viking. "I didn't know about the EZ-Off."

"Well, you might try it, although I don't understand why you would want to remove your gorgeous new celebrity lips," she said peevishly and belched again. "You know, I don't feel so good. I think I'll go back to bed, but we'll talk later. I have a good feeling about this Duke fellow."

Not happening.

CHAPTER FIFTEEN

1996

Tuesday, May 7

Phil was still in bed when Erik came in from his midday soccer practice. "You sick or something?" he asked.

"Yeah. Sick of myself."

Erik peeled off his soggy t-shirt and pitched it at the laundry bin. "You need to get over it, man. Life goes on." He opened a dresser drawer and grabbed a t-shirt.

Phil sat up, propping himself against the wall and scrubbed his hands over his dark, two-day stubble. "I'm thinking about turning myself in. Take the punishment I deserve." He squinted against the early afternoon sun glaring through the window.

Erik had one arm through the shirt sleeve and stopped cold. "Are you crazy? What good will that do?"

"At least she'll know how sorry I am. Knowing I'm in prison might help her get over it."

"This isn't just about you, buddy. You do realize that if you turn yourself in, you'll be turning me and Jake in, too. Do you have any idea what happens to guys like us in prison?"

"No worse than what we did." Phil climbed out of bed to adjust the mini blinds, then returned to his bed.

Erik snorted derisively and pulled the shirt on. "Oh, it'll be worse, all right, and we won't be drugged while it's happening. And it will be every day, several times a day. We'll be the prison bitches. Is that really what you want?"

"No. It scares the hell out of me." Phil cleared his constricted throat and whispered, "But I don't know what to do."

Erik paused a moment, staring at Phil's pathetic hang-dog face. It galled him knowing his fate lay in his goody-goody roommate's hands but knew he needed to stay cool. "I don't know what to do, either. But before you do anything, think about this. Turning yourself in will kill your parents. Do our families really deserve to have their lives ruined because of what we did? And for what? Confessing won't undo the damage, Phil." Erik pulled out a desk chair and sat backwards, resting his arms on the chair back. "Listen. I've been thinking."

"That's news."

Erik's tone became defensive. "Believe it or not, I have a conscience, too. No way would I have knowingly done that to a kid. I must've been pretty shit-faced to not realize how young she was."

"So what you're saying is, it's acceptable to drug someone over eighteen for sex, but you draw the line at," Phil finger-quoted, "*under the age of consent.* Glad you have such high standards. You do realize that no matter what age they are, when you slip a girl a roofie, it's still rape, right?"

Erik hung his head, staring at the floor, resisting an urge to get up and punch Phil in the face. "Just hear me out, will ya? I was thinking maybe we could do something nice for her, anonymously. To make amends."

"Like what?"

He raised his head and shrugged his shoulders. "I don't know. Money?"

"You really think money's going to make everything okay for her?"

"No, but it could help. By the time she's old enough for college, I'll have my trust fund. It's more money than I can ever spend, so I won't even miss it. She could go to the school of her choice. Full ride."

Phil rubbed his eyes and yawned. He was achy and exhausted. "What if she remembers? Your money won't help then."

Erik stood and shoved the chair under his desk. "I'm sick of the what-ifs. She's not going to remember because roofies cause amnesia. So technically, I don't have to do a damn thing. I'm just trying to be nice."

CHAPTER SIXTEEN

1996
Thursday, May 9

Six days after the frat party, Phil called home, asking if he'd left his jacket when he'd been there for dinner on Sunday night. It was a ruse to find out if his mom had more information about Lindsay Moore.

"I haven't seen it, honey, but let me go check the front closet." Phil heard her as she walked through the house to the entry area. The door opened and then a moment later, clicked shut.

Penny came back on the line, sounding amused. "As I opened the door, I realized the closet would be the last place you'd leave your jacket."

"Funny, Mom. Hey, anything new going on?"

"Dad and I are going to go look at RVs this afternoon. Want to come?"

"That's cool, but I can't. Too close to finals." Phil was sitting at his desk, doodling Lindsay's name on a legal pad. "Any news on that girl?"

"What girl?"

He broke the pencil lead in frustration. "The girl that got attacked." *Whoa. Lighten up, Phil,* he told himself. *Just keep it cool.* In a calmer voice, he continued, "You know, the girl you told us about during dinner on Sunday."

"Oh, yes. Lindsay Moore. Angela's spoken to her a couple more times and both her friends, too, but still hasn't come up with anything concrete, other than it was a big party in an old house with a funny sign."

"What do you mean, a funny sign?"

"Angela figures it must be a Greek symbol like you have in front of your house. She's already contacted all the fraternity and sorority presidents. Problem is, being this close to the end of term nearly every Greek house had a party last Friday. So the next step is to talk to every chapter member."

Phil gripped his cell phone and tried to control his labored breathing.

"You still there, honey? You're awfully quiet."

"I'm here. Just listening." He was so freaked out by the idea of being interrogated that he could barely hear her words now.

"It's so hard to believe that not one of them knows where they went that night. How could they be so completely oblivious to where they were going?"

"I dunno, Mom," he said, feeling hopeless.

"Just shows you how young and naive those girls are. I mean, those boys could have taken them anywhere and murdered them, for God's sake. Anyway, I think the therapist will be able to help Lindsay remember."

His mind had been wandering, but he caught the word therapist. "She's seeing a therapist?"

"Well, when you consider what she's been through, of course

she's seeing a therapist. Angela's optimistic they'll have a break-through. Her next appointment's right after school tomorrow."

"What do you mean by a breakthrough?"

"Hold on." The screen door to the backyard slammed, which meant she had walked out onto the deck to smoke. He heard the flick of her lighter and a second later, a long exhale. "Okay, much better. I'm down to four a day." She paused.

He knew she was waiting for praise. "That's great, Mom. Really proud of you."

"Thanks. It's not easy." Another puff. "So what did you ask before?"

Phil squeezed his eyes shut and tried to maintain. "I asked—"

"Oh, right. If Lindsay's mother agrees to it, Angela wants to try hypnotherapy."

Phil's pulse was thundering, making it hard to keep his voice normal. "Do you think she'll agree?"

"I know I would. If someone did this to Christy, I'd move heaven and earth to get these monsters and make them pay."

Phil felt lightheaded and clammy. *Maybe I'm hyperventilating.* "So, if this hypnotherapy thing works, they could have these guys in jail by the weekend, huh?"

"That may be a little optimistic. My understanding is, she's not going to remember the actual crime, which I think is a good thing, but the hope is the therapist will be able to guide her through the events leading up to the rape. You know, what the house looked like, the address, a good description of the boys who drugged her. And if it doesn't work, or Lindsay refuses to do it, then Angela will talk to her friends' parents about them doing it."

"But I thought nothing happened to them."

"True, but they all walked to that house, and once we know where the house is, we can get a warrant and forensics will go over every inch with a fine-toothed comb. Her clothes and body were a veritable cesspool of evidence, so it's just a matter of matching up some fibers and hairs, and then there'll be a court order for semen samples. Sorry, I know that's a little too graphic. The whole thing's disgusting and I hope they string those boys up." She inhaled her cigarette and blew out slowly. "Now where do you think you left your jacket?"

"I don't know, Mom."

———

Phil sat at his desk, relating what his mother had said to Erik and Jake. "Even if she just remembers the house, Mom said forensics would go over everything. You know, looking for hairs, fingerprints."

"Shit." Erik jumped off his bed and ripped the sheets off. "First thing in the morning I need to wash these."

"You're kidding," Phil's face puckered with revulsion. "You didn't wash your sheets after what happened? That's disgusting."

Erik tossed the sheets in the corner. "Give me a break, Martha Stewart." He looked under the bed and pulled out some dirty clothes and tossed those in the pile. A barrette bounced on the floor and landed by Jake's desk.

He leaned over and picked it up. "What's this?" He held up the pink, glittery object. "Do you think this is hers?"

Erik snatched it. "Could be anyone's." He pulled a long blond hair from it and had a sudden memory flash of her hair being clipped back. "I'll get rid of it."

Phil got up from his chair and walked to the sheets and crouched. "While you're at it, you better get rid of these, too." He pointed to a pink wad of material on the sheet pile.

Erik leaned over and peered at the object. "Shit." He stuffed the panties and the barrette into his jeans pocket.

"Could be anybody's?" asked Phil, standing up. "What else is in this room for the police to find?"

Erik checked under his bed and around the room. "Nothing."

He sat on his bare mattress and shook his head in dejection. "We're screwed if she goes to that appointment."

"Don't think your money idea's going to get us out of this," said Phil. "It's too late."

"What're you talking about? What money idea?" Jake asked.

"Erik thought we, or rather he, since he's the one with the trust fund, could send her money for college. Anonymously. As atonement," Phil answered, sitting down at his desk again.

But that was before we knew about the hypnotherapy. It was a stupid, dumb-ass idea anyway."

Jake's face lit up with a burst of hope. "No. It could work."

"How? Once she has this hypnotherapy thing, it's only a matter of time before it comes down to us."

"No. No. This really could work, Phil." Jake was excited. "If we can make her see we're not really bad guys, that it was all just a horrible mistake. We were stinkin' drunk and didn't know what we were doing." He paused a beat, building hope and momentum. "We're not that much older than her, so maybe she'll understand how things got out of control. We'll beg her for mercy. And then Erik can still pay for college or whatever."

"First off, we don't even know where she lives. And if we did, then what? Knock on her door and introduce ourselves?" Phil stood up and pantomimed the scene. "Hi, I'm Phil and these are my friends, Erik and Jake. Erik was the one who drugged you, and then we all raped you. We were really, really drunk, so we shouldn't be held responsible for our actions. Please forgive us and if you do, my buddy here," he pointed at Erik, "will pay for your college education."

"Or a car, or both. Whatever," said Erik. "Obviously, we can't go to her house, even if we did know where she lives, but—"

"You two idiots do realize that during her hypnotherapy, the doctor and her mother will be there. Right?" Phil sat back down. "Probably the police detective, too."

Jake wasn't ready to let the idea go. "But if Lindsay refuses to press charges."

Phil shook his head. "She's under eighteen."

Jake deflated and slumped over in his chair, hugging his knees. "What're we going to do?"

Erik pointed at Jake. "Fuckin' pathetic. He's the one who's going to blow this."

Phil ignored Erik and spoke to Jake. "Here's what we do. Tomorrow, first thing, we clean this room top to bottom and throw away the clothes we had on that night. Then wait it out and hope for the best."

Erik shook his head vehemently. "We'll clean the room, but we can't just sit back, twiddling our thumbs and hope everything will be fine. She saw your face, Phil, and she saw mine." He flopped down on his bed and picked up a blanket from the floor to cover himself. "Probably should wash this, too." He switched off his lamp and turned his back on them. "Let's try to get some sleep. We'll figure something out tomorrow."

Jake glanced at Phil and then averted his eyes. "No way I can sleep. Must be nice to have no conscience."

"I have a conscience, Jake. I'm just not going to let it ruin my life." After a minute Erik rolled over and said, "I talked to your sister today. About Lindsay."

"What?" asked Phil. "Why?"

"I figured they both go to Santa Lucia High, so I asked Christy if she knows her."

"You what?" Phil shouted in astonishment.

The neighboring room pounded on the wall and hollered, "Shut the fuck up."

Phil stepped over to Erik and leaned into his face. "Are you crazy? Does my mom know you talked to Christy?"

"No. I saw her after school in the parking lot."

"Didn't she think it was a little weird?" asked Jake. "You showing up out of the blue and asking about Lindsay?"

"Give me some credit, will ya?" Erik sat up. "I told her what your mom said about if we heard anything to let her know. So I said I thought it might help if I knew what she looked like."

"You don't even remember what she looks like?" said Phil. "You're the one who slipped her the roofie."

"I kind of remember, but what can I say? I was really drunk. I do remember she was a blond. Cute. That's about it."

Phil moved to his bed and sat. "What did my sister say?"

"She said that Lindsay has really long blond hair, pretty blue eyes, and waits by the flagpole everyday after school for her mom to pick her up."

"That's it?" asked Jake.

Erik continued reluctantly. "She also said she thought it was cool that I wanted to help out."

CHAPTER SEVENTEEN

1996
Friday, May 10

Friday marked one week since Phil's life had been forever destroyed by a few moments of blinding, drunk lust. If arrested, he'd be listed as a sex-offender for the rest of his life, which would be ironic considering his limited sexual experience.

The first time was with his high school girlfriend, Chloe. He'd been hopelessly in love with her and had thought they would marry someday. They dated for nearly two years, never going past heavy foreplay, and then a few days before senior prom, Chloe's father had told her he'd accepted a job in Chicago, and they would be moving as soon as the school year was over. The kids were devastated, and on the night of the prom, their tears led to passionate intercourse in the backseat of Phil's car. When she left, they swore they'd be together again, but youth, distance, and time dimmed their ardor. The last he'd heard from Chloe, she was planning to backpack through Europe with a group of friends.

The second time was with a girl he'd dated briefly the previous fall. After a few dates, Danielle was already talking marriage, and one evening, as he tried to explain that he needed to finish college and get established in his career before he could consider marriage, she had ripped off her top and shoved her hand down his pants, and he'd lost it. A few days later, a friend warned him that Danielle was already almost four months pregnant, and her parents would disown her if they found out she was an unwed mother. After that, Phil decided to put dating on hold until he graduated.

Phil showered, scouring his body roughly with a back brush, wishing he could cleanse his conscience as easily. He toweled off, wrapped the towel around his waist, and wiped the steam from the mirror to shave but found he couldn't look at himself.

He padded down the hall to his room and found his roommates sitting on the floor, sharing a joint. "I thought we were cleaning the room."

"We're working on it," said Erik. "The sheets are in the washer."

Jake inhaled deeply, savoring the calming effect, and slowly released a stream of smoke. He held out the joint to Phil, who shook his head. "I think we've come up with a plan that might work." He passed the cigarette to Erik. "It's what we were talking about last night actually. We talk to her before her appointment and beg her to forgive us."

"And pay her off?"

"Whatever it takes to ensure we all have a future, including Lindsay," answered Jake.

"So how are we going to talk to her?"

Erik took a drag, squinting his eyes as he exhaled, then passed the joint back to Jake and rubbed his hands together. "It's really very simple. Your sister said that Lindsay's mom picks her up at the flagpole everyday after school. I would assume that since she has the therapist appointment this afternoon, she'll be waiting for her mother in the usual spot. The plan is to get there before her mom does and plead our case."

"That's it? Just walk up to her and ask for forgiveness?"

"More like throw ourselves at her feet and beg for mercy," Erik glanced at Jake, who averted his eyes, "but yeah, pretty much."

"So, why did you look at Jake just now?"

"No reason," he said, glancing away.

"Is there something you're not telling me?"

Erik paused for a second, as if giving Phil's question deep thought. "Nope. Nothing I can think of."

Phil shook his head slowly in disgust. "It's an idiotic plan and I don't want to talk to her. I don't deserve her mercy."

"What are you? A priest or something?" said Erik. "Okay, you don't have to talk to her. Just wait in the car while we talk to her. Will that work for you, Father Phil?"

Phil ignored Erik's sarcasm as he pulled on a pair of sweatpants and a hoodie. "If your plan backfires, and it will, I'm turning myself in before they find us and arrest us."

"Have a little faith, will ya?" Erik chuckled at his humor. "This'll work."

Phil opened the door. "I need some air. I'm going for a walk."

"School's out at three, so be back by two," said Erik.

"Whatever," Phil shouted from down the hall.

"Okay, that actually went well," said Erik. "I was counting on him not wanting to talk to Lindsay."

"So, we're not going to tell him everything?" Jake stubbed the joint out in an Altoids tin.

"Are you kidding? He'll blow it and get us all turned in. We're doing this my way, I mean, our way, and if she freaks, we'll have to get out of town fast. I'll go to the ATM and get a wad of cash just in case."

"But if things go well, what if he *still* decides to turn himself in? I know this is eating him up. Really goes against the whole Eagle Scout thing."

Erik's dark scowl frightened Jake and his next words chilled him to the bone. "That would be a bad choice, wouldn't it? For all of us." Then he laughed and slapped his knees. "Lighten up, dude! Quit worrying about all the what-ifs. Life's too short."

———

Erik and Jake weren't around when Phil returned to the house, so he waited on the shabby, plaid sofa on the front porch. At 2:06, they strolled up the flagstone path and flopped next to him.

Erik slumped low, crossing his ankles on the porch railing. "You ready?"

Phil eyed the brown plastic bag Jake cradled on his lap. "What's in the bag?"

"Nothing—"

Erik cut in, "Got your keys?"

Phil patted his front pocket. "Why?"

"You have the biggest car, so you should drive." Erik stood and stretched. "Might as well get going then."

"What's the big rush? School's not out 'til three."

"No rush." He stuffed his hands into his pockets and shrugged nonchalantly. "I'd rather get over there and be ready to talk to her the minute she walks out, that's all." He looked sheepish. "Maybe I'm a little nervous, too. A lot's riding on this."

Phil's bronze Ford Explorer was parked a short distance down the block. When they were buckled in, Erik asked, "How's your gas?"

"Why? It's not that far to the school."

"Just don't want any delays. This is our only chance to talk to her, and it would suck if we ran out of gas on the way there. So, how's your gas?"

"I filled the tank yesterday, Mother." Phil put the SUV in gear and pulled away from the curb.

Jake spoke from the backseat. "Would you mind stopping at 7-11? I want to get a water."

Phil shook his head and muttered, "Whatever."

He parked in the shade near a blue metal ice bin and waited while Jake and Erik went into the store. After a few minutes, they returned with a bag full of waters, sodas, and snacks.

"What's all that? I thought you were just getting a water," said Phil.

"This is for all of us." Jake climbed into the backseat and set the bag all the way in the back.

"It's not like we're going on a friggin' road trip. We'll be home in an hour."

Erik pulled a flask out of his pocket, swallowed a few gulps. "Woo!" He held it out to Phil. "Want some liquid courage?"

Phil waved it away. "You think getting tanked is a good idea? Isn't that what got us here in the first place?"

"No worries." Erik put the flask back into his pocket.

"What if her mother shows up before she comes out?" Phil asked.

"Then we're out of there." Erik poked him good-naturedly in the arm. "But I'm feeling optimistic."

Phil turned to Jake in the backseat. "Are you really on board with this?"

Jake looked bleak and avoided Phil's eyes. "I don't see a lot of options."

CHAPTER EIGHTEEN

MONDAY · APRIL 15

Posted by Katy McKenna

Today was supposed to be an auspicious day—my first paycheck in my new life. A symbol of my independence from Chad, who now shall be forever known as my "was-band."

I was delivering my first freelance job since my former life, so I spent extra time dolling up. I did a twenty minute makeup instead of five, ten of which were spent trying to conceal my allergic reaction to the E-Z Off remover lotion. I gathered my hair in a loose side-braid instead of a ponytail, and dressed in a more upscale version of my regulation central coast uniform. I included a pair of cute lime green wedgies that I haven't worn in eons because they aren't very comfortable, but I was driving, not walking, so no problem. I was ready for the big day.

I wrote up a bill and scrawled "due upon receipt of work" on the top. We'd already agreed to this, but I thought it would eliminate any possibility of Wanda saying she'd send me a check. Back when I originally had done this for a living, I was stiffed more than once when the check "in the mail" never arrived.

I knew it was my lucky day when I scored a parking space in front of Acme's entrance, and the meter had thirty-three minutes left on it. I pulled my portfolio from the backseat, locked the door, and walked to the entrance. It was locked. I peered in the window —it was dark inside. I started to fume and then noticed the note on the door.

Closed for a Death in the Family

Oh, no. Had Wanda died? Then it dawned on me that if she were dead, who would pay me? All right, that was beneath me, but I had worked hard on the stupid Acme volcano. It was not my fault she'd died.

My next thought was maybe it wasn't Wanda who'd died. Perhaps it was her husband, if she had a husband. I had her cell number in my contacts, so I decided to call her and say something like, "Hey, Wanda, I'm running late." That way she wouldn't know that I already knew about the funeral. If she answered.

Problem was, my purse was locked in the car with my phone and keys inside it. Brilliant. There was nothing left to do but look for a payphone.

After walking several blocks in my wretched wedgies, I concluded that pay phones are now officially extinct. Evidently, everyone on the planet has a cell phone, even the well-dressed homeless man I'd passed a block ago.

My feet were killing me, my portfolio was growing heavier by the minute, and the thought of walking any further literally made me nauseated. I considered lying on the sidewalk and waiting for someone with a cell phone to call the paramedics, but instead I turned around and trudged back towards the homeless man, wincing with every excruciating step.

When I reached him, he was leaning on a Whole Foods shopping cart, filled with his earthly possessions—including a golf bag bungie-corded to the side. He was in the midst of an animated conversation on his phone. "You can't squeeze blood from a rock. Thanks to you, I'm flat broke, b-r-o-k-e, broke. Tell your *boyfriend* you need an eyelash perm."

I got his attention and pantomimed the universal phone gesture: May I use your phone? He looked relieved to have an excuse to get off the phone and nodded yes.

"Got to go, Nina. The attorney's calling on the other line."

He held out the phone to me. "That's what I get for marrying a hot, young trophy wife. What the hell was I thinking?"

I took the phone. "Thank you. Just need to make a quick call and can't find a pay phone anywhere."

"Tell me about it," he replied churlishly. "Damned inconvenient."

"The call is local," I continued in a fluster.

"No worries. Got the unlimited family plan." He noted my surprised look and shrugged his shoulders in resignation. "What can I say? I was downsized out of my job, alimony has drained me dry, the bank took my condo, and I lost a veneer this morning. But I have the family plan, so my kids can text me to ask for money I don't have. There you have it, my life in a nutshell. How's your day going?"

I opted not to complain about my aching tootsies. "Fine."

Mom was working, so I called Ruby. Thank goodness she answered. I asked her to meet me at Acme. No way was I waiting for her with the disgruntled homeless man, even if it meant crawling to my car.

I handed back his phone and thanked him, and in return I got asked out on a date. I have no idea what we would have done, maybe take in a meal at the local soup kitchen, but I demurely declined, feeling flattered that he thought I was hot until I heard his parting shot as I limped away.

"No more hot babes for me. No sir-ee. I have learned my

lesson. Nothing but trouble. From now on it'll be simple, uncomplicated, plain lookin' gals who are appreciative."

Hey, everyone says that in a certain light, I look a lot like Anne Hathaway. She is definitely not plain.

Three blocks later, I hobbled around the corner and beheld the glorious sight of Ruby standing beside her red '63 Triumph Spitfire.

"Grandmommy..." I lurched towards her, arms outstretched, face contorted in agony. She dodged me and I collapsed against the car.

"Good grief. What happened to you? You look like a zombie."

"My feet. They're killing me." I yanked off my wicked wedgies and rubbed a blossoming bunion.

"Cute shoes. New?"

"No, I just never wear them when I have to actually walk."

"Yeah, I can see where that might be too much to expect from a pair of shoes," said the stiletto queen.

"Well, they're going in the Goodwill bag." I tossed them onto the car floor and collapsed into the passenger seat. It felt so good to sit down.

"Maybe I'll give 'em a whirl." Ruby got into the driver's seat and we buckled up. The top was down, so she offered me a scarf from a collection she keeps stashed behind the passenger seat.

I debated a moment. Scarf hair or wind hair. Scarf hair won. "Ruby? Am I plain?"

"You are most definitely not plain. You're gorgeous. Why would you ask such a silly thing?"

Of course my grandma is going to tell me I am beautiful; that's her job. "A mean man said I'm plain," I answered glumly.

"Well, he needs to get his eyes checked. You've got my green eyes, my auburn hair——"

"Your hair's blond."

"The blond is helping me transition to gray."

"You've been transitioning ever since I've known you."

"I was prematurely going gray, and it wasn't working for me." She pulled a pink paper from her pocket and handed it to me. "Not your lucky day, huh?"

"What's this?" I glanced at it. "A thirty-five dollar parking ticket? Are you kidding me? Why'd I get a ticket? I still have lots of time left on the meter."

"Because when I got here, you didn't." She started the car, revved the engine to its maximum RPMs, and peeled away from the curb. "Let's go get your key."

I love her little sports car, a gift from Gramps when Grandma had been diagnosed with breast cancer in her fifties, but I never feel safe with just a lap belt, especially the way she drives. Fast and furious. Heck, with Ruby driving, I probably wouldn't feel safe in an Army tank.

"I should have called this morning and warned you." She shifted into third.

"About what?"

"Last night I decided to do a card reading about this Duke fellow. You know the Dial-A-Ride driver? He seems like a nice young man, but you never can be too sure. Sure would hate to set you up with a serial killer. Anyway, a couple of cards came up indicating today would have been a good day for you to lie low. But I knew you wouldn't listen, so against my better judgment, I kept my mouth shut."

I was clutching the dashboard and gritting my teeth as we zoomed through town at warp speed. "Am I in imminent danger?"

"No. I would have warned you if that was the case."

"Ruby!" I shouted frantically, slamming my foot on my phantom brake to no avail. We were about two hundred feet from an intersection. "The light's yellow. Slow down."

"Relax. We've got plenty of time. It's just a soft yellow." She floored it, and we sailed through as the light turned red. "See?"

In record-breaking time, we arrived at my house in a squeal of brakes. It took me a moment to compose myself before pulling off the scarf and shakily fumbling for the door handle.

"Hold the phone." Ruby pointed through the windshield. "Who's the stud muffin mowing his lawn?"

"Oh, that's Josh, my next door neighbor. You met him the other day when he came in through my window, remember?"

"When you wet your pants?"

"Yes," I muttered.

"Well, you'd think I would've remembered him." She smiled appreciatively or should I say, lasciviously? "He must work out. Look at those buns. Mmmm-mmm."

"*Ok-a-a-y*... I'm going to go get the key now. You wait here." I scrambled out of the car before she could scorch my ears with more smutty remarks about my neighbor's hot bod, and padded barefoot up my front walk to the door, and then it dawned on me that I didn't have a key. Rats. Why hadn't I hidden one outside after moving in? Daisy barked on the other side of the door, and I assured her it was me, which turned the barking into whining and sniffing at the threshold. Too bad she couldn't open the door.

"Hi, Cookie." The Viking sauntered across the lawn, dressed in board shorts and a tight, white tank top that enhanced his rippling, bronze muscles.

OMG. Be still my heart.

He climbed the porch steps, flashing his dazzling, toothy smile, "I couldn't help noticing you standing there, looking troubled. Are you locked out?" His eyes swept down my body to my bare feet. "Wow. What is that thing on your foot?"

"Nothing." I self-consciously set my left foot over my right foot's burgeoning bunion and then I caught sight of Ruby climbing out of the car. "Stay in the car!" I hollered, waving her back. "This'll only take a sec." I didn't want her talking to Josh. There was no telling what she might say. She ignored me and sprinted up the walk, leaping up the steps in her five-inch heels.

"Helllooo," she panted, unabashedly ogling him. "Katy, who's your handsome neighbor?"

I'll kill her later. "Josh, this is my grandmother, Ruby. Ruby, this is Josh, the, uh, my neighbor," I stammered. I'd almost said "the Viking."

Josh turned his blinding smile on Grandma. "Hi, Ruby. I remember you from the other day." He leaned forward and gave her a quick hug.

"You do?" Ruby was close to swooning. "Oh, yes. That's right. When Katy wet—"

"YUP! I'M LOCKED OUT!" I crossed my eyes and twiddled my finger by my ear. "Silly me."

"Maybe I can help you. Be right back."

He vaulted the porch railing, neatly clearing the bed of red geraniums below and jogged to his house, unaware of the immense pleasure he was giving Ruby... and me.

"Oh, would I like to play some backseat bingo with that fella." Ruby patted her chest as she watched him, then turned to me with her hands on her hips. "Tell me why you're not dating him?"

"For starters, I barely know the guy, and besides, I'm not ready to get serious about anyone."

"Oh, sweetie, I'm not talking about getting serious. I'm talking about getting laid."

"Grandmother. Really." I sounded like a Victorian prude. It was one thing for Samantha to suggest that but my grandma? Eew.

"Kiddo, if I was forty years younger—"

"Forty years ago you were married to Gramps," I righteously reminded her.

She smiled softly with a faraway look in her eyes. "Yes, I was. My cowboy."

"Gramps? A cowboy? I thought he was a high school English teacher."

She shook her head. "Oh, Katy. You don't have a romantic bone in your body, do you?"

"I used to."

She patted my arm. "You will again, sweetheart, but in the meantime... oh, here he comes."

Josh dashed up the steps, two at a time, holding an odd looking tool that he fanned out like a Swiss army knife, and bent down in front of the doorknob. "This may take a few minutes. Is the alarm on?"

"Yes."

"Hopefully I won't set it off, but I'm a little rusty at this."

"You're going to pick the lock?" I suddenly wondered who this Josh person really was. "What are you? Some kind of cat burglar or something?"

He laughed without taking his eyes off his task. "No. I'm a P.I."

"Huh?"

Ruby answered for Josh. "Private investigator. Gumshoe, flat-foot, sleuth, snoop. You know, like Jim Rockford, Thomas Magnum, Jessica Fletcher, Barnaby Jones, Sherlock Holmes."

I narrowed my eyes at her and smiled patiently. "Yeah. I know what a private investigator is, Ruby. Like *Angel* and *Veronica Mars*. I've just never actually met one before."

"I'm afraid it's not nearly as interesting, exciting, or as dangerous as the TV shows make it out to be. Same for the cop shows. Which I was," he said as he deftly inserted two different picks into the lock and slowly tested it. "Nope." He tried another combination and nothing happened.

"Why aren't you a cop anymore?" I asked.

"I was a detective. Undercover narcotics." He tried another pick in the lock. "Really hard on marriages. Mine included."

Ruby couldn't let that go by. "So you quit the department to save your marriage?"

"I wish. No, unfortunately, the marriage was over before I figured it out."

She jabbed me in the arm with her bony elbow and raised her eyebrows at me as he inserted another pick.

"Okay, I think this is the one. Oh, yeah, baby. This feels sooo...

gooood."

You can probably guess what was going through my mind as Josh was sweet-talking the lock. I looked at Ruby and she was right there with me. *Oh, yeah. Bingo!*

"Got it." Josh glanced up at me. "As soon as I open the door, run in and disable the alarm."

He opened the door and I turned off the alarm while Daisy did a happy dance.

I turned to Josh, noticing his incredible periwinkle blue eyes for the first time. And he was taller than my 5'9" by several inches. I felt petite.

"Thank you so much. I don't know what I would have done without your help." I may have batted my eyelashes.

"No problemo," he said, gazing deep into my eyes, our two souls merging into one. "Would you—"

Yes. Yes. I will marry you.

"—consider putting a spare key outside?"

Okay, it was too soon for marriage. Maybe Ruby's idea was better. Get laid. "I could get one of those fake rocks."

"No. Not a good idea. And neither is under the doormat or a flower pot. Might as well leave the door unlocked."

During this exchange Ruby had not said a word, but I caught the smirk on her face.

"Well... uh... I guess I better get my keys..." I tore myself away from his embracing eyes to get the spare key to my car.

"And shoes," Ruby added.

"I better get back to my lawn. It's not going to mow itself." He turned to Ruby. "I look forward to seeing you again."

Ruby was beside herself with glee as she attempted to break the sound barrier on the way back to Acme. "Wow. I could almost see the steam rising between you two." She was practically cackling. "And then when he said he looked forward to seeing *me* again... Well, I don't have to tell you what *that* meant."

"What?" I was a little spacey or was this horniness? I wasn't sure; it had been so long.

"He's going to ask you out." She slapped my knee and laughed. "What you need right now is a transition man. A hot he-man who'll show you a good time, and honey, Josh fills the bill nicely. Mmm-mmm."

I was way past transition and thinking about having the Viking's babies when we pulled up to the curb near Acme. I leaned over and gave her a smooch.

"Keep me posted, Katy. I want all the juicy details. I'm so excited."

I got out, grabbed my portfolio from behind the seat, and watched her lay rubber as she drove away. I'd keep her posted, but I wasn't sure about sharing all the juicy details. Oh, please, let there be some.

I was surprised to find the Acme door propped open, so I fed the voracious meter and went in.

Wanda sat at her desk behind the counter cuddling Doris, both looking forlorn.

"Hey, Wanda. I'm so sorry." I had no idea what I was sorry about, but her gloomy, mascara-streaked face crushed me. "Is there anything I can do?"

She pulled a tissue from a box on her desk and dabbed her eyes. "No." Her voice choked and she blew her red nose.

Doris creaked a long, mournful yowl.

"It's okay, baby." Wanda stroked the ancient cat. "No parent should ever be put through the agony of outliving their child."

"Oh, Wanda. I had no idea." I tossed my portfolio on the counter and ran around the counter to the chair next to her and sat down, taking her hand in mine. "Why are you here? You should be home in bed."

"Life has to go on. The living must go on. It's what he would have wanted." She lifted her head and looked around the shop. "This place meant everything to him. It will be so empty without him."

"How old was he?" I asked, without thinking whether it was any of my business or not.

She broke down into gut-wrenching sobs. "One hundred and twenty-five."

It was Dave who'd passed. Good old Dave.

"His heart gave out. I tried to revive him, even called the paramedics, but it was too late. He died in my a-a-rms."

Doris leaned forward and gave my hand a half-hearted chomp that broke my heart. I needed to let these two mourn in peace, so I told her I'd call in a few days.

———

I had the rest of the afternoon free and after hearing about Dave, I honored his memory by taking my best furry gal-pal, Daisy, to the park. We hadn't been there in a while, so when I said, "Wanna go to the doggie park?" she went berserk. Of course, using the right tone, I probably could have said anything and she would have gone berserk, like, "Wanna go to the mall and watch Mommy try on bathing suits and cry?"

Usually we go to the large regional park just off Highway One, but I changed it up and drove to the one at Lago Park on the west end of town. As I drove in, Daisy noticed the ducks hanging out in the lake skirting the road and her tail thumped against the seat in anticipation.

"Oh, darn it. I forgot my shotgun, so I guess you won't be jumping in the lake and retrieving dead ducks. Poor Daisy."

After releasing my squirming girl from her backseat tether, she dragged me to the entrance gates. The first gate was no problem, but the second was blocked by the dogs inside who couldn't wait for Daisy to enter. Finally, she was free to romp, and I collapsed on a bench next to an older man doing needlepoint.

He saw me glance at his project. "It was the one thing I simply could not give up after my sex change operation."

I had nothing to say to that, so I smiled and nodded like a bobble-head.

"I'm kidding," he said with a devilish grin. "I do needlepoint to calm my nerves. Beats the hell out of Xanax."

I looked at his project, a cute puppy chasing a ball.

"I make them into pillows and give them to kids at the women's shelter."

"How nice," I replied, thinking what a dear man he was.

"It's the least I can do," he said.

Daisy ran to me and gave my flip-flopped feet a lick, then dashed back to her new best friends.

"Nice dog," said my bench mate.

"Which one is yours?" I asked.

"Don't have a dog, just like watching them play. I used to go to the park and watch the kids, but some of the parents started giving me odd looks, like I'm a predator or something." He sighed. "I understand where they're coming from given how many I defended through the years, but I'm just a grandpa who misses his grandkids. So now I watch the dogs, soak up the sun, and do my needlepoint."

"Ever think about getting a dog?"

"One of these days, I will. This is like window-shopping for me. Right now, I'm leaning towards a Labrador. Never met one I didn't like."

I figured it was time to introduce myself. "My name's Katy and that's Daisy."

She heard her name and streaked over to say hello to my new friend.

"Hello, Daisy." He scratched the scruff of her neck. "I'm Ben."

Daisy gave him an appreciative kiss on his hand and dashed off to wrestle a Boxer.

"I take it you're an attorney."

"Was. Retired now and glad of it." He did a few delicate stitches to the puppy's nose and then continued. "I was a criminal attorney in Los Angeles for over forty years. The sad reality of the job is that most of the people you defend are guilty as sin." He paused, resting his handiwork on his lap. "Somewhere in the midst of all that, I lost my humanity. It all became a game for me. A game I had to win, no matter how heinous the crime was. My wife kept begging me to stop, said I was no longer the man she married. After forty-five years of marriage, she gave up and left me."

"Is that why you retired?"

"Yes." He cleared his throat and pinched his tear ducts under his wire-rims. "So, Katy, my dear, what is it about you that just made me unload on you?"

I considered his question a moment. "Sometimes it's easier to talk to a complete stranger about your troubles than to tell a friend."

"Or a shrink. I tried that and was given antidepressants, which made me feel worse."

"So you do needlepoint—"

"And volunteer at the women's shelter and do pro bono work. I've got a lot of making up to do." He smiled at me. "I feel like Jacob Marley dragging around a heavy chain of sins."

Daisy came to me panting and collapsed at my feet. "She's done." I leaned down and clipped her leash to her halter. "How often do you come to the park, Ben?" I asked as I stood to leave.

"Oh, three, four times a week, around this time of day. Maybe I'll see you again."

"I look forward to that."

He gave Daisy another scratch behind the ears and we went to the gate, this time to fight our way out of the park without releasing the other dogs crowding us.

Walking back to the car, I thought about Ben. Silver hair, wire-rimmed specs, goatee, snappy dresser, and somewhere around Ruby's age. That's right, I was thinking about doing a little match-making. But first I'd need a few more visits with him to see if I get any red flags.

CHAPTER NINETEEN

1996
Friday, May 10

Seventh period was study hall for Lindsay and Jenny. In Lindsay's former life, they would have been whispering, stifling giggle fits, and passing notes, but now she felt claustrophobic in the crowded, stuffy room and longed to be out in the fresh air.

She whispered to Jenny to take her backpack home, telling her she'd pick it up later, then asked the teacher's aide for permission to go to the bathroom, which she did so she wouldn't be lying. Afterward she went out to the flagpole where her mom would be picking her up in thirty minutes. She sat on the lawn and leaned against the pole, using her purple cardigan as a back cushion.

No one was out there, and Lindsay wasn't worried about getting into trouble; she figured she was due some slack after what she'd gone through. She wished it were already tomorrow when her hypnotherapy session would be behind her. She closed her eyes and tried to think happy thoughts.

The flag snapped in the light breeze, its rope clanging against the hollow metal pole. A chain-link privacy fence about thirty feet behind her shielded the swimming pool and she heard cheers and whistles blowing for a swim meet in progress.

Next year she wanted to join the swim team, but with cheer-leading and yearbook committee, it might be too much. Keeping her grades up was critical. She was thinking about becoming a vet or a marine biologist, but she really liked fashion design, too.

Lulled by the warm sun and the familiar, comforting sounds around her, she dozed off.

———

Phil drove into the high school parking lot at 2:37 and stopped under an oak tree at the edge of the lot near the street. "I don't see any empty spaces."

The school, originally built for a maximum student body of 1,500 was now educating over 3,000. Cars crowded every conceivable spot and school officials had long given up handing out citations.

"I don't believe it. There she is." Erik pointed towards the flag-pole on the other side of the lot.

Phil checked the dashboard clock. "Why is she out there already?"

"Who the hell cares?" Erik punched Phil's arm. "This is our lucky break. Let's go."

"Maybe we should wait," Jake said from the backseat. "This doesn't feel right."

"I agree," said Phil. "What if her mother's picking her up early? This is a stupid idea. We should just go." He put the car in gear.

"And lose a perfect opportunity? This could be our only chance, and we're sitting here wasting time." Erik turned in his seat, pinning Jake with an icy glare, each word enunciated slowly. "Let's just do this like we planned, okay?"

Jake squirmed under Erik's defiance. "You're probably right."

"Damn straight, I'm right." He turned to face the front. "Let's quit wasting time and do this."

Phil put the car in gear and creeped through the parking lot, slowly closing the gap between him and what he knew could only be disaster. His eyes darted around the lot, searching for a car coming that could be Lindsay's mother.

"You're driving like an old lady," snapped Erik, smacking the dashboard. "Let's move it."

"Don't really think it's a good idea to call attention to ourselves." Phil eased the Ford Explorer to the curb near the flagpole. He gazed through the passenger window at Lindsay and was surprised to see her eyes were closed. The rustle of a plastic bag distracted him and he turned to see Jake taking something out of the brown plastic bag he'd been carrying when they had met on the frat house porch. "What's in the—"

"Look at her. She's asleep," Erik whispered. "I can't friggin' believe our luck. Jake, forget those. We don't need them yet. Let's go."

Jake dropped the bag to the rubber floor mat.

"Need what?" asked Phil, but he didn't get an answer because they were scrambling out of the car.

Erik leaned back in and whispered, "Keep the motor running."

"For God's sake, we're not robbing a bank."

"True. But if her mom shows up, we need—"

"Go." Phil watched them move toward her. *This is wrong. Why did I let myself get talked into this?*

His internal alarms clanged into overdrive when he saw them skirting around her and approaching her from behind.

———

Lindsay was dozing, when she was suddenly jolted awake and roughly hauled to her feet. Her brain frantically struggled to make sense of her predicament as she found herself being dragged through the grass to a vehicle at the curb. Finally her brain connected with her mouth, and she screamed.

Erik snarled in her ear, "Shut the fuck up and get in."

From the SUV, Phil shouted, "What're you doing?"

Lindsay struggled furiously and screamed again. The back door was open and her head was forced down to the seat. Her shins slammed against the steel threshold, pitching her forward, landing hard on the leather backseat. Jake grabbed her arms and yanked her across the seat. She felt her legs shoved into the floor of the car and then something heavy settled on her back, jamming her face into the seat, pinning her head against something soft and crushing the breath out of her.

The doors slammed. "Let's go!" Erik ordered.

"No. This is wrong," pleaded Phil.

"He's right, Erik," said Jake. He sat to the left of Lindsay, and it was his thigh her head was pressing into. "I don't know what I was thinking, but I didn't know it would be like this. This is wrong. Really wrong. Let's let her go and get out of here."

"Too late now. What's done is done. Let's just get outta here before someone sees us."

The car started moving and Lindsay felt a soft bump as it rolled over a speed bump before exiting the parking lot. She struggled to raise her head to suck in air and realized Erik was sitting on her back. He punched her hard on the shoulder and told her to lie still.

"God!" shouted Jake. "You don't have to hit her."

"Erik," said Phil, "you didn't tell me you were going to grab her."

"Because you never would have agreed. Do you really think we could have stood out there and had a nice little chat with her? Seriously, Phil?"

"Oh God," said Phil. "What have you done?"

"We're all in this together so just keep driving, Phil."

Lindsay panted shallow breaths, trying to silently inhale air. Her heart rate was nearing the explosion point, her vision blurring into a sparkling mist. Starved for oxygen, she finally choked raggedly for breath.

"Erik. Get off her. She can't breathe," said Jake.

"Not while we're in town. Somebody might see her."

Erik spoke next to her ear. She could taste his whiskey breath as she gasped desperately for oxygen. "When I let you up, you gotta promise not to do anything, or I will fucking kill you."

"Erik. Cut it out," said Phil. "No one's going to hurt you, Lindsay." A minute later he said, "Okay, we're on the freeway. Let her up."

"First we have to put these on," said the voice to her left, pulling rubber masks out of the plastic bag he'd left on the car floor. "Here, Phil." He tossed it on the front seat.

"I'm not putting that on. No way, Jake."

"Do it," said Erik, "so she doesn't see your face."

"I don't care if she sees my face," said Phil. "What difference does it make?"

"If she sees our faces she can describe us," the one called Jake said. "So this is not only for our safety but for hers, too."

Erik moved to the right and jerked her to a sitting position, giving her a startling glimpse of his masked face. A grinning President Clinton.

Now able to breathe, her head cleared, and she glanced out the window. The car was on 101 heading north out of town to the grade. *Where are they taking me? Why is this happening?* The man to her left wore a hoodie with a USL logo on it, sending a new flood of terror through her. *Oh God, it must be them.* She knew instinctively not to let them know her discovery. Lindsay dropped her eyes to her trembling hands on her lap and tried to control her rising panic. Her mother's voice whispered in her head, "Focus and breathe. Focus and breathe."

As she willed her escalating blood pressure down, she remembered an *Oprah* show she'd watched with her mom a few months ago. It was about what to do when you found yourself in a dangerous situation. *What did the man say? Don't act afraid. Tell them your name so it becomes more personal.*

No one spoke as the car topped the long grade and began its descent. After a few minutes, Erik said, "Turn at Santa Sicomoro."

"What exactly is your plan?" asked Phil.

"Don't worry about it. Just drive through town and I'll tell you when to turn."

Lindsay couldn't stand it anymore and blurted, "Why are you doing this to me?"

"We want to talk to you, that's all," Erik said, his voice muffled by the grinning mask.

"Why? I don't even know who you are." *Tell them your name so it becomes more personal.* "M-my name's Lindsay."

"That's a relief," he said snidely. "It'd be a real bummer if we'd grabbed the wrong girl."

She didn't want to cry in front of them, but the tears flowed anyway. *Are they going to rape me again?* "Please let me go," she whispered, her voice choking. "I swear I won't tell anyone."

The boy in the hoodie turned to her. She shuddered when she saw the Arnold Schwarzenegger *Terminator* mask he wore. "You don't need to be afraid. We're not going to hurt you. But no more talking until we get there, okay? Then we'll discuss everything and you can go home."

"Yeah, then you can go home." Erik mimicked Jake, snuggling an arm around her thin, quivering shoulders. "Don't worry about it. Just chill." She tried to wriggle out from under his arm, which made him snicker and squeeze her tighter.

Phil saw this in the rearview mirror. "God. Leave her alone, Erik. She's just a kid."

"Not the way I remember it. She wanted it bad the other

night." His hand snaked down her front and pinched her small breast. "Didn't you, girl?"

She twisted away from him and crossed her arms over her breasts. "I-I d-don't know what you're talking about." She'd recognized Erik's voice as the creepy guy at the frat party who'd given her a Dr. Pepper.

The SUV drove slowly through the small town of Santa Sicomoro, sticking to the speed limit. As they passed several small businesses and homes clustered within the downtown limits, Lindsay frantically looked about for someone on the street. She would bang on the window and scream, and they would see the license plate and call the police, maybe even get in their car and save her, but the sidewalks were empty.

Erik noticed her eyes darting back and forth and chuckled. "No one out there to help you, *Lind-say*."

Jake slammed the front seat with his hand. "Quit screwing with her, Erik."

"Been there and done that."

CHAPTER TWENTY

1996
Friday, May 10

At 2:57, Belinda Moore parked by the flagpole to wait for her daughter. The school bells sounded at 3:00, and moments later, students poured through the gates into the parking lot. At 3:10, the school buses were leaving and she was losing patience. She wanted Lindsay to have time for a snack before her 4:00 appointment with Dr. Greenburg.

"She must be talking to friends and has lost track of time," she said aloud. She got out of the minivan, walked around to the passenger side and leaned against the vehicle, arms crossed in irritation, watching the gate.

A sudden wind gust snapped the flag rope against the metal pole and Belinda turned her head, looking up at the flag. Then she noticed a purple sweater at the foot of the pole. A split second later it struck her that it looked like Lindsay's favorite sweater. She ran to it, snatching it up, knowing instinctively that something was wrong.

She clutched the mohair sweater to her breast and rushed to the school office. The secretary was straightening papers on the counter when Belinda burst through the doors. "Have you seen Lindsay? I can't find her!"

Mrs. Watkins knew what had happened to Lindsay and when she saw the panicked look on Belinda's face, she was immediately concerned. "No, I haven't. Did she know you were coming?"

"Yes! I was supposed to pick her up at the flagpole, right after school." Belinda's shaky hand grasped at the secretary's bony hands as she fought back tears. "She knows she has a doctor's appointment."

"She probably got sidetracked and doesn't realize the time," she said in a convincing, lighthearted tone she didn't feel. "I have worried parents in here all the time looking for their kids. Often they forget and start walking home, totally oblivious."

Belinda visibly calmed down. "You're probably right. I'm over-reacting." Then she remembered the sweater she held clasped to her chest. "No, I'm not." She held out the sweater for Mrs. Watkins to see. "I found this on the ground by the flagpole. It's her favorite." She pointed at the label. "See? It has her name on the label."

Mrs. Watkins put on her black-rimmed glasses attached to a chain hung around her neck and peered at the label. "Hold on." She rushed around the reception counter and out the doors. She looked towards the flagpole, praying for Lindsay to be there now. She wasn't. She ran back into the office. "I'm not taking any chances. I'm calling the police. You stand outside and watch in case she shows up."

Belinda went outside while Mrs. Watkins dialed 911. Penny Hobart was the dispatcher who took the call and she immediately sent out a squad car.

Mrs. Watkins and the school principal, Darrell Upton, joined Belinda and together they waited for the police at the flagpole. A crowd of curious students gathered, some recognizing Mrs. Moore, and their chatter escalated as they speculated amongst themselves. Upton, a tall, barrel chested man, asked them to quiet down.

He took Belinda's hand. "I'm sorry you've had so much worry, Mrs. Moore." His innate, protective nature soothed Belinda's jangled nerves.

Jenny Farrell approached Belinda, carrying Lindsay's pink and purple backpack. "Mrs. Moore?"

Belinda turned to her, seeing the backpack. "Jenny. Where did you get that?" Her voice edged on hysteria.

At that moment, a squad car screamed into the parking lot, halting near the group. Two officers got out and Belinda ran to them, waving the sweater.

"This is her sweater! I found it on the ground over there." She pointed at the base of the pole. "I was supposed to pick her up here, right after school."

Officer Gabe Miller and his younger partner, Dan Martinez, were the officers who had found Lindsay sitting on a bench at the train station and had taken her to the hospital.

"We'll find her, Mrs. Moore," said Miller in a quiet, compassionate tone.

"I'll start questioning the students," Martinez said to Miller, as he turned towards the growing mob of kids pressing in on them. "Can I have everyone move back, please?"

A tan sedan pulled in behind the squad car and Detective Angela Yaeger stepped out.

"Angela!" cried Belinda. All at once, the police cars, the flashing lights, and the arrival of Angela overwhelmed her. It meant this was for real, that they believed Lindsay was in danger, that she truly was gone. Taken. "Oh God! My baby! Where's my baby? How can this be happening?" She sank to the ground, pressing the sweater against her womb, sobbing.

Angela knelt beside her and draped her arm over Belinda's trembling back. She almost said the empty platitude everyone says when trying to comfort someone, *it'll be all right*, but caught herself in time. Due to previous police visits to the school, Angela was on friendly terms with Mr. Upton and Mrs. Watkins, and she beckoned them to help Belinda to a nearby bench. Mrs. Watkins sat on the bench beside her and held Belinda's hand.

Angela approached Officer Miller, who was standing close by, and steered him out of Belinda's earshot. "Call Tommy. Then tape off the area."

"I've already called and they're on the way. I'll get the area secured."

Angela returned to Belinda. Upton stood up from the bench and asked her what he could do to help.

"I want to talk to her last teacher of the day, if they're still here; otherwise, please try to get them here a.s.a.p."

"I'm on it." He saw Jenny lingering on the sidelines, still clutching the backpack. "I think you should talk to her." He signaled Jenny over.

As she approached, Belinda saw her daughter's backpack again. "What are you doing with that?"

Jenny's eyes grew large with threatening tears. "She asked me to take it home with me and said she'd get it later."

"Where was this, Jenny?" asked Angela.

"In study hall. She left early and didn't come back."

Angela took the backpack. "What time?"

"Maybe 2:30?"

Angela looked at her watch: 3:35. "I want you to stay in case I need to talk to you again. You can call your parents in the office and tell them I'll get you home. Then come back here." Jenny jogged away and Angela turned to Belinda. "I'm going to empty Lindsay's backpack. If you see anything unusual, tell me." Angela unzipped the pack and spilled the contents on the ground in front of Belinda and Mrs. Watkins. A Trapper Keeper, a math book, gum wrappers, a hairbrush, cherry flavored lip gloss, two dollars, a Tiger Beat magazine, a Jolly Rancher candy stick, a half-eaten sandwich. Angela didn't need Belinda to tell her there was nothing out of the ordinary. "I'm thankful you didn't wait to call us. It's probably nothing, just a little mix-up, but we don't want to take any chances. May I have Lindsay's sweater?"

Belinda reluctantly released it to her. "Why?"

"Because it tells us she was at the flagpole, and now we have to figure out where she went, so I'm going to have Tommy, our best tracker, sniff the sweater and then we'll see what he comes up with."

"Oh my God. You think she's dead!"

"Absolutely not! But Tommy can give us a lot of information fast so we aren't wasting valuable time." Angela noted Belinda's gray, clammy pallor and was concerned she might be going into shock. She spoke softly to Mrs. Watkins. "Can you take care of her?"

"Of course. Please, don't let us slow you down."

"Go! I'm all right! Just find my little girl," Belinda pleaded.

A K-9 SUV drove into the lot and moments after, an officer leading a sleek, black Labrador joined the other officers. Angela took the sweater to the K-9 Officer, who then had Tommy smell it.

Tommy's tail wagged enthusiastically as he quickly worked the area, ending at the curb, where he became agitated and pawed the ground. Everyone knew what that meant. Lindsay had gotten into a car. But had she been forced? Tommy couldn't tell them that.

Angela returned to Belinda. "Could she have gone off with a friend or a relative?" she asked.

"No. She would never have done that knowing I was coming, and she would never have left her favorite sweater behind." She put her hand over her mouth to muffle her shuddering sobs. "Oh God, Lindsay. Where are you?"

CHAPTER TWENTY-ONE

1996

Friday, May 10

Lindsay felt the tension escalating between her captors as they drove beyond Santa Sicomoro's town limits and into the oak-studded countryside, passing ranch homes set back far from the road. Horses grazed on spring grass in the warm sun, oblivious to the frightened girl trapped in the car passing by.

"Are you going to tell me where we're going, Erik?" Phil asked.

"Just keep going."

Several miles out of town, they passed an old general store and gas station.

"We could have got supplies there," Jake said, reading a faded wood sign. "They even have ice cream and bait."

"I forgot about that old place. It's where campers load up before going to Santa Sicomoro Lake," said Erik. "How's our gas, Phil?"

"Still close to full, but it would be nice to know where the hell we're going. I've had enough of this."

A few miles later, they passed the historic "Rusty Spur" saloon, built in the 1850's. Near the road a sign was posted advertising an upcoming Willie Nelson concert.

The saloon was closed, but it made Lindsay feel safer thinking that even all the way out here, there might be people around to help her, especially if a big star like Willie Nelson would come here.

Erik glanced back over his shoulder. "Shit. We missed the turn. Go back."

Phil slowed and when he reached a wider section of road, he made a u-turn.

"See that little road just past the saloon?" Erik pointed up the road to the left. "Turn there."

After another few miles, the paved road turned to dirt, and when Phil slowed the car, Erik said to keep going.

They're going to kill me, Lindsay realized. *Why else would they bring me out so far?*

"Now I know why you were checking the gas," said Phil. "This is ridiculous."

The road dipped down and they drove through a shallow creek bed swiftly flowing with spring run-off.

"And now you know why we took your car," said Erik. "You're the only one who has four-wheel drive."

"No, I don't," said Phil.

"But it's an SUV," said Jake.

"So? It's just a glorified station wagon, that's all. You guys are brilliant, you know that?"

"Well, that's great," said Jake. "What if we get stuck?"

"Relax. We're not gonna get stuck," said Erik.

Phil yanked off his mask, tossing it onto the empty front passenger's seat.

"Hey. Put that back on," said Erik. "Do you want her to see your face?"

"It's too hard to drive, let alone breathe, with that damn thing on."

Lindsay couldn't keep quiet any longer. "You said you just wanted to talk to me," she spoke barely above a whisper. "Please don't hurt me. Just tell me what you want."

"She's right. Here's as good as anywhere," said Jake. "Let's tell her what we want, and then get out of here."

The car was climbing a steep rise and the tires were spinning and spitting loose dirt in its wake. There was a steep drop-off on the right side of the narrow road, and the SUV's rear-end fishtailed dangerously near it.

"Slow down!" screamed Jake. "Do you want to get us killed?"

"The road's in bad shape. It's a washboard, and it's really hard to drive on," said Phil. "I'm only going fifteen miles per hour. I'm afraid if I go any slower we might slide backwards and I'll lose control."

Lindsay's fear level escalated. *What if we go over the side?*

"Then gun it and let's get up this hill." Erik pulled out the flask again and tipped back several swallows.

Jake leaned across Lindsay and swatted the flask away from Erik's mouth. "Stop drinking. You're going to screw everything up."

"Worry about yourself, dickhead." Erik drank some more before putting it back in his pocket. "Come on, Phil. Let's go."

Phil thought, *the hell with it*, and stomped on the gas. The tires spun wildly, then gained purchase, causing the SUV to leap forward. It swerved crazily until he got it under control and reached the top of the rise, where he stopped the car.

"That's it. Enough." Phil put the car in park, and turned to face the backseat. Lindsay saw his troubled, angry brown eyes and recognized him as the nice boy who'd first given her a soda at the party. "This road is dangerous and we're all going to wind up dead."

Erik yanked off his mask and glared at him contemptuously. "We made it to the top without crashing, right?"

Phil didn't answer. A bead of sweat trickled down his forehead and he wiped it away with a shaky hand. He was furious for allowing himself to get entangled in this ludicrous plan, and now he could see no way out of it. He focused on Lindsay. "I'm so sorry about this. About everything. We were all really drunk and never meant you any harm."

This confused Lindsay. Maybe they weren't as bad as she thought. Except for Erik. He was horrible. Why wouldn't the other two stand up to him and let her go?

"Look, we've gone this far and we're almost there," said Erik, switching to a patient tone, as if speaking to a toddler. "It's not like you can turn around here anyway." He pointed over the seat through the windshield. "It should be right around the next bend up ahead. It's a church camp. It's not in use this time of the year, but I've been out here a couple of times, camping with friends. It's a good place to talk where we won't be disturbed."

When Erik said they wouldn't be disturbed, Lindsay's fear spiked. *Okay, Lindsay, focus and breathe.* She took a deep, shuddering inhalation, exhaling slowly. It didn't help.

Phil put the car in gear and descended the hill, picking up speed. The bend in the road turned out to be a hairpin turn and the SUV was traveling too fast to safely negotiate it. He pumped the brakes, but the vehicle was already sliding in the loose dirt as if on black ice.

A gray squirrel darted across the road. Without thinking, Phil slammed hard on the brakes. The backend spun to the right and the rear wheels slid off the road, causing the car to tip up, heave backwards, and roll out of control, crushing through the brush down the steep hill where it rear-ended with a metallic, shrieking thud into an outcropping of granite boulders.

Lindsay was not belted. On impact her head snapped back, then forward, smashing her nose against the front seat, but adrenaline shielded her from immediate pain. Stunned, she slowly straightened, gingerly touching her nose and glancing at her captors.

Jake was unfastening his seatbelt and appeared to be uninjured. He removed his *Terminator* mask and turned to her. Without his disguise, his young blond, blue-eyed looks weren't so scary to Lindsay. "Are you all right?"

"My back really hurts." It didn't hurt that much, but she said so anyway. She felt a trickle of blood leak out her nose and she swiped it away.

"Erik, what about you? You okay?"

"I'm okay, but I don't think Phil is."

Phil wasn't moving. Blood was smeared on the cracked window next to him, where his head rested. Jake clambered out of the car and slowly opened Phil's door. Still held in by the seatbelt, his body slumped towards him.

"Shit. He's bleeding bad." Jake pushed Phil's body to a sitting position as Erik got out and came around the car. "I think he's dead."

"No way." Erik felt Phil's neck for a pulse. "He's not dead, he's unconscious."

"We need to get him out of the car, before it explodes."

"The car's not going to explode, idiot. That's only in the movies."

"Oh, yeah? Well, I smell gas."

Erik stepped to the demolished rear of the car to investigate. "Yeah, you're right. I smell it, too." He crouched to peer under the car. "I can see a drip. Probably nothing, but we better get him out."

Phil was mumbling incoherently as Jake held him erect while Erik unfastened his seatbelt. While doing this, Jake asked Lindsay how her back was.

"Really hurts. Maybe I broke it."

"We'll help you in a minute. Just stay still."

"Okay," she whimpered, with a pained expression.

Jake said to Erik. "We need to move him carefully, in case he's broken his neck or something."

They gently shifted Phil's legs towards the open door and leaned in to lift him out.

"I don't know if we can do this. He's a dead weight," said Erik. "Phil. You need to wake up."

Phil lifted his head. "Whaaass..."

"I guess his neck's okay," said Jake. "Phil, do you think you can walk?"

Phil's eyes rolled up and his mouth dropped open.

"He's out again. We need to carry him," said Erik. "Hold on." He pulled his flask from his pants pocket and drank, wiping his mouth on his sleeve. "Okay, I'm ready."

They eased Phil's arms around their shoulders and lifted him to his limp feet. Phil's head flopped forward and blood trickled from his wounds, splattering in the dirt. They laid Phil on the ground, then Jake scooped him up under his armpits while Erik held his legs.

"Let's take him to those rocks over there," said Jake, jutting his chin towards a cluster of boulders about thirty yards from the vehicle.

While Erik and Jake struggled to move Phil, Lindsay groaned to cover any noise she might make as she inched her way across the seat to the side where Erik had left the door open. She slid out and crouched on the ground.

Lindsay peered back through the SUV to check the boys' progress. They still had a long way to go before they'd reach the boulders and neither was looking back at her. This was her chance.

She sprinted in the opposite direction to a grove of giant eucalyptus trees about twenty yards from the SUV and hid behind the first tree she reached. She checked the boys. They were still staggering towards the rocks with Phil, but it wouldn't be long before they returned. She moved deeper into the forest.

Lindsay wore flimsy sandals and her feet and ankles were

already scratched and bleeding as she forced her way through the nearly knee-deep, tangled carpet of peeling bark for which eucalyptus are notorious. Each step crackled and snapped as her feet sank through the coarse, woody debris. Running for cover in the trees had been a mistake. Once they came looking for her, it would be impossible to move without giving away her location.

Two minutes later, she heard the boys shouting. She squatted low and watched them, trying to think what to do.

"Lindsay!" called Jake. "Come on. We said we weren't going to hurt you."

They searched the perimeters of the SUV. Then Erik pointed to the grove of trees and they started walking toward it.

The only thing Lindsay could think to do was to bury herself under the tree litter and pray they wouldn't find her. As quietly as possible, she cleared the leaves, broken branches, and bark away, then lay on the damp, cool earth and covered herself. It was the hardest thing she had ever done.

"Come on." Erik's voice slurred. "We don't have time for this shit."

They were at the edge of the trees now, maybe fifteen yards from her hiding place.

"What a mess. She could be anywhere in there," said Jake. "How are we going to find her?"

"I've had 'nough this shit." Erik pulled the flask from his pocket again.

"Don't you think you've had enough of that?"

Erik shook the flask and the contents sloshed inside. "Apparently not."

Jake stepped into the clutter, calling Lindsay's name. She held her breath as she heard him moving closer to her hiding place. Erik took a few steps into the grove, watching Jake struggle through the debris.

"What if we can't find her?" Jake said.

Erik picked up a long roll of dry bark. "We can always burn her out."

"Are you crazy? This whole place will explode, and we could all be trapped and killed. There is no way we could get away fast enough. Especially with Phil unconscious."

Lindsay held her breath, trying not to cry out. *Oh, please, dear God. Help me, Mommy.*

"Phil's not my problem," Erik said.

Jake knew Erik was drunk, but he was still astounded. "Phil's your friend. And she's an innocent girl. I am not about to become a murderer on top of everything else."

Erik thought a moment. "Yeah, you're probably right."

Jake turned toward the center of the woods and cupped his mouth, shouting, "Lindsay! I don't know if you can hear me, but if you can… You've probably figured out who we are. I just want you to know how truly sorry we are for everything that's happened."

"Yeah, we're sorry," Erik sneered. "Real sorry."

Jake ignored him. "We never meant you any harm. We were really, really drunk that night and didn't know what we were doing. That's no excuse, I know, but it's the truth. We're still kids, not that much older than you. If you turn us in, our lives will be ruined forever. We're not bad kids, I swear." He dropped his voice and said to himself, "Really, we're not bad." He spoke louder again, "So, we want to make you a deal. Erik's rich—"

"Yeah, rich," said Erik. "Mega-rich."

"And he'll pay for your college education, if you promise not to tell anyone it was us."

Lindsay listened to Jake's bizarre plea. Did they seriously think she would go for something so stupid?

"So, what do you think, Lindsay? A college education at the school of your choice?" Jake paused. "At least then maybe something good will have come out of all of this."

"And if you don't want to go to college, I'll buy you a car. You want a car?" Erik lowered his voice and spoke to Jake, "Do you think she's listening?"

"Yes," Jake said, and then spoke to Lindsay again. "So what do you think, do we have a deal?"

Lindsay shivered in the moist menthol-scented leaves. The sun was low in the sky and she was freezing in her damp clothes. A deep all-body ache was settling in and her joints were stiff. She would wait for them to leave and when she was sure they were long gone, she would find a house where she would call her mother to come get her. Now she knew who her attackers were and could tell Detective Angela.

After a couple of long minutes had passed, Jake said to Erik, "Either she's not here, or she's just not going for it. Let's go."

"Fuck it, Jake," said Erik. "We can't just leave her here so she can turn us in." He shouted to the center of the grove, "Here's the real deal, *Lindsay*. You tell anyone, I mean *an-y-one*, who we are, and we will. Kill. Your. Mother. Got that?"

Jake shoved Erik. "What the hell? We're not killing anyone." He shouted for Lindsay to hear, "Erik didn't mean it. He's drunk. No one's going to hurt your mother. I promise."

"Do you really want to risk it, Lindsay? I'm not nearly as nice as Jake and Phil, and I've got a lot more to lose than they do, and no way am I going to lose it over a lousy, drunk fuck. So yeah, if you go to the police, I swear to God I will get to your mother before the cops get to me. But if for some reason I don't, I will pay someone to kill her. I got a lot of money, Lindsay, and I promise you, I can make it happen. Your mommy will never be safe again."

Jake said to Erik, "God, I hate you. I truly, fucking hate you."

Erik shrugged. "Hey, somebody's got to have some balls."

Overwhelming fear consumed Lindsay as she brushed away the blanket of leaves concealing her trembling thin body and called out, "Please don't hurt my mom."

CHAPTER TWENTY-TWO

TUESDAY · APRIL 16
Posted by Katy McKenna

Petition Distribution Day

First stop: Santa Lucia High School. My old alma mater. I still have nightmares about getting caught in the hall without a pass. And I can't find my locker, and when I finally do, I can't remember the combination!

The parking lot was jammed, but I found a spot at the end of the lot near the flagpole. I started for the office when a soft breeze fluttered the flag and its rope clanged against the hollow metal pole. The sound pulled me back in time to a candlelight vigil held around the pole for Lindsay after she'd gone missing. Throughout the ceremony, the rope had tapped its mournful metallic song.

This might sound a little crazy, but as I stood there clutching my petitions, I sensed an otherworldly presence join me. It was like being infused with a warm, loving, positive energy and I whispered without thinking, "I got your back, Belinda."

The office windows were decorated with posters announcing an upcoming mock rock concert. At the counter, I was greeted by Mrs. Watkins, the office manager. Her black hair was now silver, but she still wore her signature black-rimmed glasses and crimson lipstick. She was prettier than I remembered.

"May I help you?" she asked.

Thank goodness she didn't ask if I had a hall pass. "Do you remember Lindsay Moore?"

Her head dipped and she exhaled slowly. "How could I ever forget that poor little girl? Such a horrible tragedy."

I put the petition on the counter facing her. "One of her murderers is up for parole, and I would like to stop it from happening."

Mrs. Watkins read the petition, then narrowed her eyes, scrutinizing me. "Were you a student here at the time?"

"Yes, but you would never remember me. I was a shy, quiet girl. Definitely not someone you'd remember."

"Those are often the ones who go on to do the greatest things in life. The shy, quiet ones. What's your name?"

"Katherine McKenna. Katy."

"Well, Katy, we would be very glad to have your petition here. I know everyone on staff will sign it, and we'll make sure all our visitors see it, too."

Our conversation was interrupted by a bald, fragile-looking boy bursting through the office doors and dashing to the counter.

"Mrs. Watkins. I need a pass." He glanced at me and flashed an impish grin. "Sorry. I didn't mean to interrupt."

I immediately thought, *What a nice, polite young man*, and then, *God, am I getting old*. "That's all right, I'm in no hurry, but it looks like you are."

We shared a fist bump.

Mrs. Watkins peered over her glasses at him with a well-practiced stern look. "Where have you been?"

"I had to go to the doctor's. Again." He slammed a crumpled paper on the counter. "My mom wrote a note. Again."

She wrote the boy a pass and handed it to him. "Here you go, Nick. Again."

He snatched it and bolted out the door, shouting, "Thanks, Mrs. Watkins."

"What a sweet kid," I said.

"He's a sweet kid, all right, with a big problem. Leukemia. But always so upbeat. I just want to bundle him up and hug him, but these days hugging is out of the question." She pursed her lips with disgust. "Lawsuits. And let me tell you, there's a lot of kids here that sure could use a hug. Thankfully, Nick has great parents."

"This must be a hard job."

"At times it is. But I wouldn't trade my time with these kids for anything." Mrs. Watkins took the petition over to a copy machine. "We're going to need a lot of these." She slipped it into the machine and pressed the start button. "You know, Phil Hobart was a student here a few years before Lindsay. I remember him well. Not because of what happened but because he was a nice boy. An Eagle Scout." She shook her head. "I never understood it. It didn't gel with the Phil we all knew."

Her recollection took me by surprise. "He raped, kidnapped, and killed an innocent girl. How does a nice person do all that?"

"Sometimes things happen that you never meant to happen. Especially when you're young. Things get out of control and you get swept along, making one bad decision after another. I am by no means making excuses for the terrible choices he made." She waved her hands in denial. "I just know that he'd been a good kid while he was a student here."

My hackles were erupting like a bad case of hives. How could Mrs. Watkins say anything flattering about this guy? "But a mere fifteen years in prison surely cannot pay for a young girl's life."

"Nothing can ever pay for that, Katy." She paused, looking reflective. "You know, there was another girl hurt deeply by this crime. Phil's younger sister, Christy. Suddenly no one would speak to her as if it was her fault this had happened. Overnight, she became an outcast. A pariah. Eventually she tried to commit suicide and that's when her parents pulled her out of school and she never returned."

"Christy was a year ahead of me so I didn't know her, but I do remember kids talking about her. I didn't know she'd tried to kill herself. Do you know what happened to her after that?"

"I have no idea. Once she left the school, I never heard another thing. And of course we were all focused on the trial and Lindsay's poor mother." She paused in thought. "I do remember reading that Phil's dad died of a heart attack during the trial."

I hadn't considered what this had done to the Hobart family. Their lives had been ruined, too. But that didn't change my resolve to keep Phil in prison. One thing had nothing to do with the other.

Mrs. Watkins returned to the copy machine, took out a stack of petitions, and put them on the counter. "This is a good thing you're doing." She tapped the pile.

"You've given me a lot to think about. It isn't just the victim's family that suffers."

"No, it isn't. Not by a long shot. Terrible crimes like this change everyone's lives forever. If my child had done something like this, I think I would forever wonder what I could have done better, as far as parenting."

"This petition could cause the Hobarts more grief," I said, thinking aloud.

"So would his parole. These things are never truly over until everyone involved is dead and forgotten."

My next stop was the Santa Lucia police station. The charming

Spanish Revival building dates back to the 1930's. As I climbed the steps to the entrance, I paused to admire the colorful tiles fronting the steps... or was I stalling?

I introduced myself to the clerk at the front desk and explained my mission.

"I didn't live in the area when it happened, but I've certainly heard about it," he said, as he read the petition. "The chief was the lead detective on the case. I'm sure she'd be interested in what you're doing. Would you like to talk to her? I could check if she's free right now." He picked up a phone and pushed a button before I could stop him.

"I really don't want to bother her. Maybe I can leave it with you?"

Too late—he was already talking to her on the phone. He told her about the petition, paused a moment, and then hung up. "She'd be happy to talk to you. Go down the hall to the right and she'll meet you."

I longingly glanced back at the entrance door, trying to contrive an excuse to escape, but before that could happen, an attractive middle-aged African-American woman with close-cropped salt and pepper hair stepped into the lobby and greeted me.

"Hello. I'm Angela Yaeger. Officer Clayton told me you're here with a petition about Lindsay Moore."

Her warm manner immediately put me at ease. Maybe that's why she was the police chief. I was ready to spill my guts about my parking ticket right there in the lobby.

We shook hands.

"Hi. I'm Katy McKenna."

"Katy McKenna, Katy McKenna," she said, tapping her chin. "Now why does your name sound familiar?"

"My stepdad is Kurt Melby."

"Of course, you're little Katy. I remember you as a little girl at Christmas parties and picnics." She did an upsweep of my 69 inches. "Not so little anymore, huh? Let's go to my office." She started down the hall and I was obliged to tag along. "He talked about you all the time, and I do mean *all* the time. Talk about a proud papa." She ushered me into her homey office. "It's such a pleasure to meet you again. Have a seat on the sofa."

I sat and she asked, "Would you like some coffee or water?"

I watch enough crime dramas to know you should never drink the coffee at a police station, and I don't drink bottled water—got a big problem with all that plastic, plus you have no idea what you're drinking—so I passed on both.

She picked up a half empty water bottle on her desk and sat next to me. "So, Katy, tell me about your petition."

"Well, Chief—"

"Please. Call me Angela."

I held up a petition. "How can someone be up for parole after committing rape, kidnapping, *and* murder?"

"A lot of that stems from our overcrowded prison system," she said ruefully, as she took the petition. "And he had a good lawyer and no previous record. Up until the day of Lindsay's rape, Hobart had been a squeaky-clean kid, and that weighed heavily in his favor."

"I heard he was an Eagle Scout."

"Yes, he was. Let me read your petition." When she finished, she said, "This is good. Brief, well-written, and to the point."

"Should I be doing this?"

"Definitely. Someone needs to stand up for that little girl. This case is just as important now as it was back then. It caused the Alpha Gamma fraternity to be suspended until 2016, and it forced the college to adopt tough new laws to govern that kind of out-of-control partying." Her tone heated up. "But it's been a long time now, and things have slipped badly. Last fall, a seventeen-year-old freshman died from alcohol poisoning."

"I remember that. He was found in the bushes outside a fraternity house."

"Such a stupid, stupid waste." Angela cleared her throat and sipped some water.

"Will you be going to the parole hearing?

"Yes."

"May I go with you?" I asked, without thinking my question through. What was I getting myself into?

"Probably not a good idea. I don't consider Hobart to be dangerous, but he's been in the system for a long time now. He went in a scared, naive kid and now he's in his mid-thirties. God only knows what he's had to endure. That kid could have grown into someone very different. It's unlikely he's going to appreciate your efforts to stop his parole."

My wanna-be superhero-vigilante side saw me courageously standing up for justice as I approached the parole panel and set millions of signatures in front of them. But the self-preservationist, saner side of me saw Hobart jumping out of his seat and throttling me in front of the parole panel. So doing the petitions and then Angela going to the hearing while I stayed home behind locked doors was a win-win for me.

I had another question. "Whatever happened in the case of Lindsay's mother's death?"

"Belinda Moore's death is still an open case. However, it's been a few years and no new leads have surfaced, so it's pretty cold now. It always amazes me how many conflicting stories you get from witnesses. But these things happen so fast, that it's understandable when you're not trained to know what to see in a matter of seconds."

"The newspaper account said it might have been a Toyota Camry or a Honda Civic and I can see why people would get those confused. Unless it's a Hummer or a Rolls Royce, everything kind of blends together for me."

"She was a lovely, gracious woman who endured her grief with dignity. I admired her. I would love to close her case and let her rest in peace. But I doubt I ever will now."

Officer Clayton stuck his head in the door to remind Angela about her lunch date with the mayor.

"He loves Thai, and my stomach doesn't. There goes my afternoon." Angela stood up, brushing the creases out of her black pencil skirt. "I'm sorry to cut this short. If you have any more questions, feel free to call me."

We walked to the door and she gave me a hug. "I'm going to circulate your petition to all the local police departments." Angela opened the door. "We need more caring people like you in our community, Katy."

The last stop on my petition distribution list was The Bookcase Bistro, located two blocks down from the police station, so before I lost my nerve, I strolled over to face the enemy. Santa Lucia's population of 34,000-ish means that sooner or later, I will run into my ex, Chad, and *her*. I figured it would be better to break the ice on my terms rather than one day be shopping at Whole Foods, turn into the frozen food aisle, and oops. Plus, I was having a good hair day.

The bistro area was bustling. Adding it to the bookstore had been a good call on our part. Small bookstores took a major hit when the big box bookstores came to town. Now e-books are killing off those stores.

I peeked in the door and saw a young woman working the register, but no Chad, so I boldly marched to the front counter and waited my turn to speak to her.

"I'll be right with you," she said with a big toothy grin.

It was *her*. Heather. I recognized her teeth from the newspaper wedding photo, although her strawberry-blond hair hadn't been in pigtails. I hadn't anticipated her working at the store. She was, or used to be, a personal trainer. Shouldn't she be at the gym making somebody miserable? I spun around to leave, thinking... *what was I thinking?*

"Oh my God! You're *her*," she shouted at my back.

I froze in my tracks and glanced back over my shoulder.

"Oh, please don't go." She motioned me back to the counter. "Just give me a sec." She returned her attention to her customer and handed his credit card back to him along with his purchase and a thank you. I had to give her points for not telling him to "have a nice day." Then she came around the counter and grabbed me in a big hug, or as big as it could be considering her huge belly. Was she that far along? And why was she hugging me?

She backed away, holding my hands and practically jumping up and down for joy. I prayed her water wouldn't break. Wouldn't that be something? Me, delivering my cheating ex-husband's bimbo bride's baby on the bamboo floor of the business we built.

"Oh, my gosh. I have so wanted to meet you. This is so totally awesome."

Doesn't she realize she had an affair with a married man who happened to be my husband at the time? Or is she a complete dimwit? "Uhh, same here," I said, reclaiming my hands. "I really came in to—"

"Have you had lunch?"

"No."

Heather grabbed my hand and dragged me to a table in the bistro. "Look." She pointed to a chalkboard menu. "We still have your favorite sandwich. We call it 'The Katydid.' You know, with the cheese and tomatoes and honey and—"

"Yeah, I know what it is," I snapped, annoyed they were using Pop's pet name for me.

Heather's enthusiasm dropped a notch, but she persevered in spite of me. "It's super popular." She pulled out a red metal chair for me. "Sit here and I'll go order."

"What would you like to drink?" she called from the counter.

Something that would dull my senses, like a double shot of Novocain. "I'll take an iced tea."

"No problem. Is green tea okay?"

Not a fan of green tea. "Sure."

She brought two iced teas to the table and sat down, turning her ginormous belly sideways, so she could reach the table. She appeared ready to pop any minute and I was thinking we should move to a larger table.

"So... when're you due?" My curiosity winning over my reluctance to ask.

She groaned loudly. "September 5th."

I tapped my calculator fingers on my lap. May, June, July, August, September. She was only four months along. How could she be so big?

She read my mind. "Triplets. She patted her beach ball tummy. "We are so blessed. Can you believe it?"

"No, I can't," I said rather ungraciously.

"Oh God, I am so stupid. I know how much you and Chad wanted kids and how devastated he was when you were unable to conceive," she said with an oh-you-poor-thing look on her face.

Chad had told her that? It was pretty darn hard to get pregnant when your husband doesn't want kids, and he vigilantly checks your birth control pills every night and always, I mean always, wears a condom.

Heather mistook my look of shock, followed by a renewed pulse of anger and betrayal, for disappointment. "Oh, look what I've gone and done. I've made you feel bad. I am so sorry."

And then she burped. It was an amazingly long, loud, and rumbling burp, like an 8.9 on the Richter scale, followed by a few hiccups, interspersed with after-shock burps. The bistro went quiet as the other patrons waited for the inevitable explosion that was sure to follow a belch of that magnitude. Then she clasped her hands to her sternum and winced. "Oooooo... heartburn."

The next look she saw float over my face was relief, for me— that I wasn't in her shoes, but she took it as sympathy for her.

"Ohhhh. You're so sweet." She winced again and took a sip of iced tea.

Our lunch arrived and I was surprised to find myself suddenly ravenous as I bit into my Katydid sandwich. Heather had ordered spicy black bean soup. Probably not a wise choice, so I decided to eat fast and vamoose.

"So, Katy, I don't want to sound rude or unfriendly, but why did you come in? I mean, this has got to be a little weird for you." She eyed me as she stuffed a piece of jalapeño cornbread into her mouth.

It was definitely more than a little weird, and I was wondering what the heck had possessed me to come into the store. Oh yeah, breaking the ice on my terms. How stupid was that?

I put down my sandwich. "I have two reasons why I'm here. First off, I saw the wedding announcement in the paper the other day and it really hurt. Chad was still married to me when the two of you started fooling around behind my back, you know. But I'm sick and tired of worrying about running into you and Chad, like *I'm* the bad guy, so I decided to bite the bullet and face the enemy and get it over with."

Now I'd lost my appetite, and Heather looked like a pregnant nun caught in church. Her face crumpled, her eyes filled with tears, and it looked like she was having a hard time swallowing her mouthful of cornbread. Great, now I'd be accused of killing my was-band's former mistress, now extremely pregnant wifey. I handed her iced tea to her, and she drained the glass.

"I guess that was a little blunt, Heather. Confronting you was not on my list of things to do today. It never occurred to me that you might be working here. I honestly thought I would be seeing Chad."

She swiped at her tears. "I am so, so sorry. I never meant to hurt anyone. I didn't even realize Chad was married when we started dating, I swear. And then I got pregnant, and that's when he told me he was married. Gosh, I thought I would die. I'm not that kind of person."

"But you're only four months along. That doesn't add up."

"I miscarried after he left you." Her shoulders slumped and despair literally oozed out her pores. "It was a really rough time."

My indignation softened in spite of my righteous anger. *I guess I wasn't the only one who'd suffered.* "Heather, are you truly happy?"

"Yes." She paused a moment. "I admit, at first it was super hard after I found out he was married. I mean, what a jerk."

Couldn't argue with that.

"But that miscarriage did something to him. I think it made him grow up."

Finally.

"I feel so guilty about everything, but I do love Chad more than anything." She patted her belly. "Except for maybe these little ones." She beamed a Madonna smile (not that Madonna) and burped again. "But now that I've met you, my happiness won't be complete until I know you've found the right person."

"Don't worry about me. I'll be fine." It was time to change the subject. "Let me show you the other reason I came in." I handed her the petition, and she read it between slurps and burps of soup, while I wrapped my sandwich in a napkin to take home.

"Oh, wow, this is so awful," she said, when she finished reading it. "I don't even remember this."

How could she? She was probably in preschool at the time.

"I'd like to leave a few petitions here at the counter. I need to gather as many signatures as possible before his parole date."

Her eyes brimmed with tears again. "This is so noble of you. Chad never told me what a nice person you are. In fact, he said—"

I held up my hand to stop her. "Heather. It's okay." The last thing I wanted to hear was what he'd said about me. He was her problem now.

"But you're not at all what I expected. Gosh, I really feel totally bad now."

I found myself liking this dimwit and that totally annoyed me. I hoped Chad would treat her better than he'd treated me.

I made a graceful exit and went back to the parking garage

where Veronica waited. After I climbed in and buckled up, I sat a moment and thought about what had just transpired. It irritated me that I could no longer hate *her*.

"Dammit." I smacked the steering wheel. And then I remembered I'd left my sandwich behind. "Double dammit."

CHAPTER TWENTY-THREE

1996

Friday, May 10

In the deepening gloom of the eucalyptus grove, Lindsay pushed aside the layer of damp leaves she'd hidden under and sat up, only a few yards away from where the boys stood. "Please, I won't tell. I promise. Just don't hurt my mom."

Erik's lip curled into an ugly sneer. "Pinky swear?"

"When this is over," said Jake. "I never want to see you again, got that?"

"Works for me."

"Come on, Lindsay." Jake approached her. "I'm sorry about Erik. He's drunk and scared. We're all scared. We never meant to hurt you and no one's going to hurt you now, I promise." He held out his hand to help her to her feet. "Let's get out of here."

She ignored his hand, trying to stand on her own, but her back seized, forcing her to accept his help. She glanced fearfully at Erik as Jake gently pulled her to her feet. As she staggered towards the edge of the grove, she flinched with each step, emitting involuntary grunts of pain.

Erik lost patience with her slow progress and grabbed her by the arm, nearly yanking it out of the socket. "Let's move it!"

He hustled Lindsay out of the forest into the open meadow and shoved her ahead of him. She stumbled to her knees, nearly paralyzed by the excruciating cramp in her back. She didn't think she would be able to stand up again.

Jake bent beside her and whispered in her ear as he helped her up. "Try hard, Lindsay. I don't know if I can control Erik."

His gentle words gave her courage and she forced herself forward, gritting her teeth against the agony. When they reached Phil, he was alert and sitting up against a rock. His scalp wound had stopped bleeding and congealing blood covered his face, neck, and shirt front.

"Are you okay?" Jake asked him. "You look terrible."

"I'll live." Phil noted Lindsay's dirty clothes, clenched jaw, mascara-streaked face, and bloody nose. "What's going on?"

Lindsay broke into hiccupping sobs, barely able to enunciate her words. "Please. Please don't let him kill my mother."

Phil looked incredulously at Jake. "Did you say that to her?"

"Not him." Lindsay pointed at Erik. "Him."

Erik acknowledged her accusation like it was high praise. "What can I say, folks? She left me no choice."

"You're such a prick," muttered Phil.

"Yes, I am. But I think me and Lindsay have finally agreed to a deal we can both live with. No college, no car, and no dead mama... if she keeps her mouth shut." He turned to Lindsay. "Are we good, Lindsay?"

"Yes," she mumbled, averting her eyes, terrified of him.

Erik leaned toward her, cupping his ear, causing her to shudder. "I'm sorry, but I couldn't quite catch that. Are we good, Lindsay?"

"God, leave her alone!" Jake clenched his fists, desperately wanting to pummel Erik's smug face into a bloody pulp.

"Not until I can hear her answer," said Erik. *"Lindsay?"*

"Yes!" She hugged her bone-chilled body, gasping for breath.

"I think you both owe me a big apology because I just saved your sorry asses." Erik said, grinning at them in expectation.

"What? No apologies. Oh, well."

As the sun worked its way towards the horizon, the temperature dropped to the low sixties. Lindsay shivered in her damp summer clothes, crying inconsolably. Her face was grimy and splotchy, twigs and leaves were stuck in her long, tangled hair, and her swollen nose dribbled bloody snot into her chattering mouth. In her heightened state of panic, she didn't feel the urine trickling down her legs.

Erik looked at the girl with revulsion. "I must have been really shit-faced, 'cause I can't believe I actually wanted to screw you." He shoved her towards the boulders where Phil sat. "Sit down and shut up while Jake and I figure out what to do."

Erik's hard slam into her shoulder knocked her off-balance, and she pitched forward against the rock. They all heard the ominous crack of her skull when it connected with the granite. She collapsed on Phil's lap, convulsing.

"Why did you do that?" screamed Phil, trying to still her spasms by clamping his forearms over her shaking body and holding her head.

A split second passed and her convulsion stopped, leaving her deathly still. Jake dragged her away from Phil and laid her flat on the ground. "You really hurt her!"

"She's all right." Erik nudged her ribs with his shoe and she didn't move. "She knocked herself out, that's all."

Jake crouched beside Lindsay and took her wrist. "I don't feel a pulse."

Phil leaned over Lindsay and felt the carotid artery on her neck. "I don't feel anything, either."

"You know CPR, right?" asked Jake, his voice loud and shrill.

Phil hoped he had the strength to do it. "Yeah. You need to

move her away from these rocks first. I need room. Be careful with her neck."

Jake pulled Lindsay's limp body further away from the boulder. "Oh God. Oh God. Come on Lindsay. Please be okay."

Phil had injured his head, neck, and left shoulder in the car crash and movement was torture as he bent over her motionless body and checked for breath from her nose. He tipped her head back, put his mouth over hers and blew in twice, then placed his hands on her chest and compressed it rapidly several times before moving back to her mouth.

Jake hovered over her still body, nervously shifting on his feet and wringing his hands. "Oh God, how did this happen? Please Lindsay, please don't die." He looked at Erik. "You could help. This is all your fault, you know."

Erik held out his hands in a placating gesture, a look of innocence pasted on his face. "It was an accident and you know it, so what am I supposed to do?"

"You have your cell phone?"

"Yeah, so?"

"So call 911."

Erik pulled his cell from his jeans pocket and flipped it open. He had no intention of calling anyone and would have faked it, but there was no cell coverage anyway. "Crap. No bars." He strolled to the SUV and leaned against it, waiting for them to realize Lindsay was dead.

Phil continued to compress her chest, although the effort was almost more than he could bear and he feared he might collapse at any moment. "Six, seven, eight, nine..."

Jake saw her twitch and crouched beside her. "I think she's coming around."

Erik rushed over and stood behind the boys. "Are you sure? Could just be those weird muscle spasms that can happen after death. I ran over a dog once, and it flopped all over the road. It was gnarly."

Phil felt her artery again. "I think I feel something." He bent close to her face. "Yes... she's breathing."

"Oh, thank God." Jake went down on his knees and watched her face. "Should we keep doing CPR?"

"No. She's breathing on her own," said Phil, exhausted and overwhelmed with relief.

Erik squatted on the other side of Lindsay, opposite Jake and Phil. "You sure she's breathing? She looks dead to me."

Phil kept his eyes on Lindsay. "You are one lucky dude, Erik."

"How's that?"

"Because now you're not a murderer," said Jake.

"Whoa! Wait a minute. You know it was an accident. But it would've been a whole lot better for all of us if she had died, 'cause now we'll all go to prison for sure."

"But not for murder," said Phil. "It's better this way, Erik."

"God, you are such a fucking saint, you know that, Phil?"

Lindsay groaned softly and her eyelids fluttered spastically, revealing the whites of her eyes. Her hand jerked out and brushed Erik's knee.

"Oh, no you don't!" he screamed, and violently lunged forward over Lindsay.

Phil and Jake scuttled back to avoid contact and landed on their rear-ends. In the next instant, Erik's hand smashed down on Lindsay's forehead, crushing it with a stone.

"Problem solved," muttered Erik, coldly staring down at Lindsay's bludgeoned face. He leaned back on his heels and flipped the bloody stone between his hands. "Now no one's going to prison."

Jake howled an unearthly primal scream and hurtled himself over Lindsay's body, slamming Erik to the ground. He wrestled the bloodied stone from Erik's grasp and then unthinking, reared up to beat Erik with it when Phil shoved him off and straddled him to hold him down.

Jake struggled fiercely. "Please, please, let me kill him. Let me fucking kill him. Please."

"I can't let you do that. God knows, I wish I could." Phil clamped down hard on Jake's squirming body with his legs, his hand pressing Jake's windpipe to control him, and then the fight went out of the boy and they both collapsed to the ground.

Finally Jake asked, "Why? Why did you kill her? We weren't going to hurt her, remember? That wasn't the plan. We were just going to talk to her, you know, convince her..."

Erik stood up, found the stone and flung it far into the ravine beyond the boulders and turned to Jake. "You actually believed *that* was the plan?"

Jake sat up and whispered in defeat, "Yes."

"Wow. I thought you knew. I really did. I mean, come on. We abduct her and take her into the woods and then just let her go?" He snorted with a cruel laugh. "Un-fucking-believable."

"Nothing left to do now but to turn ourselves in." Phil pushed himself to a sitting position, feeling woozy. His wounds were seeping again and thick blood oozed down his face.

"Are you serious?" said Erik. "After all this, we're just going to turn ourselves in?"

Jake and Phil gaped at Erik, each silently loathing him, their mutual fear of him making them vulnerable.

For a moment, Erik wondered if Jake and Phil might gang up on him. He knew he needed to maintain the upper hand. "Look. I get it. This is awful. Really bad. But nothing we do can change what's happened."

Phil said to Jake, "Every time we listen to him, we just dig ourselves in deeper and deeper."

Erik hovered over them, his face unreadable, his tone dead calm. "And you're both going to listen to me one more time."

Jake slumped over, hugging his knees to avoid eye contact with Erik. "What?"

"I don't know about you guys, but I can't talk and look at her, so hold on a sec." Erik's tone became amiable, as he casually picked up Lindsay's feet and dragged her body several yards away.

"Guess I don't have to worry about her neck now." He dropped her limp legs to the ground and returned to Jake and Phil. "Like I said, our problem's solved. Dead girls don't talk, so we're in the clear." Erik paused, tilting his head impishly. "You can thank me anytime now." He crossed his arms over his chest and waited, wearing a self-satisfied grin.

Phil, sickened by this person who had been his friend, said, "Don't you even care what you've done?"

"Yes. As a matter of fact, I do care," he said. "I just saved our bacon."

"What happens when they find her body?" asked Jake.

"Oh, for God's sake, Jake. They're not going to find her because we're going to get rid—"

Phil gasped. "NO. No way in hell. Don't listen to him, Jake. This will get you and me in more trouble. We're not the ones who committed murder." He pointed at Erik. "He is. Let him burn."

"We'll all burn and you know it. Now we're going to do the only sane thing left to do. Bury her and go home. End of story." Erik chuckled with cold mirth. "And they all lived happily ever after." He flicked a glance at Lindsay's corpse. "Well, almost all."

Jake exhaled a slow, defeated breath. "He's probably right, Phil."

"About living happily ever after? He's a fucking psychopath, Jake."

Erik laughed. "You may be right about that, but you might want to listen to Jake, because it's your blood that's all over her, not mine. How're you going to explain that?"

"I was trying to save her and you know it."

"Yeah, because you felt real bad after you bashed her head against the rock." He put his hands on his hips and frowned with reproach. "I was shocked when you did that."

"You bastard." Phil struggled to stand and Erik put his hand on his shoulder and easily pressed him back down.

"I'll tell the police you did it!" Jake screamed, scrambling to his feet.

Erik leaned into Jake and jabbed his index finger into his chest. "Now that I think about it, maybe it was *you* who did it, Jakey. I had no idea what a nasty temper you have. No wonder you got a wrestling scholarship." He saw Jake's fists balling and moved several steps away. "No matter what, we'll all go to prison, but it'll be one of you who'll be the last to get out, if ever. Not me. My folks can get the best lawyers money can buy, and they'll make sure you guys go down for this, not me. In fact, the more I think about it, I'll probably get off scot-free. I'll be the next O.J. while you two..." He shrugged with an angelic smile. "Think about it. Jake, your family owns a small dairy farm in the middle of nowhere and Phil, you've got an accountant for a daddy and your mommy's a police dispatcher. Bottom line? Defending you will bankrupt your families. In all good conscience, how can you do that to them? They're innocent in all of this. The knowledge that their darling boys could do anything this terrible will be enough to destroy them, but you want to bankrupt them, too? What kind of sons are you?"

Phil gaped at him for a few moments, trying to process the terrible scenario that Erik had painted, then hauled himself to his feet, stumbled to Lindsay's body and crouched beside her.

"I am so, so sorry," he whispered, tenderly stroking her matted blond hair back from her forehead, his tears mingling with the ones drying on her cheeks. "I promise you, I will make my life count for something good to help make up for taking yours. I will be the best person I can be. I promise."

Erik and Jake watched, unable to hear Phil's words, and then, while still gazing at Lindsay's face, he said, "Okay, you win, Erik." He wobbled back to the boulders and slumped down against them, completely spent. "There's a blanket in the back of the car. You can use it to wrap her body."

While Erik went to the car to retrieve the blanket, Jake frantically whispered to Phil. "Are you sure about this, Phil? Everything's happened so fast. Maybe we should turn ourselves in and be done with it."

"You heard him. He's crazy, but he's right about this destroying our families. And I'm afraid he might harm them. You heard what he said to Lindsay about her mother. We have to protect them."

Erik returned with the plaid blanket. "You two done talking about me?" He spread the blanket on the ground and roughly rolled Lindsay onto it. "A little help, please?"

Jake wrapped the blanket around Lindsay's warm body and tucked it securely.

"Don't suppose you got a shovel in your car?" Erik asked.

"No," snapped Phil, looking away.

"Hey, you're the Boy Scout, so I thought, you know... always prepared?"

"You're lucky I'm not, or I'd use it to bash your head in right now."

"You need to watch that temper of yours," said Erik. "Someone might take it the wrong way and get their feelings hurt, and who knows what might happen."

Erik and Jake carried Lindsay's shrouded corpse to the eucalyptus grove. It was after six and though the days were long, the sun was ducking behind the steep hills casting deep shadows. The dusky gloom in the woods offered little light to see by as the two worked their way to the cleared spot where she had concealed herself less than thirty minutes ago.

Before they covered her body, Erik bent down briefly and said to her, "Sorry, Lindsay. No hard feelings, okay?"

CHAPTER TWENTY-FOUR

1996

Saturday, May 11

The morning after Lindsay's death, Adam Hobart was enjoying his morning coffee in his leather recliner while reading the paper and watching the Golf Channel, when Phil entered the room shortly after eight a.m.

"Hey, Dad."

Adam nearly jumped out of his skin, sloshing coffee on his plaid, flannel robe. "Holy crap! Are you trying to give me a heart attack?" He twisted in his chair to see his son. "What the hell happened to your face? Did somebody beat you up?"

"I wish." Phil moved around the recliner and slowly lowered his aching body to the end of the sofa nearest his dad's chair. He was reluctant to tell his father about the car accident, but plunged ahead, anxious to get it over. "I crashed the car and my head hit the window." He shifted to get more comfortable and stifled a groan. "I'm sorry, Dad. It was really stupid."

"Are you okay?" Adam muted the TV, set his coffee and paper down and moved to Phil's side to inspect his wounds.

"Just a little stiff, that's all." He settled back into the cushions, wincing with pain. "Or a lot stiff."

"Were you drinking?"

"No, Dad."

"How'd you get here?"

"Took a cab."

"You should have called. So what happened?"

"First, I need to take something for the aches."

Adam got up. "I'll get you some ibuprofen. Want some coffee?"

"Sounds good. Thanks." Phil had never lied to his father before. Yes, he'd told a few little fibs, maybe omitted a pertinent detail here and there, but never an out-and-out lie. But he truly feared the threats Erik had made the day before about his parents being financially wiped out if they went to trial. He also feared that if he crossed Erik, he might cause harm to his family, just like he'd threatened Lindsay. Phil believed he was dealing with an unstable psychopath and he had to protect his family.

His father stuck his head out of the kitchen entry. "Two percent milk okay? We're out of half and half."

"That's fine."

A moment later, Adam returned with three ibuprofen, a glass of water, and placed a steaming mug of coffee on the glass coffee table. Phil washed down the pills and then picked up his coffee with shaky hands. Adam settled back in his recliner and watched his son expectantly.

Phil swallowed a few reviving sips and set it on the table. He inhaled deeply and began his fabricated tale. "Jake, Erik, and I were exploring some back roads and a squirrel ran across the road and I lost control of the car and it slid and crashed into some rocks."

"Where's the car now?"

"I had it towed to a body shop. They said it might take a few weeks. The back end was crunched pretty good."

"Did you call the police?"

He shook his head. "Didn't see any reason to. It was just us and that damn squirrel, out on a quiet country road."

Penny entered the room. "I thought I heard your voice, Phil." She walked around the couch to see him. "Honey! Your face!" She rushed to his side and threw her arms around him. "What happened?"

"He crashed his car," Adam answered bluntly.

"My poor baby." She pulled back and looked at him. "Your beautiful face." She tenderly touched his wounds. "You need to see a doctor."

"I'm fine. It looks worse than it is. There's nothing a doctor could do." Phil disentangled himself from her grasp and forced his stiff body up, biting his lip to suppress a groan. He picked up his mug and went to the kitchen on the pretense of topping it off but really it was to gather his thoughts.

"You want some coffee, Mom?" he called as he poured his.

"I'll get it." She scurried into the kitchen and removed a cup from the cabinet. "You go sit and put up your feet. Wait, hold on." She pulled a bag of peas out of the freezer and wrapped it in a dish towel. "Put this on your face. It'll help the swelling. Do you want an ibuprofen?"

"Already took some. It'll kick in a minute."

Phil returned to the couch where his father waited to question him further. His mother rejoined them, sitting close to Phil. He recapped what he'd told his dad.

"Why were you exploring country roads?" asked Adam.

"Adam, leave the poor kid alone. Can't you see he's all done in?"

"He crashed his car, Penny. The car we gave him. He could have killed himself. I think I have a right to ask a few questions."

"I'm all right, Mom, and Dad's right." He continued with the story the boys had concocted the night before. "Erik wanted to show us a good camping site where we might go sometime in the summer. He said there's a stream with trout in it so we could fish, too, but we crashed before we got there. I'm really sorry about the car."

Adam's tone softened. "The important thing is you're all right. But why didn't you call us? We would have come and got you."

"The cell phone didn't work out there, so we walked to an old saloon—"

"The Rusty Spur?"

"Yeah."

"No wonder there was no cell coverage."

"Anyway," Phil continued, "there was a pay phone at the saloon, so we called a tow truck. I wanted to handle it myself and not bother you."

Penny patted his arm. "You're never a bother to us, Phil. We love you." She got up and set a sofa pillow behind his back. "I'm going to make some breakfast, and then after you eat, you should take a nap."

As soon as she left the room, Phil yanked the pillow out and tossed it to the end of the sofa. "Let your mother fuss over you, okay? In the long run, it will be easier on you than trying to convince her you don't need it. Trust me, I know. And I think we'd both feel better if you got a checkup. Make sure you don't have any internal injuries."

"I look worse than I feel, Dad."

"All right. But if you start to feel funny, we're going to the ER. Understood?"

"Okay."

"Are the other boys okay?"

"They're fine. But there's something else I want to talk to you about."

"What's up?"

"Would it be okay if I came home for a little while? I really need some peace and quiet. The term's ending and I need to concentrate on school without all the frat house distractions."

"Fine with me, if that's really what you want," Adam answered. "Your education is the top priority. But you aren't going to drop out of the fraternity are you? Those affiliations can be very helpful in your future professional life, you know."

"No. I just need a break. Things have been a little out of control lately, and I need to get myself back in line."

"You're a lot smarter than I was at your age," said Adam. "I'm proud of you, son. Maybe this summer you and I can go check out that stream and do a little fishing."

CHAPTER TWENTY-FIVE

WEDNESDAY · APRIL 17

Posted by Katy McKenna

Is two days an appropriate length of time to wait before attempting to collect payment from someone mourning the loss of their dearly departed cat? After checking emilypost.com and finding no definitive answer there, I decided it was or I'd be dipping into my nest egg again.

I called Wanda and asked as delicately as I could if she were in the mood to accept her Acme logo and cut me a check. Evidently she was because she told me to come anytime. "Anytime" was good for me, so I said adios to my coworkers, Daisy and Tabitha, and headed over.

After driving up one street and down another hunting for the elusive empty parking spot, I wound up three blocks away in a thirty-minute green-curbed zone. Loaded with my purse and portfolio, I sprinted to the shop.

A black wreath hung on the entrance door, and inside I found Doris-the-cat perched on the laminate counter next to a pewter urn that I assumed held the remains of her son, Dave.

"Hey, Doris," I said. "How're you doing?" I tentatively reached out to pet her and she hissed as I stroked her back but no bites. "I'm so sorry about your loss."

Her hisses became a low, rattling purr. We had bonded!

"Looks like you've made a new friend," said Wanda, as she came out from the office.

"Yes, we have, haven't we, Doris-sweetie-poopsie-pie?" I said in that annoying "oogy-woogy" voice that people use with babies, puppies, and ancient cats, while nuzzling her face.

And then she bit my nose.

"Ouch!" I jerked back and touched my nose. It hurt a little and so did my feelings.

Wanda chuckled. "You were doing good for a minute there, but she hates baby-talk." She inspected my nose. "That shouldn't leave a scar."

What?

She gave me a tissue from the box on the counter. I delicately dabbed my schnoz and found a tiny trace of blood on the tissue.

"Don't worry, Katy, I'm pretty sure she's up to date on her shots."

OMG. Rabies? If I get rabies in my nose, I am suing.

Wanda moved Dave's urn to the far end of the counter and placed the pissed-off cat next to it. "I'm excited to see how the logo turned out." She rubbed her hands together.

I laid the red portfolio case on the counter and pulled out her job. I hadn't looked at it for a couple of days and in spite of my pulsating nose, I found myself taken aback by the magnificence of the erupting volcano.

Wanda spoke in a hushed, reverent voice. "This, indeed, is a thing of beauty."

"Thank you," I said, feeling all glowy and wonderful. I had put my career on hold to support Chad's bookstore dream, and starting over was scary, but Wanda's praise meant I was back on track. Woo-hoo!

"Darn it," said Wanda, snapping me out of my reverie.

"What do you mean?" Was she going to weasel out of paying me?

"I planned to have this logo put on a new sign out front and on our truck, along with new letterhead, business cards, and what-have-you, but it's so darned classy that now I need to spruce up the whole place to go with it." She surveyed the large shop. "I am suddenly seeing this place with new eyes, and it's a mess. Come to think of it, it's probably been this way since my folks opened the business back in 1962, although it would've been a lot cleaner," she chuckled with a wink. "I came along a few years later and this is all I remember."

I glanced around and had to agree. Fluorescent lights flickered a dismal, gray-green light over countless bolts of fabric lining the unfinished walls, some so out of date that soon the 70's brown and gold plaid herculon would be trendy again. The concrete floors were littered with scraps and sawdust. Furniture skeletons awaited their new lives among the finished pieces ready to go home. Near the front counter was a long, scarred, plywood plank resting on sawhorses and covered with messy stacks of sample swatches.

"See what I mean?" She smacked her hand on the counter. "Darn it."

Big mistake. When she hit the counter, it spooked Doris, and she knocked Dave's urn over, spilling his ashes over the counter and the floor, creating a cloud that hit me full face and set off a sneezing attack, which further blew the ashes into a dust swirl.

"Oh, I'm so sorry," I sputtered between sneezes.

As the dust settled, an ironic smile lit Wanda's face. "You know, I was planning on scattering Dave's ashes in all the places he loved.

The dumpster out back, the fence he liked to sit on in the alley, the hood of my car, but you know what?"

"No." I sniffed back a wad of snot and swabbed my poor, slightly bloody nose, wondering if I would need plastic surgery.

"This," Wanda flung up her arms and spun around, "this is the place he loved most. Hold on." She dashed into the office and came out with a broom and dustpan. "You hold the pan, and I'll sweep him up."

How could I say no after sneezing Dave all over the place? Maybe if I'd received my check already, but I hadn't, so between more sneezes, we got the old guy tidied into a neat little pile in the pan. Then she angled the portable electric fan on the counter toward the ceiling and picked up the pan. Just as she was about to turn on the fan, I hollered, "Stop!"

"Why?"

"Perhaps we should say a few words before you blow him away, don't you think?"

"You're right." She set the dustpan down. "Wait here." She ran out the front entrance to the vacuum sales and repair shop next door, leaving Doris and me to glare at each other. A few minutes later, she returned with a dapper, bow-tied, elderly man in tow. "Katy, this is Cornelius Hembry. He's a Universal Life Church minister. He's going to say a few words before we scatter Dave to kingdom come."

Cornelius bowed and shook my hand. "Pleased to meet you, Miss Katy."

"Universal Life, isn't that an online thing?"

"Actually, Katy, I received my ordination through the mail in 1967. I can perform weddings and—"

"He did all three of mine," said Wanda with a wink. "Too bad he can't do divorces."

"—baptisms and funerals. Our motto is 'do only that which is right.'" He tweaked his small, perfectly manicured, silver handlebar mustache. "That's why I went into the vacuum sales and repair business."

I wasn't making the connection but let it go.

Cornelius eyed the dustpan. "Is that the remains of the dearly departed?"

Wanda sniffed. "Yes."

I passed out tissues from the box on the counter and Cornelius began.

"Master Dave was a good old chap. He would often visit me in the afternoons for a tea break. He was especially fond of Darjeeling and apricot scones."

Wanda's voice cracked. "That would explain the diarrhea."

"I'm reminded of the time Dave and I were helping a customer in my shop and..."

The service eventually ended and Wanda flipped the switch, blowing Dave ceiling-ward. His ashes sparkled in the sunbeams filtering through the grungy skylights and slowly descended to settle on all the newly upholstered pieces waiting for pick-up. Then Doris jumped down from the counter and leapt onto the nearest chair and curled into a purring, bony ball.

I waited for someone other than me to break the hush. Wanda said, "That was a beautiful service, Cornelius. Dave would've approved."

He bowed. "Thank you, dear lady. It was an honor. And if you didn't see the sign in my window, we are having a vacuum sale," he paused and glanced around the shop, "in case you have a need."

Between the funeral and my throbbing snout and itchy, drizzling eyes—which Wanda mistook for emotion, I'd had enough of Acme.

"Oh, darlin', you poor thing." She patted my back and handed me another tissue. "Dave's in a happier place now."

Yeah, all over your customers' reupholstered furniture. I waited a few moments, then broached the delicate subject of payment. "I have another appointment and I've got to get going, so if you have my check?"

"I sure do. Hold on."

She went into the office, leaving me alone with Cornelius. He whipped out a card and presented it to me with a flourish. "If you ever need my services. Perhaps an upcoming wedding to your beau?"

Wanda returned before I had to answer. "Here ya go." I took a quick glance to make sure it was the right amount.

"I can't tell you how pleased I am with your work, Katy." Wanda came around the counter and escorted me to the door. "I will be telling all my merchant friends. You're going to be one busy gal."

"That's very nice of you. I appreciate it."

As I was about to exit she handed me a card. "This is a little gift certificate for you. Fifty dollars off the reupholstering of an easy chair or loveseat. Anytime."

I was flattered, but that was not happening. I don't want to be haunted by the future ashes of Doris.

Out on the sidewalk, I checked my watch. I was way over the thirty minute parking time. I dashed to the car, hoping to beat another violation. Too late. The pink ticket was fluttering under Veronica's windshield wiper. Thirty-five dollars again. Could I write off parking tickets as a business expense?

I climbed into the car and inspected my nose in the rearview mirror. There were a couple of tiny puncture marks that looked like zits, which was amazing considering how few teeth Doris has left.

After depositing my check at the bank drive-thru, I stopped at the drugstore for Neosporin and found a new mascara that promises to make my lashes look fake.

At home, I checked my voicemail. Samantha had called. "Hey, girlfriend. Took the petition to the hospital and now we have them at every station. Practically everyone remembered the story and was more than happy to sign it. They think you're a rock star."

It was early afternoon and if I were a responsible person, I would have cleaned house or pulled weeds, but I wasn't feeling it. I'd distributed the petitions to everyone on my list, relieved the self-imposed obligation was out of the way, and I was solvent, so I thought it would be fun to treat Ruby to an afternoon matinee.

———

We left Veronica in the parking structure across from the movie theater where the traitor couldn't collect any more parking tickets, and with time to kill before the movie, we went into Starbucks for lattes. While waiting in line, it dawned on me this used to be Pizza-Shmizza where Lindsay had met those boys who had invited them to the frat party all those years ago. I wondered if they'd ever realized what their part in her death had been. They weren't the ones who had hurt or killed Lindsay, but they had set the ball in motion. Fate.

After the dizzying 3D extravaganza, we went to a nearby Italian bistro and over plates of butternut squash ravioli swimming in a brown butter sage sauce, Ruby grilled me about the Viking. Since there had been no new encounters, it should have been a ten-second conversation, but that didn't stop her.

"Why don't you invite him over for dinner?" she asked.

"I'd prefer a more casual first date, if there ever is a first date, that is. Like meeting for coffee."

"Boring."

"Asking him for dinner makes it sound like I want to jump his bones."

"Well, don't you?"

I took Ruby's hand across the table. "I am so not comfortable talking about this kind of thing with you. It's weird."

She put her other hand over mine. "Oh, pooh. You're just scared to get out there, that's all. By the way, I ran into Duke again, you know, the Dial-A-Ride guy?"

"Yes, I know."

"I showed him your picture."

I pulled back my hand. "Which one?" I wondered why I cared. Vanity, I guess.

"The one at your mother's fiftieth birthday party. You had on your cute pink dress. I cut Chad out of the picture. He thinks you look kind of like Anne Hathaway."

I bet Anne's grandma wasn't pushing her to have sex with her neighbors or hook up with the Dial-A-Ride guy.

"He really wants to meet you."

"Not yet, okay?" More like never.

"Did I mention he has an English accent?"

So? "No."

"English accents are very sexy, don't you think?" She leaned over the table and squinted at me. "Good grief. What's going on with your nose? Earlier, I thought it was hormonal pimples, but now it looks a little swollen."

"I got bit by a cat." I touched my nose and it felt all right. "Do you have a mirror?"

"I hope the cat had its shots. Your nose looks a little red." She dug through her purse and handed me a compact. "Have you had a tetanus shot recently?"

The dim lighting made it hard to see, so I used the flashlight app in my iPhone to illuminate my beak. It looked huge and sore. The two punctures now looked like major zits about to burst. I worked my jaw, opening wide and closing it, to make sure it wasn't about to lock up from tetanus.

Our waiter chose that moment to offer dessert menus. "You okay?" he asked, as he bent over the table to inspect my nose. "Whoa. That looks infected. Hope you don't have blood poisoning.

My brother had blood poisoning and almost had to have his arm amputated."

OMG! My rabid nose might have to be amputated? I snapped off the light, put down the mirror, and nonchalantly leaned my chin on my hand, covering my nose with my fingers. "I'm fine. Really." I enunciated each word very slowly to keep my jaw flexible.

He looked at me funny. "If you say so. Would you care for dessert?" He placed the dessert menus on the table. "Got a killer goat cheese and mango cheesecake."

"Sounds good. Just give us a moment."

"I'll wrap your leftovers while you decide."

Ruby eyeballed him as he walked away. "He's a hottie. Sure wish I was your age."

"He's a kid. Twenty, twenty-one, tops."

"So you'll be a cougar. It's very popular now."

"At thirty-one, I am not ready to join the cougar club just yet."

"It wouldn't hurt you to dip your toe in the water." Ruby was like a dog with a bone. "Is it a crime for an old woman to want to see her granddaughter happy?" She shifted in her seat and groaned. "Maybe enjoy my last few miserable years on this wretched planet surrounded by great-grandchildren?"

Ignoring her, I opened the menu. "Ooo. Chocolate tiramisu. Your favorite. Wanna share?"

She looked miffed with me and said in a pouty tone, "No, I don't want to share."

"You know too much sugar will keep you awake," I warned her. "It makes your heart pound fast. Remember how you told me to always remind you?"

She crossed her arms over her chest and shot me a sulky glare. "I don't care."

My grandmother had transformed into a petulant five-year-old who wanted great-grandchildren. Too funny.

The waiter returned to our table and I ordered two tiramisus, still coyly hiding my nose.

After dinner, I dropped off my cranky grandmother. As she made a big show of trying to pull her suddenly ancient, creaking bones out of my car, she said, "One last thing, and then I'll never say another word again."

Like I believed that.

"I may be getting old, but you're not getting any younger." She glowered at me. "Just think about that, little missy."

Ruby hadn't called me "little missy" in years. She really was mad.

"All right. You win." My stiffening jaw was running ahead of my rabid-addled brain. "I will meet this Duke guy. There. Are you happy now?"

"Yes, I am," she answered with a smug grin. She lithely leaned over and pecked me on the cheek. "This will be so much fun. Maybe we can double date—that is, if I can dig up a date."

Ruby could have her pick of the men at Shady Acres if she wanted. She didn't seem to want, so you'd think she'd understand how I felt.

"How about that cute, retired mortician?" I said.

"Very funny. You know perfectly well that Ronald's gay. Actually, now that I think about it, it could be fun. We could go dancing. He does a mean tango. I'll ask him."

I can't think of anything more fun than a dancing double date with my grandma, a gay octogenarian mortician and Duke-the-Dial-A-Ride-Guy. Count me in!

"And if you don't like Duke, there's this cute guy at the—"

"One at a time, please," I said, as she hopped out of the car.

She got halfway to her door and called back, "I'll call ya tomorrow. Toodles."

I drove home grousing aloud until the humor of the whole episode hit me and by the time I pulled into my driveway, I was in hysterics.

Daisy and Tabitha gave me a royal greeting, and I gave them a snack. In the bathroom, I inspected my nose with a 10x magnifying mirror. It definitely looked worse, so I slathered half a tube of Neosporin on it and taped a big gauze pad over it.

I crawled into bed, turned on the white noise machine to forest sounds, and snuggled into my favorite sleeping position under my cozy down comforter. Ahhh. A minute later, Tabitha and Daisy bounded into the room and hopped onto the bed.

"Wait a minute." I sat up and switched on the light. "I thought we'd agreed that you guys sleep on the couch now."

Daisy ignored me and flopped on her side of the bed, then got up and revolved about six or seven times before flopping down again in the exact same position. Tabitha wedged in against her.

I knew any further argument was useless, so I turned off the light and shifted into my sleeping position again, assuming I'd drift off momentarily, but instead I noticed I could hear my heart beating double-time in the ear pressed to the pillow. I rolled over on my back and stared at the ceiling. I felt yucky and then I heard my "dessert warning" to Ruby. *You know too much sugar will keep you awake. It makes your heart pound.* Then Ruby's voice drifted into my reverie. *You're not getting any younger, you know.*

I was wide-awake and buzzing on a sugar high. *Oh, no. I'm turning into my grandmother.*

"No way. I'm barely thirty-one, which is like the new twenty-one." I switched on the lamp and checked my alarm clock. "Who goes to bed at 9:37 anyway? Old people, that's who."

Daisy opened one eye, grumbled, and went back to sleep.

I jumped out of bed and went to the living room to watch TV. I caught the last few minutes of a show about a woman almost buried alive by her hoarding habit, then got sucked into watching people with bizarre addictions. The first story was about a woman who eats curtains. Her husband complained because they had no privacy. Jeez! Get some mini-blinds, idiot! I could have changed the channel, but I found the show disturbingly fascinating, which led me to the next show about weird obsessions. Like the woman who loved pigs so much she transformed her entire house into a pig-sty.

I'm talking the *interior*. She ought to get together with the hoarder lady. No wonder I usually only watch my recorded shows.

———

At eleven-thirty-five, I woke up on the couch, wiped the drool off my chin, and dragged myself to bed. A more respectable bedtime for a young, active woman like me.

CHAPTER TWENTY-SIX

1996
Tuesday, May 14

Phil lounged on the family room sofa, struggling to keep his eyes focused on a dry, academic history of the Roman Empire when his cell phone rang. Since moving home, he'd ignored several calls from Erik, and deleted one long-winded drunken voicemail after listening to thirty seconds of slurred nonsense. Now it was Jake calling, so he set the heavy book on the coffee table and answered.

He'd barely said hello when Jake blurted, "You need to get over here. The police are setting up interviews for this afternoon."

Phil's felt his lower back muscles instantly knot up with tension. "What time?"

"Four."

"Hold on a sec." No one was home, but to be on the safe side, Phil went outside to the back of the yard to continue the conversation. "I'll come over around three, so we can get our stories straight." As soon as he said that he realized he sounded like the criminal he now was. "How are you holding up?"

"Not good. I don't know how I'm going to get through this without breaking. I can't eat, can't sleep, can't study. They're going to take one look at me and know I'm guilty."

"Same here," Phil whispered, keeping an eye on the back door. "Remember Jake, we're not the ones who killed her."

"I know, but we let it happen."

"No, we didn't. We tried to save her. Erik's the one who murdered her in cold blood." Phil shuddered at the brutal memory.

"You're right." Jake dropped to a whisper. "But we both did the other thing."

Phil had been so obsessed with Lindsay's death, that he'd nearly pushed the rape out of his mind. It seemed almost inconsequential now when compared to murder. But the police wouldn't think that way. At the very least, he and Jake would go down for the rape and the kidnapping.

———

Phil entered his dark bedroom at the frat house and found Erik and Jake lying on their beds. For the last few days, neither had shaved or showered. The stale, airless room stank of body odor, boozy breath, and rotting takeout.

"Whoa!" Phil plugged his nose, as he raised the mini blinds and opened the window. He stuck his head out and sucked in the fresh spring air, before turning to his roommates. "It reeks in here."

"We didn't get to go home and have Mommy take care of us," sneered Erik, covering his eyes against the sudden daylight flooding the messy room.

"Have you been drinking?"

"Not this afternoon, but hey! It's five o'clock somewhere, so..." He rolled on his side and stretched for the silver flask on his desk.

Phil got to it first and held it aloft. "Do you really think it's a good idea to talk to the cops wasted?"

Erik swung his bare, dirty feet to the floor. "Maybe not." He yawned, rubbed his eyes, and scratched under his t-shirt.

Phil set the flask on the windowsill, dumped the smelly takeout leftovers in a garbage can and placed it outside in the hall. "Have either of you looked in a mirror lately? You both look like homeless bums. The minute the cops see you, they're going to suspect something's off. You need to clean up."

Jake dragged himself off his bed. "He's right." He grabbed a towel off the back of his desk chair and left the room.

Phil turned his attention to Erik. "Just keep up the drinking and you'll put us all in prison."

———

Alpha Gamma had thirty-five undergrads living in the house. The older members lived elsewhere but were coming in for interviews. By 3:55, there were over seventy young men milling about in the main floor lounge. Detective Yaeger was there with two other officers. At 4:03, she addressed the group.

"Thank you for coming. Has everyone checked his name off on the sign-in sheet in the dining room?"

Several boys left to sign in. When they returned and everyone had settled on chairs and the floor, she began again. "I'm Detective Angela Yaeger, and this is Officer Robert Harris and Officer Joanne Yee," she said.

The officers nodded to the group.

"You all know why we're here. In the early hours of May 4th, Lindsay Moore was found near here. She'd been drugged, assaulted, and gang-raped at a party that we believe was held in a fraternity house; although, it could have been a sorority house, so we've been visiting the various chapters in the vicinity where our victim was found." Yaeger's eyes swept the room. Several boys glanced away or fidgeted in their seats while others boldly stared at her. Like every fraternity she'd already visited, they all looked guilty.

"We know a party was held at this house on the night of the assault; however, there were a lot of parties that night. Go figure. Friday night? Frat houses? Mmmm. How ironic," she softly chuckled. Her remark broke the ice and much of the nervous tension left the room as the boys snickered. She paused a moment to let them quiet down. "I'm sure most of you already know Lindsay went missing this past Friday afternoon. We believe she was abducted."

One of the boys raised his hand. "Do you think this is connected to the rape?"

"That would seem likely, so please, if any of you have any information, even if it seems trivial, we need to hear it. If you've observed any strange behavior over the past week, or stranger than normal—" More laughs. "—heard any odd comments, anything, anything at all, we need to hear about it. You never know what little thing might blow a case wide open and perhaps save a young girl's life." She paused and slowly scanned the group. "Gentlemen. Lindsay's only fifteen years old. She's a good girl, well-liked by everyone because she is a nice kid. I'm sure many of you have little sisters..." She paused to let it sink in.

Phil fought back tears as Detective Yaeger brought Lindsay to life for the young men. The light mood in the room shifted dramatically. Now she was a real girl, and everyone cared and wanted to help. Phil caught snatches of whispered remarks.

"We need to find the bastard who did this."

"If anyone ever did something like this to my sister, I'd kill him."

Detective Yaeger clapped her hands to get everyone's attention. "Okay, guys, settle down. We're going to speak to each one of you in separate rooms. We'll go as quickly as we can, but it's going to take a while, so please be patient."

Officer Harris concluded his chat with Joshua Hussain and

asked him to fetch Erik Mason. As Hussain passed through the lounge, he said to Erik, "Mason, you're up. He's waiting in the parlor."

"How was it?" asked Erik.

"Piece of cake... unless *you're* guilty."

"Real funny," said Erik, as Hussain headed toward the stairs to his room. "In case you've forgotten, that girl could be dead for all you care." Erik slipped a quick glance at Phil's stony face and then left the room.

Officer Harris was sitting by the window on a straight-back chair brought in from the dining room. Another chair was placed opposite him with a small oak table in between. "You Erik Mason?"

Erik nodded, rubbing the back of his neck. "Yes."

Harris indicated the other chair. "Have a seat. You understand this is a routine interview and you are not under suspicion."

"I understand, sir."

Harris picked up a pen and glanced at his clipboard. "Were you at the party here on Friday, May third?"

"Yes."

Harris showed a photograph of Lindsay to Erik. "Do you recognize this girl?"

Erik leaned close and made a big show of looking at the photo. "No. I mean I don't *know* her, but I have seen photos of her on the news."

Officer Harris then showed him photos of Jenny and Mallory. "How about these girls? Ever seen them?"

Erik slowly shook his head, lips in a tight line of concern. "No, sir," then asked in a hushed tone, "Did something happen to them, too?"

Harris ignored his question. "Do you recall anything from the party that might be helpful in our investigation?"

"I wish, but no, sir."

Harris stood up and so did Erik. As they exited the room, the officer handed him his card. "If you think of anything, hear anything, please call immediately."

Erik took the card, shook the officer's hand, and with an expression that conveyed deep concern, he said, "Nothing would give me greater pleasure than to help you find Lindsay and bring her safely home."

Harris followed Erik back to the living room and called Oliver Russell. He didn't see the wink Erik tossed at Phil, nor the relieved grin that bloomed on his face the moment he stepped out the front door.

Forty minutes later, Phil was called to the kitchen. Officer Yee observed his healing facial lacerations and nervous agitation.

"You can relax, Phil. Have a seat. You're not under suspicion. We just need your help, okay?"

"Okay." His face flushed and he licked his dry lips.

"I can't help noticing your face. Were you in a fight?" asked Yee.

Phil touched his wounds tentatively. "No. I crashed my car. Really stupid. A squirrel ran out in front of me." He attempted a smile. "The car looks worse."

She returned his smile and placed the girls' pictures in front of him. "Recognize anyone?"

He looked at the photos carefully. His hands were clammy and under the table he wiped them repeatedly on his jeans. Sweat broke out on his forehead, which was concealed by his long, shaggy forelock. "Well, yes and no."

"What do you mean?"

Phil shifted in his seat, trying to appear calm. "I recognize this one." He tapped Lindsay's picture. "But only because her picture is everywhere. Sorry."

"No need to be sorry. Were you at the party here on the night of her attack?"

"Yes, I was."

"Do you remember anything unusual?"

"To be honest, I was really drunk," he said, looking contrite. *At least that's true,* he thought. "It's all pretty much a blur... I'm sorry."

"How old are you, Phil?" she asked with a stern edge to her voice.

"Nineteen."

"What is the legal drinking age in California?"

He dropped his chin and murmured, "Twenty-one. Are you going to arrest me?"

Her tone softened. "No. But my advice would be to cut it out. Especially after what's happened. And you can bet we'll be keeping a close eye on all the houses until the term ends."

"I already have. I'm taking a break at home right now."

"Why is that, Phil?"

"My grades have slipped and I need to focus on my classes. Frat life is getting old."

"I hear you. Pretty wild sometimes, huh?"

"Yes. And this whole thing has really gotten to me," he said, becoming animated and waving his hands to emphasize his statement. "That's not what frat life is supposed to be about."

"What's frat life supposed to be about?"

"It's like a brotherhood, you know. Making lifelong friends. Doing good in the community. At least that's how my dad described it."

What a nice kid, she thought. "How's it at home after living in a frat?"

"Quiet. I can think." Phil thought of his mother. "My mom's a police dispatcher."

"Where?"

"Here in Santa Lucia. Her name's Penny Hobart."

"You're Penny's son? Please say hello to her for me." Yee stood up and gave Phil her card. "Call me if you recall something or hear anything that might help us find Lindsay."

"Let's get right to it, Jake, so you can get out of here," said Detective Yaeger. "Did you go to the frat party, the Friday night Lindsay Moore was raped?"

"Yeah." His knee started bouncing under the table.

Yaeger removed Lindsay's photo from a folder and placed it on the oak dining room table facing him. "Do you recognize this girl from the party?"

"No." At least not from the party.

Yaeger watched him closely. Had there been a hesitation? "You are absolutely sure you didn't see her at the party?"

"Yes, I'm sure." That was true. Jake had never actually seen her face.

She pulled out the photos of Mallory and Jenny. "How about these girls?"

"No. The place was packed that night." Jake tried a smile, but it felt stiff and unnatural on his face. "People were coming and going." He shook his head. "I really wish I could be more help."

"You're doing fine, Jake. I appreciate you trying and I know Lindsay's mother will, too. This has been incredibly hard on her and I just wish we could get a break." Yaeger gave Jake her card. "Who knows? Maybe you'll think of something that will save Lindsay's life."

CHAPTER TWENTY-SEVEN

THURSDAY · APRIL 18
Posted by Katy McKenna

I placed another ad offering my services (LOL—that sounds a little sketchy) on Craigslist, then spent the rest of the morning attacking my third bedroom storage unit, which basically means I moved some boxes to the garage and stacked them along the walls. I figured if they sit out there for six months, in addition to the months they've already languished in the bedroom, and I still don't feel the need to search for anything, then it can all be tossed. It's a good theory, but we'll see if I actually do it.

My stomach announced lunchtime, so I halted the box relocation project to warm up some leftover spinach lasagna "a la Momma."

After popping a plateful in the microwave, I noticed my cell phone on the counter showed I had a voicemail from Samantha: "I'm at work, and you will never guess who just checked in. Christy Hobart. Except her last name is now Sutherland. I wouldn't have realized it was her after all these years, but her mother's here and she saw the petition and went ballistic to say the least. Talk to you later."

The microwave timer dinged and I removed my lunch and sat at the kitchen table overlooking the yard to ponder this new development. Again, doubts crept in as I considered all the people affected by Hobart's crimes and how I might be making their burdens heavier. Then I remembered the otherworldly presence I'd felt beside me at the school's flagpole. I had to quit second-guessing myself. It was too late now anyway.

I finished lunch, put the dishes in the sink, and went to the bathroom to wash up. I cautiously removed the surgical tape from my mutilated nose and pulled off the Neosporin-goopy gauze. The tip was still red, but it wasn't throbbing and I wasn't foaming at the mouth from rabies yet, so I put a bandage over it and returned to my self-imposed manual labor. I kept my cell with me, in case Sam called with an update.

———

An hour later, I was perched on a carton of old college textbooks, looking at my baby book and marveling at how adorable I was, when she called again. "Did you get my message?"

"Yes. What's going on? Is Christy having a baby?" *Stupid question —she's in the maternity ward.*

"She's in labor, and it looks like it's going to be a long one. But that's not what I'm calling about."

"You said her mother saw the petition."

"And she is mad." Sam lowered her voice, which meant she was calling from the nurse's station. "Like raving mad. In fact, I wouldn't be surprised if she *is* mad!"

"You're losing me here. I get that she's mad—"

"I do too, but this is way over the top. She's threatening to sue the hospital."

"That's probably just a reaction," I said. "Everyone says stuff like that. I feel terrible this happened to her. She's had enough pain in her life. She should be joyful about her grandchild being born, but instead she gets slammed with my stupid petition and all those horrible memories."

"I put the petitions away and brought her a cup of tea. I don't know what else I can do. At least she's not screaming louder than her daughter now. The poor father-to-be looks like he wants to bolt. Hold on."

I heard Sam talking to someone and then she came back on. "Gotta go."

I set the phone on a box and thought about Christy. Her baby's uncle was a rapist and a murderer. Someday she would have to explain that to her child. How would she find the words?

I tried to get back to work, but my motivation had flown out the window, so I decided to pack it in for the day and take Daisy to the dog park.

CHAPTER TWENTY-EIGHT

1996

Thursday, May 16

Phil was on his bed, propped against the padded headboard, playing Tetris on his old Gameboy when his cell rang. It was Jake. "When're you coming back here?"

"Why?"

"Erik's drinking a lot."

"He always drinks a lot. What else is new?"

"This is different." Phil heard the frustration and anger in Jake's voice. "It's like he's drinking to pass out as fast as he can, and I'm scared to leave him alone. I'm afraid he's going to run off at the mouth and get us all arrested."

"All right, I'll be back tonight," said Phil, and ended the call. He'd hoped never to lay eyes on either of his roommates again but knew that leaving Jake to deal with Erik was selfish.

He was gathering his things into his backpack when a car parked in the driveway. He peeked through his drapes and saw his mother and Christy coming up the front walk. Phil met her at the door and told her he was returning to the frat house.

"Why, honey? I know you're still not feeling good, so why not stay here?" She ruffled his hair. "It's been so nice having you home."

"Yeah, it's been nice for me, too, but it's wearing me out riding my bike to school from here, and it's going to be a while before my car is ready, so I need to go back."

"I suppose you're right."

"I've already got my stuff together, so I'll go get it and hit the road."

Penny was waiting at the front door holding his sweatshirt when he returned. "You better put this on, it's chilly out there. Say, did I tell you I'm down to three cigs a day now? This time I'm really going to make it."

He hugged his mother. "Really proud of you."

"You sure you can manage?" she asked, still hanging onto him. "Your backpack is awfully heavy. I could give you a ride, you know."

Christy stepped in to rescue him. "Mom. That's so awesome about the cigarettes."

She peeled Penny away from Phil and threw her arms around her in a tight embrace. "I'm proud of you, too."

Phil mouthed "thank you" to his sister and Penny laughed at them both, saying, "All right, you two. I know when I'm being worked."

———

Erik's snores echoed down the hallway as Phil grudgingly climbed the stairs to the second floor of the frat house. This was the last place he wanted to be. When he opened the door to his room, the reek of vomit hit him full-face, sparking his gag reflex. He pulled his t-shirt up to his nose before entering the room.

Jake was sitting at his desk, bare feet propped on a corner of the desk, working on a paper for his organic agriculture class while blowing out his eardrums listening to Coolio on his Sony Walkman. Phil tapped him on the shoulder, nearly sending him through the roof.

Jake slammed his feet on the floor and ripped off his headphones. "God! Give me a warning. I could've pissed my pants."

"Sorry." Phil gestured in Erik's direction. "Sorry about that, too." Erik's mouth hung open and his long, rasping snores nearly drowned out Phil's voice.

"He drinks, he pukes, he passes out, and I clean up the mess." Jake withdrew a handful of chips from an open bag on his desk and shoved them into his mouth. He brandished the bag at Phil. "Want some?"

Phil waved the chips away. The smell of taco chips mixed with stench in the room made him cringe. "No, thanks. How can you eat in here? The smell is turning my stomach." He shimmied out of his backpack, letting it drop onto his bed.

Jake opened a desk drawer and tossed a jar of Vicks VapoRub to Phil. "Put a little under your nose and it'll kill the smell. The cops on TV always do it when they find a dead body. It's not the greatest smell in the world and it kinda screws up your taste buds, but it beats breathing up his fumes."

"Nothing could stink worse than him." Lindsay's corpse came to mind and he willed the vision away. Phil opened the jar, rubbed a dab of ointment under his nose, and inhaled the strong aroma. "Whoa! Not better. Now my sinuses are wide open and it smells like mentholated vomit and piss in here. Thanks a lot." He set the jar on Jake's desk.

"I was thinking tomorrow morning," Jake said, "when he's coherent, you could talk to him. He won't listen to me. I think he's drinking to blot out what he's done, but if we can't keep him sober, it's only a matter of time before he shoots off his mouth and blows everything."

"So you want to do, like, an intervention?" asked Phil. He sat on the floor and leaned against his bed frame.

"Shit, no. An intervention means you care about someone, and I couldn't care less about him," he paused. "But we need to do something."

Phil considered that, and a chilling realization hit him. "You know, it's not going to be just until school's out. If he drinks like this when he goes home—"

"And you know he will," said Jake. "The guy's a friggin' alcoholic."

"You know, he could be sitting at a bar, five, ten years from now and start blabbing about it. We could be married with families, good careers, and suddenly everything goes up in smoke because of that bastard's big mouth."

Jake opened a desk drawer, crammed the bag of chips in and slammed it. "I hadn't thought past getting out of here. I mean, there's no way I'll ever get over this. Lindsay will haunt me forever, but you're right. This'll never end. We'll never truly be free, no matter how far away we are."

Erik rolled over to his back and belched toxic fumes of alcohol and stomach acid. Cracked, dried spittle lined his chapped, scabby lips. He turned his head towards them, opened one sticky eye and blearily slurred, "Fuck you." He reached under his pillow and pulled out a half-empty fifth of vodka and drained it while Phil and Jake watched in silent fascination.

"Last night I discovered half a case stashed under his bed," said Jake. "I got rid of it, but I guess I missed that one. This is why I needed you to come back. I won't be able to stop him from getting more liquor without your help."

Erik cradled the empty bottle to his chest and passed out. A moment later vomit gurgled up in his mouth, choking him as the bile pooled and drained back down his throat.

Jake rushed to him and turned him on his side. The sour puke poured out of his mouth and soaked the sheet.

Phil was overcome with loathing. A spoiled, arrogant, heartless drunk had ruined his life and now controlled his future. "God, we are so screwed." He stared at Erik, trying to think what to do with this loser.

"I've got an idea." Phil bent over Erik and tugged his wallet from a rear pocket and removed a credit card. "We've got to get him out of here. We'll get a hotel room and take turns babysitting him until he dries out." He brandished the credit card. "We'll use his card because his parents will never notice the charges like mine would."

"Or mine," Jake said, feeling a tingle of hope. "How long do we keep him in a hotel room?"

"Until we can make him understand what's at stake. That he has to stay sober. Forever. We'll get him to check into rehab, join AA, threaten to tell his parents, whatever it takes."

Phil snatched his backpack from his bed and placed it by the door. "I'll pack some clothes for Erik, while you get your stuff. Then you bring your car to the front of the house. I don't want to carry him any further than we have to."

"At least no one here will think anything of it. They're used to him."

Phil pulled the top drawer of Erik's dresser open and grabbed boxers and t-shirts. As he jammed them into a duffel bag, Jake suddenly yelped, "Shit, shit, shit!"

Phil spun around and saw the cause of Jake's outburst. Erik's body shook violently and his head was bent at an odd angle, slamming the wall behind his bed. His eyes rolled up and his bladder released as his limbs continued to thrash uncontrolled.

"What's wrong with him?" Jake hovered over Erik, afraid to touch him.

"He's having a seizure." Phil pushed in front of Jake and tried to hold Erik's body still. "Help me pull him down and get his head away from the wall before he knocks himself out."

Jake made no move to help.

"Please. He could bite his tongue off if we don't help him!"

"No, no way," Jake backed away and stood with his arms folded across his chest, his face set in stony resolution. "And too bad if he bites his tongue off; at least then he can't talk."

Phil straightened up from Erik, gaping at Jake. "Are you kidding?" He turned back to Erik. "Shit! He's puking again! I need to get him on his side or he'll choke." He grasped Erik's jerking shoulders and tried to pull his head away from the wall. A flailing arm knocked him sideways and he lost his footing, tripping over a skateboard on the floor, and hitting his temple hard against Erik's desk. For several moments Phil lay stunned on the floor, unable to move. When he recovered, Jake was hovering over Erik, grunting with exertion as he pinned the boy's writhing shoulders to the mattress. Erik sputtered as beige, chunky vomit gurgled and pooled in his mouth.

"What're you doing? He's choking! " Phil scrambled to his feet and struggled to push Jake away from Erik, but the muscular wrestler was stronger and blocked Phil's attempts. "Please, Jake. Please stop." He clenched his fists. "Oh God, this is so wrong."

As Erik's tremors weakened, Jake released his hand on Erik's right shoulder and pinched the boy's nostrils shut. Erik's glassy eyes opened wide as he fought to inhale oxygen, but instead sucked the sour vomit deep into his throat, blocking his esophagus.

Phil tried again to force Jake aside, but Jake angled his solid body over Erik, giving him no opening, and held fast. "Jake! You don't know what you're doing."

"I know exactly what I'm doing. He murdered Lindsay, destroyed our lives, threatened our families. Enough is enough."

CHAPTER TWENTY-NINE

1996
Friday, May 17

Angela was seated on a well-worn brown leather couch in Police Chief Paul Arnold's office. Her case notes were spread over the oak coffee table.

"We need answers fast," he said. "*Unsolved Mysteries* has contacted us and wants to do a segment on Lindsay."

Angela was surprised. "The TV show? I thought they only went after cold cases."

"So did I, but evidently they've been getting a lot of calls from our local citizens who've lost faith in us."

"I don't know what to tell you, Chief. We've followed up on every lead and we're nowhere."

"The last thing we need right now is a camera crew getting in the way of our investigation," said Chief Arnold.

Angela nodded in agreement. "And I don't want to be wasting my time babysitting those people."

"I'll do my best to stall them, but if the local press gets wind of this, it could blow up in our faces. Could look like I'm impeding justice."

"So we're damned if we do and damned if we don't."

"Pretty much. The girl was drugged and raped at a party and then later abducted. Come on. How in the hell can there be no witnesses?" Chief Arnold had asked this question umpteen times over the last two weeks.

"Oh, trust me there were witnesses, at least at the party, but they were too drunk or too stoned to realize what they saw. But no one seeing her abducted at the school did surprise me, so a few days ago I went to the school at the same time Lindsay disappeared and, yes, I can see how it could have happened. I saw one kid getting into a car at the other end of the lot but no one else."

"It would be nice if there was money in the school budget for security cameras," said Chief Arnold.

Angela laughed. "It'd be nice if there was money in the budget for art classes, or driver's education, or—"

He held up his hands in submission. "I hear you."

"Chief, we've talked to practically every kid in this town," Angela continued in a composed tone she didn't feel. "Every frat house, sorority, dorm, the high school. No one has given us anything concrete we can go on."

The chief got up from the sofa and stretched his long legs. "And her friends? Still nothing there?"

"Actually, there has been some further enlightenment as to why we have not been able to get a straight answer from those two."

"What's that?"

"I can give you the abbreviated version or you can listen to my last interview with Jenny Farrell." Angela pointed at the small tape recorder she'd placed on the coffee table when she first entered the office.

"I want to hear it." He sat down and unbuttoned his jacket and loosened his tie.

Angela pressed the play button and her recorded voice filled the office.

"All right Jenny, let's go back to the beginning."

"You mean, when we picked up Lindsay at her house or when we went for pizza?"

"When you went for pizza."

"Okay." An audible sigh was heard and then Jenny spoke. *"We went to the pizza place, next to the movie theatre, and after we got in line, Mallory said she had to go to the bathroom and told me to come with her. Lindsay held our place in line. In the bathroom, Mallory took a joint out of her purse and told me it would make the food taste way better."*

Jenny's father interrupted. *"Are you kidding? I hope for your sake, you said no."*

Angela hit pause. *"I thought I was going to lose her right then and there, but she was determined to tell her story."* She pressed play again.

"Dad, it's not like it can really hurt you... right? So I decided to try it. I only took a few puffs. It really burned, and I didn't like it, and I swear I'll never do it again. But I didn't tell Lindsay because I knew she wouldn't approve."

Her father said, *"That's because she's got more brains than you."*

"Let's continue," said Angela.

"There was some cute boys in line, and they invited us to a party. Mallory wanted to go, but me and Lindsay didn't. Mallory said it would be cool and told me I was acting like a baby. I didn't want the boys to think I was a kid, so I said okay."

Angela stopped the recording and said, "At this point, she broke down. Since she said nothing coherent, I'll fast-forward."

Angela pressed fast-forward and let it spin to the spot she was seeking. She pressed play.

"How did you get to the party?" asked Angela.

"You already know that from the last time we talked."

"Tell me again."

"We walked, but I don't remember what way we went. I was really nervous about going to the party and about smoking the joint. I was trying to act

normal so Lindsay wouldn't know, but I felt super dizzy and my chest really hurt. When we got there, there were tons of people there, and I felt stupid 'cause they were all way older than us. A nice boy showed us where to get drinks and food and then I had to go pee. When I was in the bathroom, Mallory knocked on the door, and I let her in. I had a real bad headache and felt kind of sick, and she said she had some medicine that would get rid of it, so I took it."

"What?" shouted Jenny's father. *"She hands you a pill, and you just take it, without asking what it was?"*

"I thought it was headache medicine, like Tylenol. She said it would make me feel better."

"What was it?" asked Angela.

Jenny's voice dropped to a whisper. *"Ecstasy."*

"Turn that thing off," demanded Farrell.

"Please, Mr. Farrell. Lindsay's missing out there somewhere," said Angela. *"We need to know everything that happened that night."*

"Do we need a lawyer present? Jenny just admitted to using illegal drugs, for God's sake."

"Please, Daddy." Jenny was sobbing. *"I know I screwed up big-time."*

"How do you know it was ecstasy?" asked Angela.

"She told me."

"When did she tell you?"

"Right after I swallowed it. She thought it was funny. I got really scared then."

"I swear I am going to kill that girl!" screamed her father. *"Feel free to arrest her, for all I care."*

Angela said quietly. *"Jenny, what happened next?"*

"I got scared, and I didn't want Lindsay to know, so I didn't go back to her. After a while my stomach felt weird and rumbly, but then I started feeling really good. Like really, super happy. I felt totally awesome."

"That's it. I'm going in the other room," snapped Farrell. *"I can't listen to any more of this crap."*

"Daddy, I am so sorry. I didn't know."

"Well, Jenny, that's not exactly true, is it? You knew you smoked pot. And

you knew you took ecstasy." His voice faded as he left the room. "_And you knew all of this from the beginning but chose not to tell anyone until now._"

"_I'm sorry!_" she screamed.

"_Too little, too late!_" he yelled from the next room. "_This is going to kill your mother._"

"_God, I really screwed up,_" Jenny said. "_My parents will never forgive me._"

Angela waited for Jenny to compose herself. "_Tell me what happened next, Jenny._"

"_I'm not really sure. I was dancing and having fun. Then I kinda remember feeling super cold, and my jaw clenched up, and my headache came back really bad. I don't even remember going home._" There was a pause. "_I'm so sorry I didn't tell you this before. I was really scared. Will I have to go to juvie?_"

Angela turned off the machine.

"Well, shit," said the chief. "This just gets better and better, doesn't it?"

CHAPTER THIRTY

Erik's death was ruled accidental and for the first time in over two weeks, Phil slept through the night at his parents' house and woke with a ravenous appetite. He found his mom in the kitchen nursing a cup of coffee at the kitchen table and reading the newspaper.

"Morning, Mom."

Penny glanced up from the paper. "Well, good morning to you too, sleepyhead."

Phil poured himself a cup of coffee. "I thought I'd make some breakfast. Want some?"

"Breakfast sounds great."

Penny pulled the newspaper closer. "Still no leads on Lindsay Moore's disappearance," she read aloud. She looked up from the paper. "The TV Show, *Unsolved Mysteries*, wants to do a segment."

"You're kidding. Here in Santa Lucia?" Phil's hand started

shaking and he carefully set his mug on the counter with two hands.

"That show's had a lot of success solving crimes and we can use all the help we can get. Lindsay could be anywhere by now. Maybe brainwashed in some cult like the Moonies, for all we know. But a nationally televised show might actually help to jog someone's memory. I'm sure everyone on the central coast would be watching." She sipped her coffee. "The sad reality is, in all likelihood she's lying dead somewhere out there and her mother will never know what happened to her."

Penny saw the stunned look on Phil's face. She knew Erik's death weighed heavily on him and talking about Lindsay had stirred that up again.

"Honey, I'm sorry. I realize how terribly hard these last few days have been. Losing your friend so suddenly." She shook her head, biting her lower lip. "I can't even begin to imagine what Erik's folks are going through. But you've got to realize there was nothing you could have done." She got up and hugged him. "And I know this girl's attack and disappearance has affected you, too. You can't help it. You're a caring person." She pulled away and looked into Phil's eyes, smiling gently. "At least Erik's parents will have closure."

Phil could not meet his mother's eyes. *I thought it would stop with Erik's death, but it isn't. And her mother needs to know.*

———

In his bedroom, Phil picked up his flip-phone and pressed Jake's speed-dial number. After a few rings, it went to voicemail. Relieved he didn't have to speak directly to Jake, who surely would have tried to talk him out of it, he said, "Jake, it's Phil. Listen, man, I'm really sorry about this, but I'm going to tell my parents. I can't live a lie anymore. I'm so sorry." He shut his phone and laid his head on the desk.

"Phil?"

He lifted his head and saw his mother standing in the doorway, holding a stack of folded towels.

"What was that all about?" she quietly asked.

"What do you mean?" He didn't want to tell her like this.

"I heard you say you're going to tell us something. That you can't live a lie anymore." She entered the room and sat on his bed, still clutching the towels.

"Please call Dad to come home. I need to talk to both of you."

"Phil, you're scaring me." Penny's eyes welled up with tears. "What is it?"

———

Penny and Adam sat with Phil at the kitchen table, waiting for him to tell them the dreadful thing that was bothering him. Phil was still uncertain. If he did this, everything would change forever. Then he remembered that *Unsolved Mysteries* wanted to do a segment about Lindsay. Sooner or later, he was going to get caught. In the end, it would be better for everyone if he turned himself in now.

His mother said, "Phil, whatever it is, we'll get through it."

"Your mother's right. You're a young man with your whole life ahead of you. Just tell us what's wrong and we'll deal with it." Adam took a breath, exhaled, and forced himself to ask the words no parent ever wants to ask. "Phil, did you get a girl pregnant?"

Penny groaned. "Oh, my God. Is that it? You got someone pregnant?"

Phil smacked the table in frustration. "No one is pregnant."

They waited for Phil to continue and he forced the life-altering words out, "I know where Lindsay Moore is."

"How do you know? Who told you?" Penny shoved her chair back and stood up. "We have to call Angela and get that girl home."

Adam watched Phil's reactions. "Penny, stop. Sit down." He spoke slowly. "Phil, how do you know where Lindsay is?"

Phil swallowed hard, fighting the bile crawling up his esophagus. "Because I put her there."

"What do you mean?" his father said softly. "Are you saying you're hiding her?"

Penny clutched at Phil's arm. "Why would you be hiding her? Why?"

He pulled his arm from her grasp and put his trembling hands in his lap. "May I have a glass of water, please?"

Adam went to the sink, poured a tall glass of water, and placed it in front of him. Phil took a shaky sip.

His father sat down. "Why don't you start at the beginning."

Phil told them every sordid, damning detail. He told the story straightforward with no attempt to sugarcoat his participation in the crimes. Throughout the long narrative, his parents remained silent, except for his mother's suppressed sobs and hiccups. Tears rolled down Adam's face unchecked, his face was flushed and a vein twitched on his forehead as he stared at his son. The only thing Phil held back was Jake suffocating Erik.

Phil had not seen his father cry since he had been a child and was in the ER, suffering an asthma attack. When he finished speaking, he waited for their response. They were stunned, speechless.

"Please say something," Phil said.

After a time, his mother spoke. "Why, Phil? For the love of God, why?" her voice choked. "Why would you tell us something like this? It can't be true. It just can't be."

Adam rose from the table and went to the sink. "I don't even know you." He poured a glass of water and brought it to Penny.

"You didn't mean to do it," cried his mother. "It was a terrible accident. You're not a bad boy." Her voice cracked and she wiped her streaming eyes with a paper napkin. "It's not your fault. You're a good boy." She pounded the table with clenched fists, screaming, "You're a good boy. You've always been a good boy."

Adam crouched by her chair and held her until the storm passed. Phil had never seen his father show such deep love for her. He knew he had broken their hearts.

Adam straightened and stated in a dead, defeated tone, "We'll need a lawyer. I'll make some calls, and then you'll have to turn yourself in."

"Wait!" Penny grabbed his hand. "Why does he have to turn himself in? What good will it do? It won't bring Lindsay back, and you know he didn't mean to do it. Look at your son, Adam! He's already suffering."

"Phil has to do the right thing. He knows it; that's why he told us." Adam turned to leave the room.

Penny stood up and clutched his arm. "Please. Please don't call."

He took her sagging body in his arms and spoke gently. "I'm not calling the police, Penny. I'm calling the lawyer. Do you want to lie down?"

"No. I want to stay with Phil. He needs me."

Her pathetic voice ripped Phil's heart. Was it worth it? Was this truly going to help anyone?

Adam left the kitchen to call the family attorney. In the home office, he closed the door, sat at the desk, and stared sadly at a framed family photo taken last Christmas. After several minutes, he opened the address book and looked up Dave Holloway's number. He was an estate attorney, but unless you were a member of the mob, what ordinary middle-class family had a criminal lawyer? Over the years, Dave had taken care of the Hobart's estate planning and had become a trusted friend and golf buddy.

After a short, difficult conversation, Dave suggested a criminal attorney in his building. Adam asked if he would call for him.

Holloway put Adam on hold while he rang Jeri Slater's line and gave her a brief run-down, then came back on the line with Adam. "I gave her your number and she'll call in the next few minutes. Phil will be in good hands, Adam."

At 1:10, Jeri Slater held open the Santa Lucia Police Headquarters main door and ushered the Hobart family in. She told the desk clerk that Angela Yaeger was expecting them. A few moments later she came out to greet them.

Slater stepped forward. "Angela, I'm Phil's attorney and will be representing him in this conversation."

"It's nice to see you, Jeri," said Angela with a frown, mystified as to why Phil needed an attorney. She noted Penny's swollen, red-rimmed eyes and Adam's stony demeanor. "Why don't we go into one of the conference rooms where we won't be disturbed."

In the room, the group clustered in a corner until Angela closed the door and told them to be seated at the long, rectangle table. A moment later, Officer Yee entered and took a seat.

Angela activated the tape recorder sitting in the middle of the table. "Phil, I gather what you have to say is of a serious nature, so I will be recording our conversation. Is that all right?"

He glanced at Slater for approval. She nodded and placed her own recorder on the table.

"Yes, ma'am.

Angela switched the recorder on and clasped her hands on the table. "I am Detective Angela Yaeger of the Santa Lucia Police Department. Today is Tuesday, May 21, 1996. The time is 1:27 p.m. I am speaking with Phillip Hobart. Phil, please state your full name, age, address, and today's date."

Phil spoke softly, "Phillip Adam Hobart."

"Please speak louder," Angela directed.

"Phillip Adam Hobart."

Within the first sixty seconds of his narration, Angela realized he was confessing to Lindsay Moore's rape and murder.

CHAPTER THIRTY-ONE

FRIDAY · APRIL 19
Posted by Katy McKenna

I woke at dawn with Christy Hobart on my mind. It was too early to get up, so I tried various positions to fall back to sleep, but just as I'd start to float off, she'd drift into my thoughts and snap me awake again.

Mrs. Watkins, the school secretary, had told me how Christy had been shunned by her friends, as though her brother's crimes were her fault. Guilt by association. The poor kid had even tried to commit suicide. Somehow she'd survived that rough time and now was married and having a baby. That and an extreme need to pee got me out of bed. Daisy and Tabitha were not having sleep issues and took no notice of my exit.

As soon as I had a few swallows of caffeine under my belt, I sat at the kitchen table and called Samantha. It was 5:55 a.m. She'd be up savoring some moments of quiet and a cup of tea before the pandemonium of getting the kids off to school commenced. She answered on the second ring.

"You're up early," she said. "What gives?"

"I woke up thinking about Christy. Did she have her baby?"

"Not on my watch. She was at five centimeters when I left at five-thirty last night."

Knowing next to nothing about the birthing process, I asked, "How many centimeters do you need to deliver a baby?"

"Ten. So she had a ways to go. These things can drag on and on, or they can suddenly shift into high gear and it's baby time. That's how I was with Casey. Went from three centimeters to ten in about thirty minutes. Hopefully by now she's cuddling her little newbie."

"How was her mother when you left? Had she calmed down about the petition?"

"Seething but keeping it under control. The doctor made it abundantly clear that if she wanted to remain with her daughter during labor, she was not to upset her." I heard Sam sip her tea, so I did the same. "I went in to say goodbye to them before leaving, and Mrs. Hobart walked out into the hallway with me and asked if I knew who'd started the petition."

Without thinking, I blurted, "Oh, no. You didn't tell her, did you?"

"Are you kidding?" She was dumbfounded and rightly so. "Do you honestly think I'd do that to you?"

"I'm sorry. That was stupid of me."

"Yes, it was, but you're up way early, so I'll give you a pass. Hold on." She took another swallow. "I told her I had no idea who'd made the petition."

"Yesterday you said you thought she might be a little crazy."

"How do I put this?" Samantha paused. "I understand that she was stressed out with her daughter being in labor and all, and it had to be very upsetting to see the petition, but I think most people would've chosen not to call attention to themselves considering what he was convicted for. But I definitely think there's a screw loose. There was a look in her eyes that was really off. She gave me the willies."

"Are you working today?" I asked, hoping it was her day off.

"Unfortunately, yes. I hope no one on staff told her I was the one who brought in the petition."

"What will you do if she confronts you?"

"Well, it's pointless to lie if she already knows, so I guess I would tell her that most people feel her son hasn't paid his debt, and that's why I brought the petition in. With any luck, it won't come to that. Hold on." She put me on hold for a few seconds. "Spencer's on the other line. He's in Albuquerque. Talk to you later, okay?"

I dumped my coffee in the sink, no longer able to stomach it, and showered and dressed in my daily ensemble, topped off with my favorite pink floral scarf.

It was 6:20. I curled up in the chair by the French doors and thought about Mrs. Hobart. Had I put my best friend in danger? A shiver ran down my spine and I chided myself about watching too many of those "women in peril" movies on the Lifetime channel. Mrs. Hobart had to realize the community was not going to welcome her son back with open arms. My thoughts started to drift, so I pulled a throw over me and snuggled into the cushions and closed my eyes for a quick power nap.

———

Daisy nudged me awake, begging for brunch since breakfast time was long past. It was almost 11:00 so I fed my girls and rummaged in the fridge for something to satisfy my rumbling tummy, but nothing was inspiring me. I decided to go by the hospital and see if Samantha could take a break for an early lunch with me in the cafeteria. Yes, I know. Hospital food? Really?

Truth be told, my curiosity was getting the better of me. I

wanted to know what was going on with Christy and her mother. I thought I might quit worrying once I saw them—from afar. I couldn't think of any good reason for Penny Hobart to know who I was.

The maternity ward is on the second floor. I went to the nurse's station and asked the nurse staffing the desk to tell Samantha I was there and then sat in the waiting area. I thumbed through a *Parents* magazine and felt my heart tugging at the smiling babies looking adoringly at their mommas.

I want one of those. I chewed a nail that was threatening to grow, dreaming of my own perfect someday-baby. My musings slid to Chad and Heather's impending triplets, and an intense spike of jealousy slammed me in the gut. It should have been me—but with only one baby, not triplets—no way could I handle that. And certainly not with Chad-the-cad. I tossed the magazine on the table just as Samantha buzzed through the locked door.

"I saw that," she said, standing with hands on hips. "Your time will come, and you are so lucky you didn't have any babies with Chad. The marriage wouldn't have lasted, and you would've been tethered to that loser for years to come. Birthdays, holidays, weddings. Look at Spencer and me. Chelsea's mother couldn't care less what her daughter is doing, but even though Spencer has full custody, there she is, constantly stirring up trouble and confusing Chelsea. It just drives me up the wall." She stopped abruptly and sat down next to me. "Claudia is such a bitch."

An elderly woman sitting in a corner chair knitting something pink cleared her throat and cocked a reproachful eyebrow at us.

Sam saw her disapproval and apologized, then turned back to me. "She called and told me she's breaking her promise to take Chelsea to Disneyland when school lets out, and I get to be the one to tell her. So not fair."

I stood up and slung my purse over my shoulder. "Maybe we can move this to the cafeteria and get something to eat. Sounds like you could use something sweet."

"I could use some cake. Preferably chocolate." A hint of a smile crossed her lips as she stood up to join me. "What's going on with your nose?"

I touched the bandage covering it. "It's actually a funny story and I'll share it with you over cake."

We walked down the hallway to the elevator. The doors opened and we stepped aside to allow the passengers to exit.

"You!" screamed a gray frazzle-haired woman in the elevator, pointing at Samantha. "You bitch! You lied to me. You're the one who brought that vile petition into this hospital. How dare you?"

"Oh God," muttered Sam. "It's Penny Hobart. Guess she hasn't calmed down."

The other passengers quickly distanced themselves from the angry woman, although a few stopped to record the scene on their smartphones from down the hall.

Mrs. Hobart rushed at Samantha swinging a humongous, red patent-leather purse. Sam ducked and deflected the blow with her forearm.

I yanked the heavy purse away from the wacko and flung it across the floor shouting, "I did it. Not her."

Hobart turned to me. "Who the hell are you?"

That was where I lost all reason as I dredged up my righteous, stupid indignation and declared, "Katy McKenna. Someone who wants to make sure your son pays his debt in full. Someone who knew Lindsay Moore—a sweet kid who died because of your son. Someone who doesn't think fifteen years in prison can even begin to right that wrong. Some—"

Her eyes bulged, her lips curled back revealing ugly brown, smoker's teeth, and she lunged at me shrieking, "Shut up! Shut up!"

She shut me up by grabbing the pink silk scarf looped around my neck and yanking it into a lethal hangman's noose. I tried to dig my fingers under the cloth, but she had a death-grip on it and jerked harder. At that point, everything was in blurry slow motion, but in my surreal fog I heard Sam screaming for help, while Hobart kept shrieking, "Shut up! Shut up!"

Sam punched Mrs. Hobart in the chin just as a burly security guard ran up and grabbed Hobart from behind. The tenacious crazy woman still gripped my scarf, jerking me toward her like a dog on a choke chain. White sparkles twinkled around me as I sank to my knees. Sam finally pried the scarf from Hobart's locked fingers and I crumpled to the floor, sucking in delicious oxygen as she removed the killer scarf from my neck.

I peeped up from my sprawled position on the cold terrazzo floor, afraid to make eye contact with the lunatic lady. I was relieved to see the security guard had her restrained. Samantha was right. Penny Hobart was nuts.

Sam helped me sit up, and with the assistance of another nurse, they got me on my feet and to a bench on the wall.

"Mom?" A beautiful, ivory-skinned, raven-haired woman wearing a blue satin robe approached the group. "What's going on?"

"Christy! She's the one who brought the petition here," Mrs. Hobart hissed, glaring at me. "It's all her fault."

Samantha was sitting next to me checking my pulse, but she corrected Hobart. "No. I'm the one who brought it here, not her."

"But *she* said she did it," said Hobart, jutting her scraped, swelling chin at me.

"I..." My voice cracked, and I cleared my throat and squeaked, "I made the petition."

"And I brought it here because I agree with her," said Samantha. "Fifteen years is not enough punishment for killing Lindsay. Not by a long shot."

Christy was a little wobbly and sat on the bench next to me.

Hobart screamed at her daughter, "Get away from that bitch-liar."

I tried to speak to Christy, but my voice was raspy. "I'm sorry

223

for all this. I read the news article about your brother's parole and remembered Lindsay and—"

"I can barely understand you." She put her hand over mine. "But I know what you're trying to say and it's okay. I get it. But my mother never will."

"Do you want to press charges?" the security guard asked me.

Hell, yes! "No," I croaked. How could I do that to Christy? "I don't think she really meant to hurt me."

"Like hell I didn't!" Hobart snarled as the guard released her. "You and your lies are the reason my son's in prison!"

"Mother!" shouted Christy. "The reason Phil's in prison is because of the crimes he committed." She dropped her voice. "Please, Mother. Just let it be."

Mrs. Hobart stepped closer. I involuntarily cowered behind her daughter and pulled my cardigan up over my nearly-garroted throat. Sam stood, shielding me with her body as the guard moved towards Hobart, ready to grab her if she went berserk again.

She leaned into her daughter's face. "You have never understood what my poor baby went through. You and your father. Both the same. Have you ever, ever given one thought to what it has been like for your brother? Ever?"

Christy didn't flinch under her mother's icy glare. "Dad's dead. Remember? He died from the stress of the trial." She narrowed her eyes and returned the glare. "Have you ever thought about what it was like for me? Your daughter? Ever?"

Hobart straightened up and adjusted her sweater. "You were fine."

Christy laughed as she teared up. "That must be why I tried to kill myself when I was sixteen. Because I was so fine."

Samantha whispered to the security guard, "She needs to leave now, but before you escort her out of the building..." She turned to me. "Are you certain you don't want to press charges? She assaulted you." Sam bent and whispered in my ear, "Katy, she's certifiable."

"How long can they hold her?"

"Seventy-two hours, I think."

"Then she'll *really* be pissed off," I said. "Take a look at your arm. She assaulted you, too."

There was a nasty red welt on the underside of her forearm caused by the gold buckle on Mrs. Hobart's tacky purse. Samantha twisted her arm around and inspected it, and then flexed the sore, grazed knuckles that had connected with Hobart's chin. "Against my better judgment, I'll let this go." She moved close to Hobart, locking eyes with her. "You need to understand how lucky you are that we're letting you go. But understand this—you are barred from this hospital. If I see you in here again, I will have you arrested."

"Oh, yeah? Well, maybe I'll sue you for hitting me. And the hospital, too." Hobart swiveled her deranged eyes over to me. "And you most of all. This is all your fault."

Sam pointed down the hall. "You leave now, or I'm calling the cops."

The guard took Mrs. Hobart's arm and she tried to jerk away. "Let go of me."

"Please, Mother," said Christy. "You've done enough damage, please just go."

"All right, Christy, I'm going. But don't think for one minute you can keep me away from my grandson. I have grandparental rights, you know. You'll probably be a lousy mother and I'll sue you for custody of Baby Phil."

Sam followed the guard and Mrs. Hobart down the hall. I watched until they were out of sight, then croaked to Christy, "I don't know what to say. If I'd known this could happen, I never would have done the petition."

"Your poor throat." She swiped at the tears dribbling down her cheeks. "As far as my mother goes, there's nothing left to say. Phil was the light of her life, and his imprisonment broke her. The trial, losing all her friends," she shook her head, "My father had a heart attack during the trial and died. And then I tried to kill myself with aspirin—so stupid..." Her voice faltered, and she paused to collect herself. "Phil tried to make her understand that he deserved to go to prison. That he *wanted* to go to prison, but in her mind, it was everyone else's fault. Not his." She pulled a tissue out of her pocket and blew her nose. "This is supposed to be a happy day." A shy smile lit her face and she whispered, "I have a baby boy."

"Oh. This *is* a happy day," I said, suddenly hit with a rush of pure delight for a woman I'd just met but already felt close to, in spite of the odd circumstance. "What's his name?" I knew it couldn't be Baby Phil.

"Neo," she said, beaming. "Neo Adam Sutherland. It means 'gift' or 'the one.'"

Her eyes shifted to the hall and her smile widened. I looked to the source of her smile and saw a cute, nerdy guy wearing horn rims and a goofy grin approaching, lugging an enormous teddy bear. Samantha followed behind him with a wheelchair.

"Hey, little mama." He kissed her cheek, and then backed away and scrutinized her face. "You been crying?"

"I'm fine now. Devin, this is Katy and..." She looked at Samantha who was pushing down the footrests on the wheel chair. "You remember Samantha from last night?"

"Hi, Samantha. Didn't see you behind me. Have you met Neo yet?"

"Not formally. Why don't we wheel Christy back to the room and you can introduce us."

Christy climbed into the chair and said to me, "If you're feeling okay, I'd love it if you came, too."

Devin looked perplexed. "Why do I feel like I missed out on something here?"

Christy said, "Mother."

Devin frowned and nodded. The love in his eyes for Christy touched me, and in that moment, I knew what I would be looking for in a man. Someday, when I finally see that love shining in a man's eyes for me, I'll be done looking.

After my near-death experience at the hands of crazy Penny Hobart, I was too rattled to get behind the wheel, so Samantha took a break and drove me home.

She settled me on the couch and while Daisy bestowed soothing kisses on my face, Sam fetched me a whopping glass of cabernet. I attempted a sip and sloshed half the glass down my shirt. "Guess I'm a little shaky."

Sam dashed to the kitchen for a towel as I tried to set the glass on the coffee table and wound up chipping the base. It was a super expensive Waterford crystal wedding gift, so no biggie. My post-war, I mean, post-marriage Pier One glasses are more my style.

As she blotted my shirt, I thought about investing in a set of sippy cups for special occasions like this.

"I really hate to leave you alone."

"I'll be fine," I spoke through chattering teeth. "It's freezing in here."

"You're a little shocky. Let me help you change." She hustled me into my bedroom and I didn't argue. Would have been a waste of energy, anyway. She got me into sweats and warm, woolly socks. I was still icy cold. "You'll warm up when the shock wears off." She plunked a beanie on my head.

"I'll throw the shirt in the wash before the wine sets, while you rest on the couch with Daisy and Tabitha."

I heard the washing machine filling and Sam called, "I might as well do a full load."

The lid thudded and a few minutes later she handed me a plastic cup—filled halfway with chardonnay. "We never had lunch, so I'll get you a snack before I leave."

Daisy's ears perked to attention at the magic word "snack" and Sam assured her there'd be something tasty for her, too.

I leaned into the cushions and sipped my wine, though swallowing was painful. That was okay. The pain meant I was alive.

"This'll go down easy." Sam set a bowl of yogurt and sliced bananas on the table, and gave Daisy a dog cookie. "You don't have any ice cream, so you'll have to make do. Do you want soup?"

"No, I'm fine. You need to get back to work."

She covered the kids and me with the comforter from my bed and handed me the TV remote. "Knowing you, you have an old movie recorded."

"Sam. I'll be okay. Go back to work."

Her big blue eyes reddened and brimmed with tears. "It's starting to hit me, how close I came to losing my best friend. I can't imagine my life without you in it."

I choked up (bad choice of words) and shared a good, grateful cry with my dear best friend.

———

I always keep a few favorites recorded on the DVR for rainy days, and though it was a sunny, cloudless day, I sure felt dismal. I had a choice between *Rebecca*—an old Alfred Hitchcock movie, *Bridget Jones's Diary*, and *Roman Holiday* with Audrey Hepburn.

Rebecca won. It is a gloomy, romantic mystery set on the rocky coast of England. I have watched it countless times and can practically recite the dialog line for line.

"Tabitha, you're in for a treat, huh, Daisy?"

Daisy gave me a patient look and settled her chin on her paws with a long sigh, while Tabitha burrowed her noggin into my thigh and purred. I pressed play and settled back to relax.

During the opening credits, the doorbell rang and Daisy went ballistic, leaping off the couch and tearing to the door like Santa Claus was on the porch. Tabitha followed at a more dignified "who cares" pace.

I hit pause, grumbling about being interrupted, and then had an unnerving thought. *What if it's Penny Hobart and she's come to finish me off?*

I stood at the door wishing I had a peephole and too afraid to look out the shuttered side window when Mom shouted, "Hey, honey. It's Mom and Grandma."

Relief washed through me as I opened the door and burst into tears. "Mommy. Gramma."

"Samantha called us." Mom set a grocery bag on the entry table before group-hugging me with Ruby. Daisy and Tabitha did their best to scrunch in between our legs for the love-fest.

Mom pulled back and inspected my wounded neck. There wasn't much to see since Samantha had bandaged it, but a rainbow of bruises was blooming on the exposed skin. "My poor baby."

"That bitch could have killed you," said Ruby. "Did you report this to the police?"

"No," I sniffled. *Should I have?*

"Why the hell not?"

"She was extremely upset about the petition and her daughter just had a baby." I spoke in a whisper, touching my tender neck. "It was in the heat of the moment, and I'm sure she didn't actually mean to hurt me."

"In the heat of the moment is how most people get murdered," said Ruby. "It's called manslaughter."

"Your grandmother's right. I don't care how upset she was, she had no right to attack you," said Mom. "I've been upset many times in my life, but I've never choked anyone."

"There were times when I wanted to strangle Bert. The way that no-good bastard treated you, Marybeth, I would've gladly—"

Mom cut her off. "Mom—not in front of Katy. Bert's her father."

I wiped my snotty, sore nose on my sweatshirt sleeve. "I'm not a child anymore, Mom, so you don't have to protect me. Besides, Kurt's my dad, not Bert. He's always been too busy racking up trophy wives to care about me. In fact, the only communication I've had with him in months is a Facebook friend request, which I turned down. So as far as I'm concerned, he probably deserved to be strangled."

"Amen to that," said Ruby. "Thank goodness, you're all right, sweetie. We could be at a funeral home right now, picking out your casket." She was really worked up.

"Maybe you should get a restraining order," said Mom.

"Oh the hell with that! How's a piece of paper going to protect Katy? She should get a shotgun!"

They were really freaking me out. "She doesn't know where I live, but if anything else happens, I promise to report her. And remember, I have a security alarm system that Pop insisted I get when I moved in here. State of the art. So I'll be fine."

"Is it set now?" asked Mom.

"No. But when you leave I promise, cross my heart, I will set it." I needed to change the subject. "What's in the bag?"

"Goodies." Mom looked past me into the living room. "Looks like you got yourself all set up in there. What's Daisy doing?"

She was guarding my bowl against any would-be "yogurt thieves" that might be lurking. My guess would be Tabitha.

"I was about to watch an old movie. *Rebecca*. Want to join me?"

"Ahhh...Lawrence Olivier and Joan Fontaine. One of my favorites," said Ruby. "I've lost count of how many times I've watched it and it never gets old."

Mom led us into the kitchen. "Ruby, how about pouring some wine, while I unload this bag and set up a tray. I don't want the ice cream to melt."

I looked hopefully at her.

"Mint-chip for you and chocolate for us. Today, my iPhone told me the meaning of life is chocolate, so we've got plenty, and dark chocolate pairs well with cab."

"Shaky hands do not pair well with cabernet, so I'll stick to chardonnay." I was feeling weak-kneed again and leaned against the counter for support.

"Come on, kiddo." Ruby guided me to the couch, then went for the wine bottles and glasses.

After we settled in, we raised our glasses, and I squeaked out a simple, heartfelt toast. "I love you guys."

"I love you too, honey." Mom turned to Grandma. "I love you, Mom."

"Right back at ya both. Bottom's up." She flicked a stray tear away and said, "Now start the movie already."

I pressed play and we all recited the opening line together. "Last night, I dreamt I went to Manderley again..."

CHAPTER THIRTY-TWO

1996

Tuesday, May 21

~PART TWO~

After an intimate midnight conversation with his fiancée, Jake had turned off his phone and then overslept, barely making his 11:00 class. Afterward, he grabbed a cheeseburger at a café on campus and parked himself under a shady tree to enjoy it.

A surge of pure joy flowed through him. Erik was dead, and he was free to move on with his life. Yes, his parents would be disappointed if he didn't finish college, but they'd get over it when they held their first grandchild. He decided to call Heidi and ask her what she thought about a fall wedding.

He grinned, anticipating his sweetheart's warm, sexy voice as he turned on his cell phone. Before hitting her speed dial number, he checked his voicemail. He had messages from his mother, Heidi, and Phil.

"Why's Phil calling?" he muttered aloud, feeling a pang of

anxiety. He listened to the message. *"Jake, it's Phil. Listen, man, I'm really sorry about this, but I'm going to tell my parents. I can't live a lie anymore. I'm so sorry."*

"Shit! Shit! Shit!" Jake slammed his forehead repeatedly with the closed flip phone.

Students nearby stopped talking and watched his meltdown.

"Sounds like you got bad news," said a boy, sitting with a group of friends.

Jake scrambled to his feet and set off at a dead run to his car.

"Dude!" shouted the kid. "You forgot your backpack."

Jake kept running. He was reacting with no plan in mind. When he got to his dusty green Nissan, he fumbled with his keys, dropping them three times before getting the car door open. Inside the hot, airless car, he leaned his head against the steering wheel and tried to think.

Phil had called over two hours ago. He'd be confessing by now. What next? They'd come to the frat house looking for him, so he couldn't go there. What next? Phil would take them to Lindsay's body.

He leaned back against the leather seat, not feeling the searing heat burn through his thin t-shirt. "Think, you stupid fuck!" He pounded on the steering wheel.

His mind raced. *What to do? The minute they find her body it's all over. But what if there is no body?* He forced himself to concentrate on that thought. *No body. No crime.*

He checked his watch. He still had a chance. Slim, but better than none. He hadn't come this far to give up now. He started the car and tore out of the campus parking lot. A few minutes later he was on U.S. 101, driving north.

Once he topped the long grade going north out of Santa Lucia, it was only a few miles to the Santa Sicomoro exit. Like that other day, he was mindful of the speed limit. This was his last chance. If he blew it now because of a stupid speeding ticket, he would have to run for it.

Jake glanced in his rearview mirror. No cops. A few more miles and he passed the general store and then the saloon where they had called the tow truck. He realized he'd missed the turn and drove past the saloon again and turned at the first road on the left.

He'd been sitting in the backseat the last time he was on this road. *What if I can't remember?* The pavement gave out to dirt and he pressed on. Ahead was a shallow creek bed. As the car dipped through it and began to ascend the other side, everything felt familiar. Jake could hear Lindsay's voice in his head. *"Please tell me what you want from me."*

The hill was steep and he drove slow to avoid sliding out of control like the last time. *"Gun it and get up this hill!"* Erik ordered from beyond. Jake slowed instead. He crested the hill and remembered Phil stopping there, refusing to continue. As usual, Erik had controlled the decision and Phil had knuckled under.

Jake saw the bend up ahead. "It's just around that bend," Jake whispered Erik's words and felt a chill. He was sure he was close to the crash site. Halfway through the sharp curve, he pulled over, got out, and walked along the road, searching for flattened bushes and tire tracks. When he found the break, he listened for approaching cars. He went back to his car and drove half a mile past the break and parked out of sight.

Staying alert to oncoming cars, he jogged back to the bushes and slid down the hill to the boulders that had halted Phil's careening SUV.

The grove was twenty or thirty yards from the rocks. He ducked behind the granite boulders and again listened. When he felt safe, he dashed for the trees. Near the edge of the forest, he crouched in a clump of sage to gain his bearings.

"God, where is she?" Jake said, visually searching the area. He looked back to the boulders and mentally drew a line. "There."

He stepped out into the open and sprinted to the point of entry into the grove, then zigzagged through the dry leaves. He worried that if anyone were approaching from the road, they'd hear the crunch and snap of the dry woodland clutter under his feet from as far away as the boulders. And then he heard flies buzzing and his heart shifted to warp speed. He eased towards the sound and he picked up a rank odor mingled with the cloying, medicinal aroma of the eucalyptus. He recognized the sick-sweet smell from when he'd found a rotting cow carcass in a gully back home on the farm. He batted at the swarming flies as he bent and cleared the debris.

Flies attacked his exposed skin and the fetor of decaying human flesh sickened him as he fought back involuntary gags. "I can't do this!" He clamped a hand over his mouth. Hot vomit spewed through his fingers and dribbled down his forearms.

He straightened and glanced wildly around. No one was coming. "I don't have a choice." He resumed the horrifying task.

"Please don't hurt me," Lindsay murmured in his ear.

"I'm so sorry. Never meant for this, Lindsay. I swear to God."

The red and yellow plaid blanket peeked through the leaves and the reek overwhelmed him. His stomach reeled and bucked, but he didn't stop. He cleared the area around her body and saw the blanket had been chewed through in several spots. Her exposed feet had lost several toes to hungry woodland creatures. He shut his eyes and fought to regain control.

It would be impossible to drag her body through the leaves, so he would have to carry her. Breathing through clenched teeth, nervous sweat stinging his eyes, he knelt beside her and slid his arms under her shrouded body. The jostling caused her fragile bloated corpse to sigh gaseous sounds as the skin split under the blanket. Wet, noxious body fluids seeped onto his bare arms. The blanket fell away from her once pretty face, now consumed by flesh-eating maggots.

"Oh God! Oh God! Oh God!" he screamed over and over, as he jerked his arms away and fell backwards, clamoring away from the remains.

Slimy, plump maggots squirmed over his arms and pants. Trembling violently and sputtering convulsive gasps, he swept them off while tiny, ravenous flies attacked his sticky flesh, digging at his eyes and crawling up his nostrils. His stomach shot its contents until he could no longer stand.

"I have to do this. Please, please God, give me the strength to do this. It's my last chance."

He crawled back to Lindsay.

CHAPTER THIRTY-THREE

1996

Tuesday, May 21

~PART THREE~

Following Phil's confession, Officer Yee escorted him to a police car where they waited for Detective Yaeger. Several minutes later, she joined them, sitting in the passenger seat. Another squad car followed as they drove out of the station parking lot.

Phil had already told them the route during his confession, so they rode in silence, occasionally broken by radio dispatches. He looked out the window, remembering the last ride north on 101 and wished he could go back in time and make different choices. If only he'd stood up to Erik and Jake the moment he saw them grabbing Lindsay at the school flagpole, he wouldn't be leading the police to her corpse now.

They took the Santa Sicomoro exit, and at the east end of the small town the county coroner's van and two county deputies in a four-wheel drive SUV waited along the roadside. They pulled out as the squad cars passed by.

Finally Angela said, "Up ahead is the Rusty Spur Saloon. Where do we turn?"

Phil peered through the barrier separating him from the front seat. "Slow down. It's just before the saloon, on the right."

"How far is it now?" Yee asked after making the turn.

"We still got a ways to go." Phil shuddered, realizing he was echoing Erik's words.

The asphalt ended, and they were driving on dirt. A few miles further, they passed through the creek bed.

"We're getting closer," said Phil. "Keep going."

"This road's in terrible shape." Yee gripped the wheel. "Sure wish I was driving a four-wheeler like those deputies."

They reached the crest and Phil heard Erik's voice in his memory. *It should be just around that next bend up ahead.* "There's the bend in the road up ahead. Be careful," Phil warned Yee, "it's a really sharp turn."

She eased into the one-eighty degree turn. Angela found herself holding her breath, as she gazed fearfully over the edge into the steep ravine.

Less than a minute later, he said, "I think we're pretty close to where my car slid off the road."

Yee pulled to the side, and both women breathed a sigh of relief. They got out, leaving Phil locked in the car. The other vehicles parked and the Santa Lucia police officers joined them. Angela told them to find the location where Phil's car had gone down. The two deputies from the county sheriff's office, and the coroner and deputy coroner were approaching Angela when an officer called out. "Over here!" Approximately thirty feet away, a young male rookie stood pointing beyond the roadside. "All the bushes here have been crushed. I see tire marks in the dirt."

Angela told Yee to fetch Phil. When he was at her side, she walked him to the break in the bushes. "Is this the spot?"

He answered through pressed, trembling lips. "Yes, ma'am."

"Okay, everybody. Let's go, but please take a wide berth and be mindful not to disturb the tire tracks," said Angela.

The coroner, Janet MacDonald, stepped close. "Steve and I will get our gear and meet you down there."

"I'm surprised to see you here, Janet. I know how," she paused, "overloaded—"

Janet grinned. "You know you were going to say buried, right? Like I haven't heard that one before."

"Sorry. I'm not very original, but I am surprised. I know you're understaffed and our victim's been dead for nearly two weeks now, so I assumed we'd only see Steve today."

"This one really got to me, Angela."

"To both of us." Steve's dark condemning eyes glanced at Phil for a split second. "I have a girl about the same age."

They spoke as if Phil were invisible. A nonentity. He stared at the ground, burning with shame.

"I'll head back to the van now." Steve's voice caught and he cleared his throat. "You'd think I'd be used to this sort of thing."

"I want two officers to assist Hobart down the hill," Angela called to the other officers.

Phil had not been arrested yet but understood Yaeger's meaning; he had no intention of running. The rookie and Officer Danen took Phil's arms and guided him down the hill. The dirt was loose and Phil's trembling knees caused his feet to slip out from under him several times, but the officers kept him upright. Before they reached the boulders, Angela stopped the group. "Phil, are those the boulders where your car crashed?"

"Yes, ma'am."

"Where did Lindsay hit her head?"

He nodded his chin. "Those boulders over to the right."

"Okay! Let's get this area secure," Angela said.

Phil stood with his eyes bolted to the ground, too ashamed to make eye contact with anyone. He desperately wanted this day to be over.

Several minutes later, Angela spoke grimly to Phil. "All right. It's time to take us to Lindsay."

Phil lifted his head and pointed towards the eucalyptus grove. "Over there."

"You lead," she said through tight lips.

Officer Danen kept a firm grip on Phil's arm. "Don't even think about running."

"Would you kill me if I did?" Thinking that could be his escape.

Danen realized that might be what the kid wanted. "No. I'd just make you miserable."

At the edge of the dark, densely wooded grove, they halted. "Now where?" asked Angela.

Phil surveyed the woods. "I didn't bury her, but I think they would have gone towards the middle."

"Everyone! Spread out and step carefully," said Yee. "Take your time."

Angela stayed with Phil on the edge of the trees, watching the officers step gingerly through the dead branches and leaves littering the ground.

Officer Yee shouted from behind a wide, three-trunked tree. "Over here!"

Angela called to the officer closest to her, the rookie, "Officer Walkin. Please stay with Hobart."

"It's really bad," Yee warned in a thin, quivering voice. "Really bad."

Danen stepped out from the multi-trunked Eucalyptus Globulus and called, "Over here, Detective." His voice dropped, "Jake Werner is here, too."

Angela quickly worked her way around the massive tree blocking her view of the other officers. Halfway around, her nose caught the overpowering, noxious odor of rotting flesh.

Seventeen years on the force hadn't prepared her for the grisly scene she beheld. Jake was sitting on the cleared ground with Lindsay's disintegrating corpse draped across his lap. The blanket hung open, revealing the putrid remains of nature's recycling process. Maggots spilled from Lindsay's body, squirming on Jake's arms and legs, while flies poked his eyes and ants swarmed his entire body. And yet, the most frightening thing of all was Jake's eyes. He was alive, but his eyes were dead.

CHAPTER THIRTY-FOUR

SUNDAY · APRIL 21
Posted by Katy McKenna

Today, with a heavy heart, I put every scarf I own in a paper bag and set it by the front door to take to the Goodwill store. It wasn't easy. I've been collecting scarves since high school and I have a color to go with everything, in an array of fabrics from nubby to silky. I'll feel half-dressed without them, but they have to go. I cannot be wearing lethal weapons around my neck. If I ever have any second thoughts, and find myself being lured by a vibrant, multi-colored scarf that will go with absolutely everything in my closet, all I have to do is look at the photo of my semi-garroted throat in my phone.

———

Although I slept through most of yesterday, I still felt wrung out when I finally dragged my tush out of bed at nine-thirty this morning, so I thought it would be a good day to catch up on shows piling up on the DVR. I'd missed the last two *Pop Idol* episodes. Usually I watch it the night it is on so I can vote, but it's down to the final five —all girls—and all so good, I can't decide who I want to win—so I don't feel the need to vote.

The performances were stellar and I cried when they booted Jackie on the results show. Then I cried through two old *Army Wives* episodes. And I cried through a *Modern Family* repeat. It was definitely time to get out in the sun and soak up some Vitamin D.

My neck looked too nasty to go anywhere—swollen and scraped raw where the fabric had dug deep into my skin, with swirls of blue, purple, red, and green around the circumference. Between my neck and nose, I'm a ghoulish sight to behold, so I decided to attack the overgrown geraniums around my front porch.

I plugged ear buds into my cell phone, opened the iPod app and spun through the menu looking for a playlist suitable for gardening. I chose Shania Twain's album, "Come On Over." Cell phone safely jammed in my denim pocket and clippers in hand, I cranked up the volume and opened with "Man, I Feel Like a Woman." Of course, I was singing along, or more like croaking along.

I know snatches of the song, so when a line came that I knew, I squeaked it out as I mangled my poor geraniums. And when listening to a tune like that, who can resist dancing? So I danced.

I did a spin and spotted the Viking standing at the edge of my lawn, watching the crazy lady show along with a Great Dane walking an elderly couple, and a boy on a skateboard with his cell phone aimed at me, which probably means I'll soon be the next YouTube star.

I paused the music and bowed to my audience. Yes, I was embarrassed, but I was dancing in my yard, not laying in a casket, so what the heck?

Josh clapped as he strolled across my yard. "What do you do for an encore?"

"Got any requests?" I said in my new deep, gravelly voice.

His smile faded as he came towards the porch. "What happened to your neck?" He moved closer to inspect the growing collage of gruesome bruises. "There's only one thing that could cause this, Katy."

I nearly swooned when he said my name. Katy. Who knew my name could sound so lovely? *Kaa-tee.*

Josh tilted his head and frowned. "Are you all right? You look a little sick. Maybe you should sit down."

I plopped myself on the porch steps. Shania's lyrics twisted in my head to—*I feel like an idiot.*

He sat next to me, a paragon of concern. "So what happened?"

I gave him an abbreviated version of the petition story and the scarf attack at the hospital.

"I didn't live in the area in 1996, but I'd like to hear the whole story. Do you know Suzy Q's?"

"It's one of my favorite restaurants," I said. "Their mac and cheese—"

"Is killer. I've tried to replicate it at home and failed miserably. "Why don't we go for dinner and you can tell me everything?"

He cooks. He gardens. He picks locks. What can't this man do?

"Sounds great." I touched my neck and winced. "But I don't have a thing to wear that'll cover my neck, and I sure don't want people staring at me, and I will never, ever wear another scarf."

"Don't blame you, and I don't like the idea of people looking at me and wondering if I'm a wife-beater." He snapped his fingers. "I have a turtleneck you can wear. Be right back." He dashed across the yard before I could say anything.

Had I just been asked out on a date? I wasn't sure. Should I call Samantha? *Sam! Guess what? The Viking has asked me out. I think.* How juvenile. So I didn't call her. I texted.

A few minutes later, Josh returned with a sweater. "A little out of season, but it'll do the job." He held up a hideous Christmas sweater adorned with appliquéd felt reindeers outlined in white against a green background. The middle deer had a large red fuzzy ball attached to his nose and a jingle bell on his tail. "A gift from my Aunt Arna in Minnesota." He handed the sweater to me, with a sheepish grin. "I know. It's pretty ugly and way too big for you, but you're so stylish, you'll make it work."

OMG! He thinks I'm beautiful, I mean stylish. Whatever. I clutched the adorably ugly sweater to my chest. "Ugly Christmas sweaters are very popular now."

Josh laughed. "Especially in April." He looked at his watch. "How about I meet you here in half an hour?"

"Yeah." I didn't move. I was grinning, which hurt my neck, so it may have been more like a grimace, but I couldn't stop.

"You sure you're all right?"

So considerate. "Yeah." Grin-grimace.

"Oo-kay then. See you soon." He turned and strolled away and at the edge of the yard, looked back and waved.

"Yeah." I waved back, and he disappeared around a Pyracantha bush.

Suddenly it dawned on me. I had a date, I think. My first maybe-date in my new, wonderful life. And then I freaked out. I only had half an hour!

CHAPTER THIRTY-FIVE

WEDNESDAY · MAY 1
Posted by Katy McKenna

It's been quite a while since my last post and so much has happened. It has been crazy! I'm going to break this down into segments, because my elbow really aches and it's hard to type, so I'm trying a new dictating app. I have to walk, I mean *talk* really slow, but it seems to be working yell, I mean *well*.

Monday, April 22—Part One

I checked to see if there were any responses to my Craigslist ad (nada) while my coffee brewed and Daisy brought in the newspaper. That chore done, she went back to bed, evidently zonked from getting up, and I settled in the living room to catch up on the news.

The big feature on page one covered an unfaithful, senior senator on trial for trigamy. Page two featured a story on a spoiled Hollywood star whose name I won't mention, just in case I ever share this blog online, but let's just say she needs to get her act together and quit the drinking and the drugs, and for God's sake, somebody needs to take away her driver's license before she kills someone. I read the first paragraph concerning her latest self-inflicted dilemma, super annoyed that she still gets acting jobs and gobs of money, then lost interest and turned to the local news.

Page one of Section B had a story about a concerned local who was gathering signatures to keep a convicted felon in prison. I read the woman was me, Katy McKenna, residing at 539 Sycamore Lane, former co-owner of The Bookcase Bistro. The article applauded my efforts and evidently I had been unavailable for comment.

I flung the paper down, completely astounded. How could they print a story about me without asking? Isn't there a law that prevents such things, like invasion of privacy or something? Then I calmed down as I rationalized that nobody reads the newspaper anyway. These days, most people get their news from those show-bizzy "news" shows where everyone looks like a movie star. The average Joe on the street will recognize a photo of Kim Kardashian and be totally stumped when shown a photo of the vice president.

I was still fuming when Samantha called to find out how my dinner date with Josh had gone. I knew she'd waited until later in the a.m., in case I was "busy." I could have called her, but it was more fun leaving her in suspense.

"Hi," she asked in an exaggerated whisper. "Can you talk?"

"Yes!" I shouted, which was not a good idea with my sore throat.

"I take it he's not there?"

I have never been the kind of girl (all right, amend that to "never was," since it has been a hundred years since I've dated) who hops into bed on the first date, if this even was a date. Still not sure.

"Tell me everything," said Samantha, "from the beginning and don't you dare leave anything out."

I decided to start at the good part. "He thinks I'm stylish."

"Why would he say something like that?"

That miffed me. Doesn't Samantha think I am stylish?

"Because he lent me a really ugly turtleneck Christmas sweater to hide my neck. He said I'm so stylish, I could make anything look good." Close enough.

"Did you?"

"I belted it and wore leggings, my cowboy boots, and the leather bomber jacket we found at that thrift shop in San Francisco. It worked. Kinda. A scarf would have helped."

"That sounds cute until you take off the jacket. So tell me about the date. No wait, hold on a sec."

In the background I heard little Casey whining. He is a cheerful little four-year-old, so when he is cranky it usually means he is coming down with something. Then I heard Sam say, "blow," and he did for all he was worth. She told him she would read him a *Thomas the Tank* story in a few minutes and that seemed to appease him.

She came back on. "He's got a little cold, but I think it may be going into his ears, as usual. Now tell me the rest."

"You sure? We can talk later when he's napping."

"No, tell me now. I was up half the night with him, so I plan to take a nap, too. But I can't do that until I hear about your date."

I walked out onto the backyard patio and settled in a lounge chair to enjoy the gorgeous spring day. "I'm not sure if it was a date or just a friendly get-to-know-ya kind of a thing, but I had a nice time."

"That's how most relationships start, Katy. Go on."

"We walked to Suzy Q's and it was busy when we got there, so we had a glass of wine while we waited for a table."

The dog door slapped and Daisy strolled by on her way out to the lawn, where she laid down and rolled over to wriggle all the itches out of her back, moaning in doggy ecstasy.

"Then what happened?" she asked.

"Once we were seated, I started telling him the petition story. He asked a lot of questions and seemed genuinely interested. I think he was impressed with me."

"Well, he should be. And it'll take the edge off of when you peed your pants in front of him."

I winced at the memory. "Thanks for reminding me, as if I'll ever forget."

"Hey. What are friends for? Someday we'll laugh about it. Actually I already am. What else did you talk about?"

"Not that much really. The petition story took up most of dinner." I thought a moment. "I wanted to know about his ex, but it didn't feel right to ask. I did ask if he had any children."

"And?"

"No. Loves kids and it's a someday thing when he finds the right person." I smiled, feeling all glowy inside, thinking what a great guy he was and how beautiful our children would be.

"Well, that's good. No strings. So you walked back home and *then?*"

"I was so nervous. I was afraid he'd try to kiss me, or maybe even want to—uh, you know. I was also afraid he wouldn't." I stopped and left her in momentary suspense.

"Jeez. Just tell me what happened."

"Okay, okay. Joshie, that's what I call him now, walked me to my door and waited while I unlocked it. He was standing behind me, so close I could feel the heat radiating from his body..."

"Yeah? Yeah?"

"Then he got upset when he realized I hadn't set the alarm."

"Shame on you. And then what?"

"Hold on, I'm watching Daisy."

Daisy was done scratching and now hunting for lizards. A couple weeks ago she spied a blue-belly sunning on a rock, and since then, she has devoted a portion of every day to hunt for the elusive little critter.

Samantha cleared her throat. "I'm waiting."

I sighed orgasmically. "He looked deep into my eyes, our two souls merging and then..."

"And then? And then?"

"And then he... Oooo..." *I'm so awful.*

"WHAT? You're killing me!"

"He made me promise to set the alarm as soon as I closed and locked the door. I said good night and closed the door, then locked it and set the alarm. The end."

She snorted with disgust. "Well, that's sure exciting—not."

"Hey, have you read this morning's paper yet?"

"Who has time? I'm not a woman of leisure like some people I know. Hold on." She held the phone away and called to Casey, "Yes, buggy-boo. Mommy's coming." Then back to me, "I gotta go. Keep me posted."

CHAPTER THIRTY-SIX

THURSDAY · MAY 2

Posted by Katy McKenna

I'm loving this dictating app. Typing is so mold-school—I mean *old*-school.

Monday, April 22—Part Two

This is my favorite time of year. The days are getting longer, the daffodils are blooming, and it's time for Nordstrom's annual spring shoe sale. Against my better financial judgment, I decided to take a stroll through the shoe racks to sniff the divine aroma of fresh footwear.

I gathered my things and set the alarm. Before stepping off the porch into the wide open, I peeped around the trumpet vine to see if Josh was in his front yard. I felt confused and shy about our "date", and if I'd seen him, I probably would have ducked back inside. How seventh grade was that?

The coast was clear, so I dashed down the steps and jumped into Veronica. At the stop sign about a block from my house, a cute blue Prius appeared behind me and for a split-second, I wished I had one. And then I felt a twinge of guilt. Veronica has been my trusty steed for as long as I've been driving, and before that, she and Mom had safely transported me to preschool, gymnastics, soccer, ballet, school... I patted her dusty dashboard and said, "Shame on me. How could I think such traitorous thoughts?"

On a sudden whim, I detoured past the dog park to see if Ben were there. It was close to four in the afternoon, the right time of day for him, and if he were, I had concocted a diabolical plan.

He was getting out of his car when I drove into the parking area. I stopped near his car, cranked down my window, and called, "Hi, Ben."

He waved. "Hello, Katy. What're you up to?" He peeked in the backseat window. "I don't see Daisy in the car."

"I was in the neighborhood and thought I saw you. Are you going to be around for a while? If so, I'll go get her."

"Got nothing else planned, so I'll be here for a while."

"Okay. See you soon." I put Veronica in gear and drove away.

When I was out of sight, I stopped to call Ruby's cell. It rang several times before she answered. I pictured her digging through her bottomless-pit faux Prada purse, searching for her elusive phone and cussing a blue streak.

"Hello," she snapped.

"Hey, Ruby. I need a favor."

"What?"

"Whoa. Somebody sure is snippy."

"I just got a big shipment of E-Z Lips in and now no one wants their order. Hold on." She took a breath and I could almost hear her counting to ten in her head to calm herself. "All right. Better now. What do you need?"

"Actually, it's—"

"Stop. Not better." I heard a long, slow, cleansing exhale. "Okay, go on."

"Daisy needs you." Now what do I say? My plan had not been fully concocted when I dialed, so I was winging it.

Her voice took on a concerned tone. "What's wrong with Daisy?"

"Uh... She's depressed and needs to get out and I am absolutely swamped with super important errands, so I was wondering if you would take her to the dog park."

Silence. She was probably counting to ten again. She's crazy about Daisy, so I was pretty sure she'd cave. "My car's not big enough."

"No problem. I'll come get you. Then all you have to do is sit on a bench at the park with her and enjoy the beautiful day."

Silence.

"She's so sad," I added, then continued in a hoarser, poor-me voice, "and I'm still not feeling so good after my near-death experience." I adjusted the rearview mirror to look at my neck and noticed another blue Prius parked along the road about fifty yards back. *Those things are multiplying like rabbits.*

I heard an annoyed huff. "When?"

"Now. I'll be right over. Bye." I pressed the End icon on my phone before she could reply, threw it on the passenger seat, and peeled out.

I pulled into my driveway in record time, ran to the front door, unlocked it screaming for Daisy, who was already at the door. Where else would she be? A split second later, the alarm went off and she started howling.

"Darn it." I punched in the code to shut the annoying thing off, then hurried to the laundry room with Daisy on my heels to get her halter and leash. My amped behavior had set her into hyper-mode, so it took some wrangling to get the halter on her.

"Let's go." I was breathless and Daisy was panting with excitement as we raced through the house to the front door. When I flung it open, we barreled into the Viking. Overjoyed, Daisy jumped up and planted her paws on his chest, forcing him back against the porch rail, and smacked him on the lips.

"Daisy! Leave the poor guy alone." I scolded as I dragged her off. I could learn a thing or two about kissing from my dog.

"I heard the alarm. Are you okay?" he said, peering through the front door for bad guys.

"We're fine." I slammed the door. "Gotta go. Huge rush. Daisy, let's go bye-bye."

I dropped her leash to avoid being catapulted off the porch by her, as she bounded down the steps to the car. I opened the back seat door and she hopped in. Backing out of the driveway, I glanced back at Josh. He didn't look happy. As soon as I rounded the corner, I stopped and tethered Daisy, because she likes riding shotgun and I prefer her safely tucked in the back.

A block from Ruby's house, I gave Daisy a command to lie down and stay. "Try to look depressed, Daisy." I spoke in a boo-hoo tone and she dropped her head on her paws and sighed. The rest of the way down the street I kept saying, "Oh, poor, poor Daisy. She's so sad. So, so sad."

Ruby was waiting outside her cottage, arms crossed, dressed in ratty, gray sweats. I had no idea she owned anything so ugly.

Daisy's tail thumped and she started to sit up. "No, Daisy. Lie down. Remember, you're so, so sad."

Her tail froze and she whined forlornly and collapsed.

Ruby got in and I blurted without thinking, "Is that what you're wearing?"

"No, it's not what I'm wearing. It's an optical illusion," she said rather churlishly. "Geez Louise! We're going to the dog park. Should I have worn my tiara?"

"No, I'm just surprised, that's all. I've never seen you dressed so... casually."

"Well, get used to it. I'm stuck with 350 bucks worth of E-Z

Lips. This could bankrupt me and pretty soon K-Mart sweats will be all I can afford."

Daisy whimpered in the back seat for attention, and Ruby twisted to see her. "You look fine to me."

Daisy lost it and attempted to leap over the front seat, but her tether held her back. So much for obedience.

"That's because she loves her sweet grandma," I said. "Just seeing you has perked her up."

Daisy stood up on the seat, wagging her tail in agreement. I could hear her tongue lapping air-kisses at Ruby.

"Yes, I love you, too." Ruby reached around to scratch Daisy's head. "Drive slow, Katy. George's on duty and he's got a new radar gun."

I drove a sedate fifteen mph past the empty security booth. George is the skinny, nerdy head of Shady Acres security and is on a perpetual crime-stopper-power-trip. He loves reporting me to the office, who in turn report me to Ruby, who in turn yells at me.

"Watch out! There's that sneaky son-of-a-gun." Ruby was pointing at the bushes lining the right side of the road.

George was crouched in a Bougainvillea bush aiming the radar gun at us, looking like he was about to holler, "Freeze, turkey!"

I slowed to five mph as Ruby rolled down the window. "You better be careful, George. With those knobby old knees of yours, you could get a leg cramp." She rolled the window back up. "Not to mention a bunch of thorns in his skinny butt."

I watched George in the rearview mirror, wrestling the bush to de-snag his sleeves and pants. Thank goodness it was just a radar gun that he was waving around like crazy or Veronica would have been riddled with holes.

Ruby turned her attention back to me. "So what are all these important errands that can't wait?"

"Business. I am swamped with work. Wow. It is *cr-aa-zy*."

"You're lucky to have work in this crappy economy." She was

quiet for a few minutes, probably worrying about her E-Z Lips. "Maybe I need to get a job. I'm sick of being an independent sales-person." She shifted in her seat to face me. "Maybe I could help you."

"Doing what?"

"I could be your assistant. Run errands for you, type up invoices, get coffee."

Was she kidding or was she serious? I didn't know how to play this. "Uh, I don't think I'm *that* busy." Immediately, I knew that came out wrong.

She harrumphed and turned away to stare out the window.

"I mean, I'm doing okay, but I can't afford an *executive* assistant yet." I did not want Grandma Ruby as my "Gal Friday."

Mollified by the word "executive," she sat up straighter. "I gotta think of something." She paused a moment. "Say, how's your dreamboat neighbor? Anything going on yet?"

No way was I ready to get into that discussion, so I said, "I'll keep you posted." Not a lie, an omission. Big difference.

She sat back and didn't say another word until we got to Lago Park. I parked and Daisy's tail thumped a drum solo on the back-seat as I untethered her.

"I'll get you guys settled and then I'll dash," I said as Daisy dragged me to the gate.

Ben was on a bench, engrossed in his needlepoint. Ruby scur-ried to catch up with me.

"*Psst!* Katy!" she whispered. "Look at that old man over there."

I played dumb. "What old man?"

"The weirdo with the goatee doing embroidery on the bench over there. He must be gay."

"It's needlepoint," I corrected her. "And he's not gay." Oops.

"How do you know?"

"I've talked to him once or twice. He's nice. I'll introduce you."

Her eyes narrowed and I could see she was suspicious. "Why are you giving me that look?" I scooted her and Daisy through the gate and marched them over to Ben without waiting for an answer.

"Hey, Ben. This is my grandma. She's going to babysit Daisy while I run some really important business errands."

Ben set his needlepoint aside and stood up, extending his hand. "It's a pleasure to meet you."

"Oh, my goodness. Where are my manners?" I drawled like a Georgia peach. "Ruby, this is Ben. Ben, this is Ruby." I released Daisy and handed the leash to Grandma. "I'll leave you two to get acquainted."

"If I didn't know better, I'd say this is a set-up." Ruby shifted into her own vocal version of Scarlett O'Hara. "But I know my darlin' Katy would never do something so underhanded as that to her dear old grandmother."

Ben saved me with his good manners. "Then we'll just call this a happy serendipity." His eyes traveled to my black and blue neck. "My God, Katy. What happened to you? Who did this?"

I knew he was remembering all of those wife-beaters he'd defended. "It's not what you're thinking, but it's a long story and I'm really in a hurry and—"

"You skedaddle and I'll tell Ben what happened." Ruby settled on the bench.

I pecked her cheek. "Thanks. I won't be long." I hightailed it out of there, shouting over my shoulder, "I'll be back as soon as I get my important business done."

I pointed Veronica in the direction of the mall for the shoe sale, hoping to score 95% off some Jimmy Choos. One could always hope.

I was driving on the narrow side road that runs along a few acres of strawberries valiantly growing between the shopping mall and the freeway. The radio was blasting 80's oldies and I was singing along to "Girls Just Want to Have Fun," when I was nearly catapulted out of my seat by a hard rear-end thud. Veronica bounced and narrowly missed going into the drainage ditch. My first thought was I had a flat tire—more like a tire explosion. I stopped on the shoulder of the road, put the car in park, and took a moment to collect myself before getting out to inspect the tires. I looked in the mirror to check for oncoming traffic and saw another blue Prius, sitting about ten yards back.

My heart started pounding as my brain went on high alert. I nervously laughed at myself. "Get a grip, Katy. It's a harmless little Prius, for gosh sake. Gangsters do not drive Priuses. Especially pretty sky-blue ones."

I checked the mirror again and the car's front bumper was badly damaged. Had they rear-ended me?

"Crap." I shouted and banged the steering wheel. I tried to put a plausible spin on what was going on. *Maybe they don't have insurance, and now they're waiting to see what I'll do. So there's no point in even trying to talk to them because I'll still have to pay the deductible if there's any damage.*

I gripped the wheel. "Okay, I'm way overthinking this. I'm just going to get out of here." I put Veronica in drive and pressed the gas. I peeped in the mirror and saw the Prius was coming up fast.

"Oh, shit." I stomped on the gas and Veronica laid rubber, careening down the narrow road with the Prius sniffing her tail. Less than a quarter of a mile further was a metal barricaded dead end, and no way out except for a three point u-turn. Coming up on my left was the final turn into the mall parking lot. I had to take it, but knew I was going too fast to make it without flipping the car. I slowed and my rear bumper took another hit from the Prius.

"What's up with this guy?" I screamed. Unlike me, Veronica didn't lose her cool. She took the turn, keeping her tires pinned to the ground, and we sped into the parking lot with the Prius in hot pursuit.

We raced past shops, department stores, and big box stores, whipping around light posts and honking at pedestrians who dashed out of the way, angrily waving their fists and flipping out their cell phones to take videos. "Call the freaking cops, you idiots!" I shouted.

Several times the Prius from hell closed in on me and rammed my Volvo, causing my seat belt to snap me back hard against the seat. It didn't release and I could barely breathe, but still that damned blue car kept coming at me. I was heading down an aisle that led to a towering, concrete fountain in an outdoor pedestrian plaza in front of Barnes and Noble. The turn at the end of the aisle was sharp–doable at ten mph, but not at forty-five. People saw me coming and scattered. Crashing into the fountain wouldn't be in my best interest, so I hit the brakes hard and prepared for major whiplash. My pursuer must have come to the same conclusion and hit his brakes, too, then spun his wheels in the opposite direction, squealing around a meridian and out of sight.

I ignored the hostile glares from the plaza people and drove to the opposite end of the mall and parked under a tree near Bed, Bath & Beyond between a minivan and a SUV. I turned off the engine, grabbed my purse, and jumped out, crouching on the other side of the minivan, waiting and hyperventilating.

A Chihuahua in the minivan's driver seat yipped nonstop, as if screaming, "Hey, killer Prius, she's over here!" and a couple of people passing by gave me funny looks, but the Prius was a no-show.

I waited a full five minutes before getting up the nerve to check my car's rear end. There were blue-smeared dents in the chrome bumper but no body damage. I knew the damage to the other car would be extensive, and that gave me some satisfaction, but why had someone tried to hurt me? Thinking back over the last few hours, I counted up the sightings and realized they'd been stalking me. Due to its tinted windows, I had no idea if it were a man or a woman behind the wheel, and I'd been too rattled to even think about license plates.

I thought about calling the police, but then what? An evil blue Prius had stalked me all over town for who-knows-why, a report would be filed, and I would still have to pay the damned deductible.

In the meantime, I needed to calm down before picking up Ruby. Shoe shopping was out of the question, but a strong dose of caffeine would help. As luck would have it, a Starbucks was two doors down from the linen store. I sat outside in a shaded corner of the patio, sipping my double espresso while scanning the parking lot for blue Priuses. I counted three parked close by and surreptitiously glanced around at my fellow java junkies. No one appeared to be watching me watching them. In fact, I was the only one not staring at a cell phone, a tablet, or a laptop.

Eventually my heart rate settled down, while the coffee cleared my head enough to think rationally. I tried to conjure up a reasonable motive for what had happened. In all likelihood, it was just some wacko with anger issues. Maybe I'd cut them off earlier in the day without realizing it. I know there's been times I've been mad enough to chase after people and slam into them but not weird enough to actually do it.

———

Ruby and Ben were deep in conversation and didn't acknowledge my approach until I was practically standing in front of them. Daisy was passed out under the bench and Ruby had Ben's red cardigan draped over her shoulders. Ahhh.

"Hey, guys. I'm back."

Daisy wagged her tail but made no effort to get up. Guess she'd had a good workout.

"There she is," Ben said. "How's our girl?"

Yes. My plan had worked. Was it too soon to call Ben *Grandpa?*

"Well, it's about time," Ruby scolded. "It got chilly and this poor man had to lend me his sweater. What took you so long?"

I didn't want to worry her about my freaky car-chase, so I made a big show of looking at my watch. "It's only been an hour or so."

"Did you get all your *important* errands done?"

"Almost."

She stood and returned Ben's sweater. "Thanks for letting me use it."

"My pleasure." He winked at me.

I leashed Daisy and started for the gate. Ruby lagged behind and I heard her say, "I look forward to tomorrow."

What? I stopped and listened.

"I'll pick you up at five," Ben replied. "That'll give us plenty of time for dinner before the concert."

What? I spun around.

"Benny's has great early-bird senior specials," said Ruby in a coquettish tone.

No! Not liver and onions. So not romantic.

"I have something a little nicer in mind," said Ben.

Thank God.

"Well... Until then," said Ruby, toodling her fingers at him.

I drove my suddenly giddy-girlish granny home, while constantly checking my rearview mirror for rogue Priuses, and at her door she invited me in for a glass of wine. After a long drink of water, Daisy sagged in a pooped-out heap in the living room.

"I don't know what I'm going to wear," Ruby said as she poured two Pinot Grigios.

"Let's take a look at your clothes and I'll help you pull an outfit together," I said, remembering the Viking had said I was stylish.

She shook her head in doubt. "I don't know if I've got *anything*."

Ruby's closet is the entire second bedroom of her house. She keeps up with the trends while keeping it age-appropriate and classic. The age she has determined appropriate for her seventy-four years is fifty-ish. It works.

We spent the next hour trying on various outfits. The keepers I set aside for further consideration.

"It's been a while since I've been on a date and I want to look absolutely fabulous." She sat on a silk brocade slipper chair by the window. "Especially after Ben seeing me in *those*." She kicked at the sweatpants lying on the floor. "How could you have let me wear sweats?"

Because I couldn't let you know I was setting you up. "You know what? You need something new. Nordstrom is having a sale."

"I can't go shopping. I'm almost destitute." She slumped in the chair, surrounded by a multitude of lovely ensembles that had not passed muster.

"Just this one time, okay? This is an emergency."

"You're right." She stood up and pulled her sweat pants back on.

"How about first thing in the morning? It's getting late and I'm tired and Daisy hasn't had her dinner."

"Okay." She gathered me in for a hug. "That was pretty darn shifty of you, kiddo. Setting me up with Ben like that."

I gave her a contrite grin. "I know."

"No matter what happens, I forgive you. But don't think I've forgotten about your promise to meet Duke."

CHAPTER THIRTY-SEVEN

FRIDAY · MAY 3

Posted by Katy McKenna

Monday, April 22—Part Three

After leafing rupee—no, I mean *LEAVING RUBY* surrounded by a mountain of first bait—no, FIRST DATE—jeez—what is wrong with this thing? Darn it! I forget what I was saying, or yeah—FIRST DATE REJECTS, I rowed home—crap—keeping my eyes peeled for menacing rude Princesses—no, I mean, *Pri-us-es*—blue ones, darn it—I so hate this dictating app! It was working fine before! Okay, calm down. I have to speak *slooowly* and *eenunceeaaate*. Let me try again.

———

After leaving Ruby surrounded by a mountain of "first date" rejects, I drove home, keeping my eyes peeled for menacing blue

Priuses. I took a few quick, evasive turns just in case. Once satisfied I wasn't being tailed, I turned onto Sycamore Lane. Rolling down the quiet, tree-lined street, I saw Josh-the-Viking getting out of his BMW. He didn't see me and I wasn't ready to see him. I pulled into the garage and hit the garage door remote as soon as Veronica had cleared the door. Then I remembered I needed to pick up my birth control pills at the pharmacy (like I really need those—ha, ha), so I let Daisy into the backyard, figuring that would give Josh enough time to get into his house before I backed out again.

When I got home, Daisy did not greet me when I entered the house through the garage door, so I figured she was in the yard attending to business.

In the fridge, a bottle of Chamisal Stainless Chardonnay was calling, make that screaming, my name. My plan was to veg out on the couch, savoring my wine and the second to last episode of *Frantic Hausfraus*. I poured a glassful and set it on the coffee table, queued up the show, and then checked to see if Daisy was ready to come in, but she was still busy in the bushes.

There'd been no sign of Tabitha, so I went looking for her because I wanted everyone settled before the show started.

"Tabby. Where are you, sweetie?" I called as I walked down the hall toward my bedroom. I figured I'd find her cat-napping on my bed but no luck.

"Come on. Where are you?" I heard a muffled mewing but didn't see her. I pulled back the blankets on my unmade bed, that's right, unmade—and no Tabitha. She called again and I realized she was in the closet. I opened the door to a very unhappy cat. "Poor baby. Did Mommy leave you in the closet all this time?" I scooped her up and cuddled her. "I am so, so sorry. What a bad mommy you have." Her fur was up and she was moaning low. "How about a little dinner? That should make you feel better." I carried her to the kitchen, and when I put her down to fill her bowl, she darted out of the room, presumably to sulk. "When you're ready to forgive me, I'll be in the living room."

Daisy still hadn't returned, so I sat on the couch to wait and impatiently sipped my wine. *I'll just watch the intro rehash and then we'll settle in.*

Just as I pressed "play" on the remote, I heard a soft, shuffling noise behind me. "Is that you, Daisy?" I twisted to look behind the couch. "What took you so darn—"

It happened fast and my recollection is sketchy at best. I saw a person looming over me, swinging something toward me. One thought flashed through my mind in that millisecond.

This isn't going to be good.

Whatever it was, it connected with my head and it was lights out.

———

When I came to, my first thought was, *God, what a horrible migraine. I need to take something.* I moved to get up and couldn't. The pain was beyond awful and I was so groggy that I couldn't fathom why getting up was not happening. I tried a few times and then hung my poor head in despair.

"My head hurts," I whimpered, and tried again to get up but was stuck. My muddled brain wasn't connecting. All I knew was moving hurt. Talking hurt. Thinking hurt. Breathing hurt.

I forced myself to focus (focusing hurt) and found my arms and chest were tied to a kitchen chair. My restraints looked familiar. *Are those my scarves? Why am I tied up with my scarves?* And then I saw my pink, floral scarf lying on my lap and my panic button was officially pushed.

"Well look who's back," a woman said in a freaky, singsong voice.

Lifting my head to the voice shot piercing darts of pain through my head. A woman was kneeling in front of me, and there was a seeping, bloody gash across her cheek. It took a moment to connect the dots, and when I did, my terror ratcheted up several notches.

"What are you doing here?" I swallowed my ramping panic and spoke as softly as possible to avoid jarring my scrambled brain.

She pulled a chair up to me and sat. "You've been a naughty girl and I'm here to punish you." My skin crawled as she carefully looped the pink scarf around my neck. "There, now don't you look pretty?" She tilted her head and flashed a smile that didn't extend to her glassy, off-kilter eyes.

Oh no! Was she going to strangle me again, only this time finish the job? I forced myself to speak. "Why?"

"For making my little Philly go to prison." Blood dribbled off her chin as she spat the words at me, tugging the scarf tighter with each word.

Talk about your lunatic fringe. Penny Hobart was nutso and my life and scarf were in her hands.

"I didn't make him go to prison. He raped and killed a girl. That's why he's in prison."

"Lies! Lies! Lies!" Penny got up and went to the living room and returned with my iron skillet.

No wonder my head hurt.

"This thing sure is heavy." She gripped it with both hands and spoke like a semi-normal person. "You're probably going to need an MRI. You really should get some stainless non-stick pans, you know. So much easier to clean. Of course, I know you're not ever supposed to wash these things. So how *do* you clean it?"

"I–I..." Why was she asking me that? Oh yeah. Because she's a loon. So I answered, "I rinse it out with a scrub brush and put it on a burner to dry it."

"Wrong!" The crazy voice was back. "That's not how Alton Brown does it." She brandished the pan in front of me. Was she going to clobber me again?

"You put kosher salt in it and scrub that around and then wipe it out, you dummy. Water ruins the pan. Don't you know anything?" She flung the pan across the kitchen and it crashed through the picture window facing the backyard. The glass shattered and spilled to the floor. "Oh, dear. Now look what you made me do." She stared at the gaping hole a moment, shook her head, and then spoke in a saner tone. "What a mess. Make sure you don't walk barefoot in here. You don't want to get glass in your feet."

Penny sat down again, visibly calmer, which terrified me even more. "I'm sorry. That was uncalled for." A sob burbled in her throat. "It's just been so hard."

I heard Daisy outside the broken window, whining in a pathetic voice I'd never heard before. Something was wrong with her. Had she been hit by the flying skillet?

"Why don't you tell me about it," I replied, to distract Penny from the sound.

"My Philly is such a good boy." She met my eyes and beamed with a mother's pride. "He's an Eagle Scout, you know. And in the Honor Society. He's been accepted at USL and he's going to be a teacher, even though Adam wants him to be a lawyer."

What year was she living in? Didn't her husband die from a heart attack? Yes. Christy said he'd died during the trial.

"People keep doing mean things to him. They put him in prison and that horrible woman told me she was going to make sure he never gets out."

Did she mean me? "I never said that. I just said—"

She smiled spooky-sweet. "Not you, you silly ninny. I'm talking about the mean lady who spoke at my Bible study luncheon. She said my Philly was a murderer." Tears mingled with the blood on her face and oozed down her cheeks, dripping onto her arms. "She said he raped and killed her little girl. She said she would fight every chance for parole he ever gets so he won't be able to kill any other girls. How could she say that about my Phil?" Mucus drained from her nose and she swiped at it, smearing a revolting blend of blood, snot, and tears across her face. "She asked everyone to sign a petition that she will present when Phil's first parole hearing comes up."

I really wanted to take a nap, which probably meant I had a concussion, but I forced myself to speak. "What did you do?"

"I stopped her," she answered, tilting her head and giggling childishly.

Loony-toons. "How?"

"I poisoned her dog food."

What? "People don't eat dog food."

"Not her, silly. Why are you so confused? Your stupid dog. I poisoned her. That's why she wouldn't come in when you were calling her. I had to cover my mouth so you wouldn't hear me laughing. Can't you hear her crying out there? She's dying." She turned her head and screamed, "Shut up, stupid dog!" She turned back to me. "Oh, boo-hoo, so sad. Your doggy's dying."

Oh, no. Not Daisy. Not my baby. I thought my heart would break, which made my head ache even more, but I knew if I lost control, I wouldn't have a chance of surviving this.

"Your stupid cat wouldn't eat it." She pulled up her sleeve and showed me a long, nasty, red slash down her arm. That also explained her shredded, bloody face. *Way to go, Tabitha.*

"I hate cats. They're so uncooperative."

I love cats! I didn't know what to do, but in the crime shows, they always keep the bad guy talking until someone rescues them, so I asked, "What about the woman?"

She looked perplexed. "What woman?"

"The one who spoke at your church luncheon. The mean lady with the petition." I thought if I could convince her that I had nothing to do with a petition, I might survive.

"Oh, her," she laughed. "The idiot was crossing the street and so busy talking on her cell phone, she never knew what hit her." She sighed contentedly. "When I looked in the rearview mirror, I saw her petitions blowing away in the wind. That was the end of that." Her smug, satisfied look faded and she refocused on me.

"Until you came along." She cocked her head and sighed. "Hey, how do you like my Prius? Cute, huh? You should get rid of that old orange crate you drive and get one like mine."

I heard a soft noise and gazed beyond her shoulder at the gaping hole in the wall. Daisy was attempting to climb into the room. Normally the eighteen-inch wall under the broken window would have been no problem, but in her feeble condition, she was having a difficult time and I was afraid Penny would hear her and finish her off.

NO! NO! I willed Daisy to hear my thoughts. *Stay!* She ignored my mind-melding attempts and kept struggling to get in the room. So I kept talking to distract Penny. Beyond that, I had no plan.

I winced with each word as I nearly shouted to cover Daisy's noise. "What do you mean, until I came along?"

"You found her petitions and you were going to use them to make Phil stay in prison. So now I have to stop you—Katy McKenna, 539 Sycamore Lane." She frowned at me like I was a petulant child. "When Phil is released, I'm going to retire and everything will be wonderful. Phil can teach and I'm going to write a cookbook."

Daisy had her front paws planted on the glass-strewn wood floor and was painfully dragging a hind leg over the wall.

Penny's gaze drifted to my vintage white O'Keefe and Merritt stove. "My parents had a stove like that."

Daisy was hauling her other back leg in the room. I was terrified for her.

"Oh really?" I bellowed. "I love mine!" *Please don't see Daisy!*

Daisy was in the room. I watched her in my peripheral vision while trying to keep Penny distracted. "So, uh, where'd you grow up?"

Daisy's ears laid flat against her head. Her muzzle twitched and puffed as her lips wrinkled back baring her long, sharp canines. The muscles in her back quivered and the hair along her spine stood rigid. Her tail slowly wagged while a low menacing growl rumbled deep in her throat. My sweet girl had shape-shifted into Cujo.

Penny's eyes shifted towards the window just as Daisy bolted across the room and lunged at her throat, knocking her off the chair to the floor. The element of surprise was on Daisy's side and even in her weakened state, she was doing serious damage. My baby's teeth were clamped on Penny's scrawny throat, shaking her like an old rag doll. Penny was struggling and her bloodcurdling shrieks escalated Daisy's adrenaline infused canine frenzy.

I seized the opportunity and bounced my chair out of the kitchen toward the front door, shouting encouragement at Daisy along the way. "Kill her! Good girl! Kill the wacko, Daisy!"

Each bounce ricocheted through my cracked skull, and several times the chair legs grazed down the back of my ankles, but incredible adrenaline was propelling me and I made it to the front door. It wasn't locked, and after several attempts I was able to push the door handle lever down with my foot and coax it open.

As soon as it swung wide, I started screaming, "HELP! Somebody help me!"

I tried to jump the chair over the threshold, but it toppled and I fell out onto the porch, landing hard on my side, which I felt in spite of the adrenaline. The damned scarves held me tightly bound to the chair, but I kept screaming.

From a distance, Josh yelled, "What's going on?" He raced up the walk and pounded up the wood porch steps.

"My God, Katy. Are you all right?"

No, you idiot. I'm tied to a chair, lying sideways on the porch, with a skillet-flattened skull. "I'm fine. Help Daisy. In the kitchen." He raced through the front door to the kitchen, as I warned, "Be careful."

A split second later, I heard him shouting, "Daisy, stop! It's okay, girl. You can let go of her now."

Daisy wasn't ready to relinquish control and she snarled like a hungry wolf protecting her prey from scavengers.

"Daisy, please. Let go of her," Josh spoke in a calm, soothing voice. "It's all right now, girl. Let go. Come on, let go of her throat. That's a girl. You did good."

A moment later, she lay next to me and rested her bloody muzzle on my thigh.

"Daisy. Thank you," I murmured. "You are my brave, brave girl."

The adrenaline rush was officially over, and we both slipped into oblivion.

CHAPTER THIRTY-EIGHT

SATURDAY · MAY 4

Posted by Katy McKenna

Tuesday, April 23

I was released from the hospital in the late morning. My left elbow was broken and encased in a half-cast, and I had a concussion. No surprise there.

My folks took me to their house and ensconced me on the sofa in the sunroom, where I had a view of the garden and the sixty-inch flat screen. Almost perfect.

"Are you hungry, Katydid?" Pop set a cup of my favorite tea, Murchie's No. 10 blend, on a tray next to me.

"No, thanks." I took a sip, placed it on the side table, and settled my aching head into the down pillows. I closed my eyes, listening to the birds twittering outside and counting my blessings.

I opened my eyes to a pair of beautiful brown eyes gazing into mine. Daisy was on the couch wedged between me and the back cushions, her head on my chest, her breath tickling my chin. Samantha, Ruby and my folks stood nearby.

"We were trying to keep her off the couch so she wouldn't wake you, but she wasn't having it," said Mom.

Now everything was perfect.

———

Police Chief Angela Yaeger came to see me late in the afternoon. She'd brought along her sidekick, Lieutenant Joanne Yee.

Mom led them into the sunroom, offered coffee, tea, or soda, which both declined, and then excused herself. Before they sat on the rattan chairs near the couch, they peeked at the back of my head, even though it was covered by a bandage.

"You poor thing," said Angela. "How many stitches did you get?"

"Eight."

"That must be why they had to shave so much hair off," Yee observed.

"I'm bald?" I shrieked and instantly learned that shrieking hurt. "MOM!" Ouch.

Mom ran into the room. "What's wrong?"

Due to my pounding head, I whisper-screamed, "You didn't tell me I'm bald!"

I caught the apologetic glance that Yee shot my mother, and knew that meant it was bad.

"How big is the bald spot?" I demanded.

Mom gave me a it's-not-that-bad smile. "Maybe an inch or so."

"Or so? What does 'or so' mean? Five, six inches *or so*?" I raised my arms to check the back of my head, momentarily forgetting my left arm was no longer operational. Agony shot through my elbow and curled my toes.

"Two inches at the most." She and Angela exchanged a quick glance. Liars. Traitors.

"I saw that! Two inches, ha! More like the entire back of my head. Might as well shave the rest of it off and be done with it."

"Honey, you have a severe scalp wound and it needed stitches. The doctor had no choice. She had to shave the area. It's hair. It'll grow back. I can give you some layers and it won't even show. It'll be cute."

"I hate layers," I whined like a spoiled, pissy child. "It's too hard to put your hair into a ponytail."

Angela laughed. "You certainly are the plucky one. By all rights you should be dead now, and here you are, having a fit over your hair."

"You won't be getting your hair into a ponytail for a while, anyway, with your broken elbow," said Mom, using the reasonable tone that had never worked on me when I *was* a pissy child.

"I think your hair will look cute." Yee unconsciously flipped her long black braid over her shoulder.

I hunkered down in the couch and muttered, "Yeah, right."

I'd pushed Mom's last "patient button" and she lost her cool. "In the last few days, you were attacked twice by a crazy person. It's amazing you're even alive. Why don't you try to be grateful, instead of whining about a patch of stupid hair. I could have lost my child last night, who by the way is not a child, but a thirty-one-year-old woman, even though sometimes I wonder."

"Actually it was three times."

Mom put her hands on her hips. "What do you mean, three times?"

"She crashed into my car at the mall yesterday afternoon, too."

"What? Why didn't you tell me?"

"Because I was unconscious at the hospital and it slipped my mind until now."

"You know, come to think of it, a cup of tea would be nice," said Angela. "Don't you think so, Lieutenant?"

"Yes. Tea would be lovely." She made a show of opening her notebook, and setting a digital recorder on the coffee table.

Mom started to leave for the kitchen, but I stopped her. "Sorry, Mom. I'm acting like a jerk."

"I'm just glad you're alive so you *can* act like a jerk."

"Last night you had no control over anything that happened," Angela said to me, "so it's understandable to overreact now. You're only human. And it's your *hair.* Come on."

"Actually, that's not quite true," said Mom, her tone back to normal. "You did take control of your situation last night. You kept a cool head and got yourself saved."

"Thanks, Mom, but it was Daisy who saved me."

Daisy was still tucked in beside me, recuperating from being poisoned by that wacko, but thumped her tail when she heard her name. Angela and Yee leaned from their seats and petted the hero.

Mom fanned away threatening tears. "I'll go get the tea now."

Angela straightened up. "We went to the hospital last night, but you were in no condition to answer questions."

Yee snickered. "You were sawing logs."

"I was trying to be delicate," Angela chuckled. "But now, we really must go over everything while it's still fresh."

I'd been avoiding thinking about it, literally blocking it out by sleeping most of the day. The pain meds had made that easy, but she was right. Time to talk. "What about Penny Hobart? Is she in jail? Please say yes!"

The women were silent. Did that mean she was on the loose? Yee frowned and my fear spiked.

"You're scaring me." I glanced out the windows, expecting to find the skillet-wielding wacko lurking in the shrubbery.

Angela leaned from her chair and closed her warm hand over mine and steadied me with her compassionate, brown eyes. "It's okay, Katy. She can't hurt you now. She passed early this morning."

I was stunned. "You mean Daisy killed her?"

At the sound of her name, my sweet girl lifted her head, her gentle brown eyes flicking between us.

"Yes. She saved your life, no doubt about it. Totally amazing, considering the condition she was in."

"Do you know what poisoned Daisy?"

"Antifreeze," said Angela.

"Lucky you're a vegetarian and your dog isn't," said Yee. "Hobart laced a plate of lentils with it and Daisy only ate a small amount. There was no internal damage and she will have a full recovery."

"Thank God." I hugged my girl. "I don't know what I would do without you Daisy."

Angela released my hand and stroked Daisy's back. "What a brave girl you are." Her voice caught, and she cleared her throat. "We knew how hard everything had been on Penny. Her son being convicted and sent to prison. Her husband dying of a heart attack during the trial. Her daughter having so many troubled years."

"So much grief," said Yee, "and yet, she continued to do a stellar job at the station, and over time she seemed to be her old self again."

"That's right," said Angela. "It was years ago and we thought she'd gotten past it. Especially the last couple years. Like the huge weight had finally lifted when Christy got married and found happiness. Penny was so excited about her daughter's pregnancy and becoming a grandma."

"Yeah. She was even trying to quit smoking," said Yee. "Always saying how second-hand smoke wouldn't be good for the baby."

"Then I come along and stick my nose in and ruin everything." I said. "Was it worth it?"

"How could you have known?" asked Angela. "You were trying to do the right thing. Most people wouldn't bother. They'd rather just complain about the system than actually get involved."

"Yeah, well I will have to think long and hard before I get involved again, that's for sure."

Angela turned on the digital recorder. "Now, Katy, tell us what happened. Take your time, starting with the mall."

Reliving the experience was highly emotional and my tears flowed freely. It was hard to believe that my lovable doggy had killed Penny Hobart. As I was telling them about Daisy struggling to climb through the broken window, I abruptly stopped, shocked at what I suddenly had remembered.

"Penny Hobart killed Belinda Moore!"

CHAPTER THIRTY-NINE

SUNDAY · MAY 5

Posted by Katy McKenna

Wednesday, April 24

I was lounging under a shady Chinese elm in my parents' yard and lusting over Kevin Costner in *The Bodyguard* on my laptop, wishing I had a handsome knight in shining armor who would protect me. In my peripheral vision, I detected someone approaching and hit pause, expecting to see a parental unit bearing snacks. Instead it was the Viking, limping in a plastic aircast, followed by my furry bodyguard, Daisy.

I slapped my sunglasses over my mascara-free eyes and tried to fluff my hair over the bandage wrapped around my head. "What happened to you?"

"It's nothing." He collapsed in the chaise lounge next to me and hoisted his jean-clad leg up on the cushion with a groan. Daisy stood next to him, and he unconsciously scratched her head.

"Doesn't sound like nothing. Tell me."

His eyes swept the length of my sweats-attired body, taking in my injuries: backs of ankles scraped raw by the chair legs while bouncing to safety, broken elbow, bandaged head covering my stitches, a black eye—hidden by my sunglasses, grazed cheek and swollen nose from my face-plant on the porch, and, last but not least, my gruesome neck.

"The short story is—I slipped in Hobart's blood and sprained my ankle."

I shut my laptop and set it on the table next to me. "Like I haven't heard that one before. Tell me the long version."

He pulled his troubled eyes from my face and gazed at the billowy clouds floating by. "I was trying to stop the flow of blood from her neck with a towel, when she grabbed my hair and yanked me into her face. Caught me completely off guard." A muscle bunched in his jaw beneath his blond stubble. "My feet slipped out from under me on the bloody floor and I fell on top of her." Josh shuddered a full body shiver and my heart went out to him. "I had to head-butt her to get away. In the struggle I wrenched my ankle."

"God. How awful." There was probably more to it than what he'd told me, but it was more than enough for me. I already had enough fodder to fill my nightmares for years to come. "I'm so thankful you came when you did."

"Daisy had things under control. Hobart was all but done when I got there." Josh was quiet a moment, then he softly chuckled. "You know, if I was still on the force, I'd never live this down. I mean, come on! I'm six-three, 198 pounds."

All muscle. Sure would like to check that out to make sure. Then I mentally slapped myself. *Stop it! The man is injured.*

He continued, oblivious to my steamy musings. "And she was five-three–five-four? Maybe one hundred and ten? And half-dead at the time."

"But it was a lunatic one hundred and ten. You should have

seen her throw that skillet through the window. I can barely lift it with one hand."

Josh reached over and picked up the hand attached to the good elbow and encircled my wrist with his big, strong fingers. I curled my fingers so he wouldn't see my chewed up nails and almost passed out in a lust rush.

"That's because you have such dainty wrists." Then he noticed the watch on my dainty wrist. "Whoa! I've got to go."

In my drunken state of horniness, I slurred, "Where?"

"I have a date. My first in months."

Date? What? "Oh? Who?" I tried to sound casual. And what did he mean by that crack, *My first in months.*

"Don't know. It's a blind date a friend of mine set up. He convinced me it's time to get back on the horse and ride."

Ooo. Bad choice of words.

He set my limp wrist down and gave me a playful punch on the arm. "Wish me luck, buddy!"

Buddy?

After he made a hasty exit, I sat there feeling pretty darn stupid and more than a little disappointed. I'd already picked out our kids' names, Barbie and Ken.

Oh, well, maybe it's for the best since he lives next door. But he's so darned hot. And a nice guy, too. But what if it didn't work out? It could be awkward. Maybe he could be a friend with benefits. A boink buddy. Oh jeez, Ruby was right. I needed to get laid. I shifted on the chaise lounge and sharp pain slammed through me, leaving me breathless and immediately putting the kibosh on my lusty reveries. What I really needed was more pain meds. And ice cream.

I heard the screen door slap and saw Mom approaching with the house phone. "It's your father. Are you up to talking?"

Not really. I took the phone and said hello to bio-father-Bert.

"Hey, kitten. How're you doing?" His voice boomed so loud, I didn't need to use the speakerphone.

"Fine."

"Not according to Marybeth. She told me you got hit with a frying pan."

"No big deal."

His voice dropped to a quiet, concerned level. "Sounds like a big deal to me, Katy."

"It *was* pretty scary. And it sure hurts. And I have a bald spot." Those were the most words I'd said to him in months. Maybe years.

"Is your beautiful face all right? You know I'm pretty good at what I do," said my Palm Springs plastic-surgeon-to-the-stars father.

"She got me in the back of the head, so not to worry."

I heard him sigh with what sounded like genuine relief. "Listen. I was thinking when you're feeling better, you and I could do something special."

My father has been married five times since Mom, and every time he is going through a breakup, he starts thinking about what a lousy no-show father he's been. Then he wants to make amends by spending quality time with me, but usually before we actually do anything, he gets hooked up again and that's the last I hear from him, except for his requests to be a Facebook friend. I haven't even met his current thirty-three-year-old trophy wife.

"How's Bridgette?" I asked, not really caring and already knowing the answer. There was no point in even remembering the wives' names.

"She's great. For someone so young, she sure has an old soul. She'd like to get to know you, but this get-together needs to be just you and me. I was thinking I could drive up there and take you to Carmel for a few days."

Should I call his bluff? Yes, I should! "How about in a couple of weeks or so? I should be feeling pretty good by then."

Now came the part where he would say he'd check his calendar and then in a few days he'd call back and tell me he had too many facelifts and boob-lifts and butt-lifts scheduled.

He called my bluff instead. "Perfect. I was hoping you'd agree, so I went ahead and booked us a two-bedroom suite with an ocean view at The Highlands Inn."

CHAPTER FORTY

MONDAY · MAY 6

Posted by Katy McKenna

Saturday, April 27

"I'm afraid," I whispered. I stood on the porch, feet rooted to the spot, unable to step over the threshold into my once-cozy, safe refuge. Daisy glanced up at me, gave me a reassuring smile, and trotted in.

Pop put his arm around my shoulders. "It's not the house that hurt you, Katydid. It was Penny Hobart, and that poor, demented woman is at peace now. But you *will* remember to always to lock the door and set the alarm from now on, right? I don't care how big a rush you're in."

"I will."

"And I want to get you a gun."

"No way," I said, wincing. "Guns scare me."

"And they should, but remember your old man was a cop. I will teach you how to shoot and safely handle a gun. We'll go to the shooting range—"

"Kinda like a father-daughter thing?"

"Yeah. It'll be fun. And once you're back to full steam, let's get you enrolled in a self-defense class."

That was definitely a good idea. I peeked inside toward the kitchen, thinking about Josh slipping in the blood.

"Everything is back in order. Come see for yourself." He guided a reluctant me through the door.

The broken picture window had been replaced and the floor looked pristine—actually better than before—I guess that's what a good scrubbing can do. Thank goodness she'd died in the hospital and not on my kitchen floor. The last thing I needed was Penny Hobart's restless spirit working on her phantom cookbook in my kitchen.

"We had a disaster team come in and clean up, and now you have a dual pane window."

At least one of the windows in my old house won't be drafty. "Thanks, Pop."

I heard Tabitha before I saw her. She was loudly scolding me as she scurried through the house. She slammed full-tilt into my legs and went into purr overdrive. I scooped her up and went to the living room sofa, forgetting that Hobart had clobbered me there, and by the time Tabitha finished telling me off for leaving her alone, I was lovingly coated in gray cat hair.

CHAPTER FORTY-ONE

FRIDAY · MAY 10

Posted by Katy McKenna

Today was "petition gathering day." My last stop was The Bookcase Bistro. My earlier decision to face the enemy on my terms had fizzled after my first visit to the store. Now I just wanted to get in and get out as fast as possible.

Chad was always a creature of habit, so I timed my arrival to coincide with his usual three o'clock afternoon break. Luckily he'd only changed wives, not habits, and was nowhere to be seen when I sneaked in and hid behind a bookshelf to recon the shop before approaching the counter. Heather was sitting on a stool behind the register engrossed in paperwork and hadn't noticed me skulking about.

"Hi, Heather."

Her face lit up in a genuine smile. "Katy." She struggled to get her rotund self off the stool.

"No, please. Don't get up," I said, waving her back down. "I mean there's no need to get up on my account. I'm just here to pick up the petitions." The poor thing is massive and still has at least three months to go.

"Oh, pooh." She trundled around the counter and sideways-hugged me. "You're so sweet. Really, I'm fine." She pulled back and gazed at me. "But how are you? I read what happened in the newspaper online."

She reads the newspaper? Maybe I've been a little hasty in labeling her an idiot.

"You're like a hero. And you solved a cold case. I'm so totally impressed."

I *had* solved a cold case. Hadn't been trying to, but nevertheless I had.

"I have your petitions here. We have, like, over six hundred names. Six hundred and thirteen to be exact."

She handed me the hefty stack and made me promise to come back and visit. Like I want to be pals with my ex's wife. How weird would that be? But I promised anyway, because Heather is pretty darned hard to refuse.

She was hugging me again when Chad walked in and weird took on a whole new meaning, except for Heather, who dragged us into a brief, group hug. Very brief.

"Hey, Chad," I mumbled, disengaging and thinking, *His hairline is receding. Ha. His waistline is expanding. Double ha.*

"Hello, Katy. Heather showed me the newspaper story about you. I'm glad you're all right. Pretty scary stuff, huh?"

I shrugged nonchalantly, rocking on my sandaled heels. "Yup, pretty dangerous, all right. But it goes with the territory, you know. Helping the police department solve cold cases and all." I flaunted the petitions. "At least we'll be keeping *one creep* where he belongs." I looked directly into his eyes, but he was too dense to catch my drift. What had I ever seen in this guy?

It was time for me to shut up and vamoose, so I started backing away. "I guess I'll get going now." I wanted to bolt for the door, shouting something brilliant like, '*Cheater, cheater, pumpkin eater, had a wife and couldn't keep her,*' but that would have been immature, so I kept my cool vibe going.

"Let me walk you out." Chad took my good elbow, guiding me toward the door. I glanced back at Heather and she was grinning like she had solved the world's problems with a hug.

As we walked, he whispered, "You look so sexy with your new hairstyle."

It's official. I hate layers. Thanks a lot, Mom.

"God, I've missed you, Katy. I didn't know if you'd ever speak to me again, but when I heard you brought the petition in, I knew you felt the same way." He leaned close and murmured, "I've missed your scent. I'm obsessed."

What? That line actually gave me shivers—not the good kind. I scuttled through the entrance with Chad hot on my heels. As soon as we cleared the glass doors and were out of Heather's sight, I spun around. "What the hell is wrong with you? You're about to have three babies." I held up three fingers and considered bending back two of them.

"I know." He hung his head and murmured, "I know. I'm the world's biggest fool."

"No. You're the world's biggest ass."

Chad shook his head, staring down at the sidewalk. "What have I done?" He looked up, reaching for my hands and I stepped back, cradling my sore elbow protectively. His eyes raked over my body and he groaned. "Katy. Leaving you was the biggest mistake of my life. I still love you."

To say I was astounded would have been an understatement. I was gobsmacked. "Too little, too late. Heather is a sweetheart, and you better take good care of her and your incoming kids, or you will have me to deal with, got it?"

"God, you're so sexy when you're mad." He groaned again. "Remember how good make-up sex was?"

Oh puke!

"I swear I'll do right by my children, but I'm going to win you back, Katy McKenna. I can't live without you. You are my soulmate and I was too stupid to realize it."

It was like being trapped in a cheesy soap opera, except it really hurt. I had no snappy comeback, nothing cerebral or cutting. It just plain hurt. And now I was hurting for two. Heather and me, or five if you counted the kids.

"Drop dead, Chad." I turned and walked away, knowing the sleazeball would ogle my tush, so I sashayed. Not for him. For me.

———

Final destination was the police department to turn in the petitions. The desk clerk checked with Angela, then sent me down the hall to her office. I stuck my head in her open doorway. She sat at her desk and appeared busy. "Hi. Okay if I interrupt?"

"Katy! Come in. Sit down—no, wait. Your hair! Spin around so I can see the back."

I did as told, inwardly grumbling about my new do.

"Kind of has a gypsy vibe to it. Very cute and still long enough to get into a ponytail. Love the bangs. They make your eyes look so big. I never realized they're green. Your mom really knows her stuff."

I unconsciously fluffed my hair and caught my reflection in the window. Okay, maybe I could learn to like it. Maybe.

"Thanks. Still getting used to it." I plunked my stack of petitions on the desk next to the impressive pile already sitting there and sat down. "Nine-thousand, eight-hundred and forty-two."

"Wow! I was just counting what we have here, so let me add up these numbers. She punched the figures into a calculator. "Are you ready?"

"Yes! I can't wait."

"Drumroll, please."

I drummed a rapid one-handed staccato on the edge of her oak desk.

"Fifteen-thousand, one-hundred and twenty-seven signatures!"

"Woo-hoo!" I shouted and we high-fived.

Angela straightened the thick stack and placed a paperweight on it. "Can you believe it? When this all began, I had no idea you'd wind up with this many. It's way beyond my expectations."

I laughed with a satisfied blend of pride and delight. "Way beyond mine, too."

Angela stood up and leaned over to shake my hand. "Well done, Katy. Well done."

She sat down again and held up a folder for me to see. "This is Belinda Moore's file. Thanks to you, it's now a closed case. Lindsay's mom can finally rest in peace."

A warm glow surged through me. I'd made a difference and it felt good. Maybe I could expand on this experience and become a force of good, like Wonder Woman or Mother Teresa. Selfless, caring, an advocate for all mankind.

Angela broke into my virtuous reverie. "Katy? Have you ever thought about joining the police force?"

EPILOGUE

~ 1996 ~

After Jake was found with Lindsay's corpse in his lap, he never spoke another word. The horror of his actions had culminated in a complete disconnect from reality and a few days later, he committed suicide.

That left only Phil Hobart to stand trial for the rape, abduction, and murder of Lindsay Moore. The public outcry and the ensuing media circus made a fair trial in Santa Lucia County impossible, so it was relocated to Monterey County. As the trial unfolded, it became apparent Erik had been the catalyst behind the crimes and had ultimately caused Lindsay's death. The fact that Phil had tried to revive her weighed heavily in his favor. In determining punishment, factors taken into consideration included his age, his lack of prior criminal record, a good academic record, being an Eagle Scout, and that he had been well-regarded by various community leaders. Therefore, he was sentenced to life in prison with a possibility of parole.

Hobart was sent to Folsom State Prison in Sacramento and

released into the general population, where for the first year he lived a nightmare beyond anything he ever could have imagined.

~ Now ~

Two weeks after the parole hearing, I received a letter from the state of California Board of Prison Terms.

Dear Ms. McKenna:
Re: HOBART, Phillip Adam F-1067

This will acknowledge your petition concerning Phillip Hobart.

The Board of Prison Terms is required by statute to conduct parole consideration hearings for persons serving life sentences with the possibility of parole, and it must consider the comments of all persons concerned with the granting or denial of parole to a prisoner.

According to our records, on July 12, Phillip Adam Hobart was found unsuitable for parole and denied further consideration for five years. We are forwarding your petitions to Mr. Hobart's file at the institution so that your petitions will be considered by the next Board panel who hears this case.

You may be assured that your petitions will be given appropriate consideration in future hearings.

Sincerely,
Edmund K. Greene
Chairman

———

Bio-dad Bert came through on his promise to take me to Carmel. Maybe it's never too late to grow up. I now have thirty-five Facebook friends.

One more thing before I close. Samantha, along with my folks,

Grandma Ruby, and a few other close friends, begged me to let them read my blog after I told them I'd written about everything that happened during my petition misadventures, so I decided to share it with those closest to me. They've all given their solemn promise not to be mad at me after they read it. I hope I don't live to regret it.

I'm glad I listened to Sam when she suggested the idea of keeping a blog. She was right. It really *is* cathartic. Who knew? I think I'll keep doing it.

In 1996, Congress passed the Drug-Induced Rape Prevention and Punishment Act, as an amendment to the Controlled Substances Act. This amendment established federal penalties of up to twenty years imprisonment and fines for anyone convicted of committing a crime of violence, including rape, by administering a controlled substance without the victim's knowledge or consent.

AFTERWORD

Dear Reader,

Many years ago, I read a newspaper article about an upcoming parole hearing for a man who had raped, kidnapped and murdered a young girl in our community. Like Katy, I was incensed that someone could *ever* be eligible for parole after committing such heinous crimes—let alone after only fifteen years.

In the ensuing years, the girl's mother had died and there were no other family members to speak for her at the parole hearing, so I decided I would speak for her. After researching the crime to ensure that there had been no miscarriage of justice, I started a petition and gathered thousands of signatures.

When it was time for the parole hearing, I wanted to attend, but the District Attorney told me it was too dangerous. He did not want this man to know my identity.

Years later, when I finally sat down to write a story loosely based on my experience, I knew that I wanted my protagonist to be fun and quirky because I plan to spend a lot of time with Katy in upcoming books.

But I had no idea that the criminals would turn out as they did

—that's one of the weird phenomenons of writing—characters tend to take on a life of their own, and the writer tags along. According to everyone I interviewed at the time I did my petition, the real criminal had no endearing or redeeming qualities what-so-ever.

I am happy to say that he is still in prison all these years later.

Respectfully yours,
Pamela Frost Dennis

———

If you enjoyed this book, I would be eternally grateful if you left a short review on Amazon.

Indie Authors get very giddy when
we get a good review.
Thank you!

Dead Girls Don't Blog

If you're reading an ebook, this easy link
takes you directly to the page
for leaving a review.

ABOUT THE AUTHOR

I live on the California Central Coast with my husband, Mike, and our furry canine writing muses. I enjoy gardening, reading, yoga, riding my bike, playing guitar, binge-watching TV shows (especially British ones), and playing with our three awesome grandkids.

Pamelafrostdennis.com

Recipes from the book
are on my website.

Try the Sugar Cream Pie from
Better Dead Than Wed.
It's to die for!

THE MURDER BLOG MYSTERIES

Additional Books in the Series

BETTER DEAD THAN WED
Book #2 in the Murder Blog Mysteries

Katy McKenna has had enough near-death experiences and heartache to last a lifetime. Now all she wants to do is get her career back on track, find a nice guy, and live happily-ever-after. But when she hears about a man maliciously exposing innocent young women to HIV, she is compelled to put her plans on hold to stop him.

Meanwhile, Katy's mother is forced to reveal a shattering childhood trauma that has come back to haunt her; her obnoxious baby sister is moving in, and her scuzzy was-band is stalking her.

And she's beginning to wonder why every rotten person she has recently heard about has suddenly dropped dead. Is it divine providence? Or is it murder?

COINS AND CADAVERS
Book #3 in the Murder Blog Mysteries

While battling a furry vermin invasion in the spooky attic of her old house, Katy discovers a vintage wooden chest hidden behind a wall. Although everyone assures her the box is legally hers, its incredible contents compel Katy to search for the rightful owner.

Meanwhile, she takes a temp job assisting her hunky P.I. neighbor, Josh Draper. The assignment: Trap a sleazy wife-cheater. Something Katy knows about all too well from personal experience. During a cozy stakeout in Draper's two-seater, things get awkward as the sizzling tension builds. Who will make the first move?

Since she's already been searching online for past owners of her home, Grandma Ruby asks Katy to use her sleuthing skills to discover what happened to her bigamist great-great grandfather. Katy's quest leads her to find an extended family she never knew existed.

Family secrets are revealed,
for better or worse....
Romance blossoms,
for better or worse....
And Katy's good intentions lead her
into a terrifying
dilemma she may not survive.

WAS IT MURDER?
Book #4 in the Murder Blog Mysteries

In the latest Murder Blog Mysteries novel, Katy finds herself at loose ends. She's jobless, but not penny-less thanks to a recently discovered box of rare coins in her attic. But she's clueless as to what her next career will be. Plus, her sizzling romance with Josh, is doing a fast fizzle since he left town to continue nursing his ex-wife through her cancer battle.

Just as Katy is settling in for an extended pity-party of weepy old movies and tubs of mint-chip ice cream, her mother calls with tragic news. A dear family member has met an untimely end. Now Katy and her grandma must travel to the scenic Cotswolds of England to sort out legal matters. When they arrive, they're overwhelmed by the friendly villagers who offer help and moral support.

However, when Katy and Ruby become the target of vandals, they realize that not everyone in town is pleased about their presence.

Is murder next on the list?

———

I hope you enjoy the first two chapters of
Better Dead Than Wed
on the following pages.

BETTER DEAD THAN WED - CHAPTER 1

THURSDAY · JUNE 6
Posted by Katy McKenna

After nearly getting myself killed while solving a cold case a couple months ago, Police Chief Angela Yaeger asked me if I'd ever considered a career in law enforcement. Nope. I'm a graphic artist. Make that an out-of-work graphic artist, because my broken elbow was collateral damage in solving that old case.

While my elbow has been healing, I've had time to weigh my career options. I love being a freelance graphic artist, but there are some drawbacks, like: If I'm sick—no paycheck. Injured—no paycheck. No client—no paycheck. Vacation—who can afford a vacation? Benefits—what are those?

Fortunately, I made a tidy profit selling the grandiose house that Chad, my "was-band," had to have, or I'd be back in my old bedroom at my folks' house watching cat videos and blogging about my boring life. Oh wait, I *am* blogging about my boring life, and I *love* watching cat videos. Who doesn't?

Back to the law enforcement idea. My stepdad is a retired cop with a good medical plan, a nice pension, and a monthly disability check for taking a bullet in the knee. I don't want to be shot in the knee, but Pop told me that in over twenty-five years with the Santa Lucia Police Department, he didn't draw his gun until his last day on the job. So the odds would be in my favor. Of course, your first day on a cop job has the potential to be your last day. But a steady paycheck and a medical plan paid by someone other than yours truly sure would be nice.

Yesterday I called the chief and told her I was seriously thinking about what she'd said, and she suggested I go on a ride-along to get a realistic feel for the job; so today, I went to the station to sign up. I was sitting in the police department lobby with a clip-boarded waiver on my lap, pen in hand, ready to sign. Then I read it.

I acknowledge that the work and activities of the Santa Lucia Police Department are inherently dangerous and involve possible risks of injury, death, and damage or loss to person or property. I further understand such risks may arise from, but are not limited to, civil disturbances; explosions or shootings; assaults and/or battery; vehicular collisions; and the effects of wind, rain, fire, and gas. I freely and voluntarily assume all possible inherent risks, whether or not they are listed herein.

That gave me pause. I'd pictured something a little different. Like going for donuts, helping little old ladies cross the street, getting a cat out of a tree, lecturing a truant kid, throwing the town drunk in the hoosegow. In other words, a ride-along with Sheriff Andy in Mayberry.

I stepped to the counter and slid the clipboard under the office clerk's nose. "Exactly how often do people get killed in ride-alongs?" I tapped the waiver. "This says there could be explosions and riots, terrorist attacks, car crashes, and possible death."

"Well…" She glanced at the form through red, half-rimmed specs. "Ms. McKenna."

"Katy."

"Well, Katy. I don't see anything here about terrorist attacks——"

"These days you never know."

"True, but this form is merely a formality to protect the department from potential lawsuits. I can assure you we've never lost a ride-along passenger in all the time I've worked here."

That was reassuring. "How long is that?"

"Almost four months now."

Not so reassuring.

The waiver included an area where you checked off a box indicating which days and shifts you preferred. I preferred Monday, eight a.m. to noon. I figured more crimes were committed on the weekends and criminals liked to sleep in on Mondays. Better safe than sorry, I always say.

BETTER DEAD THAN WED - CHAPTER 2

TUESDAY · JUNE 11
Posted by Katy McKenna

Yesterday I arrived at the police station at 7:45 a.m., latte in hand, and dressed according to the ride-along guidelines. Nice pants, cute pink top, a cardigan to ward off the chilly overcast day, and semi-practical shoes.

After checking in at the lobby counter, I took a seat on a bench. A few minutes later, Chief Yaeger greeted me. "Katy. So good to see you." We exchanged a hug, then sat.

"Wow. You look fabulous," I said. "I love your hair that way."

Angela had let her hair go totally gray since I last saw her, and her new close-cropped hairstyle looked stunning against her warm, ebony skin tone.

She patted her hair. "I got tired of fighting the inevitable. I'd let it start to go gray, then I'd hate it and color it again. I finally got it all cut off and I'm loving it. Should've done it a long time ago."

She paused, giving me a concerned look. "You okay?" she asked. "You look a little tense."

"The waiver I signed the other day kind of unnerved me. You know, car crashes, shootings, explosions."

She chuckled. "You know, we wouldn't have the ride-along program if there were a big risk of endangering our civilians." The woman's motherly smile calmed me.

"Yeah, I know. Just too many cop shows, I guess."

She patted my knee and stood. "Come on. Let's go meet your partner."

I followed her down the hall and out a door to the squad-car parking area. Shifts were coming in and departing. A brawny Latino officer leaned against his car, gazing in my direction. The thought of spending the next four hours cruising the town with that police-calendar stud gave me goosies.

"Is that him?" I said, feeling a mixture of hopeful dread.

"No." She snickered. "Talk about danger. That bad boy would eat you alive, girl."

And that would be a bad thing? Since my divorce, Grandma Ruby has been pushing me to get a rebound man. In other words, my sweet old granny thinks I need to get laid.

"There's your ride." Angela ushered me toward the squad car parked at the end of the lot. "Just to warn you, Katy. Your partner may seem a little rough around the edges, but he's very good at his job and you'll learn a lot, so try not to prejudge him."

A ruddy-faced man who barely met the minimum height requirement and was pushing the maximum weight limit ambled toward us. He stopped a moment to hoist up his pants and cock his hat at a jaunty angle.

"Sergeant Crowley," said the chief. "This is Katy McKenna. Your ride-along partner."

"Howdy, ma'am." Crowley tipped his hat. "Bob Crowley at at your service. I hear tell you're thinkin' about a career in law enforcement." He rehoisted his pants.

Was this a joke? It had to be. It were as if he had stepped out of one of those old *Smokey and the Bandit* movies that my dad loves. I glanced longingly back at stud-cop, but he was too busy flexing his perfect triceps to notice.

"Sergeant Crowley does all our ride-alongs. He's our top field-training officer," Angela said. "Katy is the daughter of Kurt Melby."

"Ya don't say. Good man and a fine officer. Darn shame about his knee."

"Katy's responsible for closing the case on Belinda Moore's murder."

"Chip off the old block, huh? Your daddy must be mighty proud."

"I'll leave you two to get acquainted." Angela turned to me, giving me a look obviously meant to remind me not to prejudge the sergeant, and told me to come see her after my ride.

"Well, little lady," said Crowley, "before we roll, let me give you a quick tour of my office."

I followed him to his car. "This sweet ride is a Dodge Charger." We stood at the front grill, and he caressed the gleaming, black hood. "She's got a 5.7 liter hemi—"

I nodded, acting like I cared.

"—V8 and 370 horsepower." Crowley moved toward the back of the car, running his fingers along its side. "She'll do zero to sixty in 5.4 seconds." He popped the trunk. "We got your first aid kit, your portable defibrillator, your fire extinguisher, your shotgun, your tools." He lifted out a Kevlar vest and handed it to me. "Put this on."

I slipped it on, made a few admiring noises, and then began to shuck the ponderous thing.

"Nope. You need to wear that during our shift. Department policy. That's an old one." He smacked his vest. "Now we wear load-bearing vests so we're not carrying all our gear on our belts, which was killing my back."

"What all do you carry?"

"A sidearm, two loaded magazines," he said as he patted each item in his vest, "a radio, a body camera, couple of cuffs, flashlight, pepper spray, baton, a Taser, and what-have-you."

"Don't you get hot?"

"I prefer sweat to dead. Besides, if I get killed on duty and I don't have my vest on, the little woman won't get her full benefits." He laughed, shaking his head. "LuAnn would whoop my ass for sure."

Crowley slammed the trunk lid, then opened the front passenger door. "Plunk yourself down, and we'll get rollin'." He went around the car and settled into the driver's seat with a grunt. "You look a tad jumpy, Katy. Don't be. Nothin' ever happens on this shift."

The muscle car rumbled out of the lot onto Chestnut Street. "Now if you really wanted to see some action, ya shoulda rode on a Friday night. It's a college town, so we get a lot of drunk-and-disorderlies. Sometimes a pot bust. If we're lucky, maybe a burglary."

We left downtown and cruised to a seedy neighborhood near the industrial area. Crowley told me that junk cars in the front yard were usually a good indication that there was a meth lab operating inside the house. There were a lot of rusty cars in the weedy yards.

Up ahead, a scraggly bearded man wearing gravity-defying pants held up with one hand, stood at the edge of a thirsty looking yard, waving at us to stop.

"Probably havin' a tiff with the wife. Stay in the car, Katy. That's an order. Domestic calls can get real ugly."

"Officer. You gotta help me." The scrawny man was hopping around like his feet were on fire. "That bitch's crazy!"

Crowley approached slowly. "Calm down, sir, and tell me what the problem is."

"I'll tell you what the problem is!" screamed a chunky dishwater blond on the porch, aiming a shotgun in our direction. "That piece of slime molested my little baby, that's what the problem is!"

The slimy guy hollered, "No way would I touch Jasmine. I love my little girl."

"She ain't your little girl, and you are one sick pervert. The world is gonna be a better place without you in it." She stepped off the porch, advancing toward the quivering man.

"Ma'am, please put down your weapon." Crowley used an amiable tone, sliding his hand toward his gun.

"No! I'm gonna kill that son of a bitch once and for all." She pumped the shotgun and swung it in Crowley's direction. "Please take your hand off your gun… and… and put 'em behind your head. I got no quarrel with you, but there is no way in hell I'm gonna let that piece of shit walk away from this."

Crowley did as told, and she turned the gun back on the man, aiming at his crotch. "I caught you in the act, Leon, so don't bother denying it." She hiccupped a sob. "This is all my fault. I should've listened to my mama and never married you. She said you was trash."

"Please, Tanya. I'm begging you. Don't kill me. It's not my fault. I got a sickness. I need help so I can get cured."

"That's a joke, Leon. The only cured pedophile is a dead pedophile." A mangy calico cat curled around her legs, and she gently nudged her away with her foot while keeping the shotgun dead aimed on Leon. "I want you to take the officer's gun and bring it to me."

Leon sidled up to the sergeant, and with the hand not holding his pants; he slid the gun from Crowley's holster.

"Hold it by the barrel," Tanya ordered, "and remember—the closer you get, the bigger the hole in your chest will be."

I rolled up the car window and slumped low in my seat, keeping an eye on Crowley. He wore a police radio on his shoulder but didn't dare move to activate it. His eyes locked with mine. He seemed to be telling me something. He tilted his chin, looked at his radio, and then back at me. Call the police!

I scrunched down so no one could see me, dug in my purse for my cell, and pressed the Home button, and whispered to Siri, "Call 9-1-1."

"I'm sorry. I did not understand that."

"Call 9-1-1."

"Calling 9-1-1."

A moment later a woman answered. "9-1-1. What is your emergency?"

I peeped out the window. Leon was inching his way toward the squad car, aiming Crowley's gun at Tanya.

"I don't want to hurt you, Tanya!" Leon shouted. "Just let me go, and I won't shoot you."

No! Go the other way! I silently screamed. *Oh shit! Can a shotgun blast go right through the door and kill me?*

Tanya laughed. "No way you'll hit me, you low-life meth-head."

"What is your emergency?" The dispatcher spoke in a placid tone that made me want to strangle her.

I whispered, "I'm in a police car and a crazy woman has a shotgun."

"What is your location, ma'am?"

"I'm in Santa Lucia."

"Where in Santa Lucia?"

"God, I don't know. Can't you trace this call or something? It's a crummy area near the freeway."

"Ma'am, try to stay calm. Can you see a street sign?"

I raised my head just enough to look out the window, hoping my head wouldn't be blown off. Tanya had raised the shotgun, aiming at the car.

"Oh shit! She's gonna shoot!" Ducking my head between my knees, I heard Leon fire off a shot at Tanya from behind the car. Then the shotgun exploded, and the car shivered as a billion bullets slammed into it. Something thumped hard on the hood, but I kept my head down.

Crowley ordered the woman to drop the weapon and lie down,

but she kept screaming she was going to finish off the good-for-nuthin' dirtbag.

I stayed down, praying to anyone out there who might be listening. "Please don't let me die. Please don't let me die."

The dispatcher said, "Please remain calm and tell me where you are."

"Stop telling me to stay calm!"

The driver's door opened and Leon dropped into the seat, still clutching Crowley's gun. His entire body seemed to be oozing blood.

"Get out!" we screamed at each other.

The coppery smell of blood mixed with Leon's reeking BO made my stomach lurch as I fumbled to unfasten my seat belt. I heard the *chung-chung* of the shotgun racking and glanced out my window. Tanya was advancing, presumably to finish Leon off as promised, which did not bode well for me.

I rolled down my window. "Please, Tanya! Don't shoot me!"

"Then, girl, you best get outta the car pronto."

I wailed pathetically, "I'm trying, but I can't get the seat belt off."

Leon had the motor running. "Shit, I can't see a fucking thing outta the window!"

The thump I'd heard on the hood had been Leon, and the windshield was spray-painted red with his blood. He flipped on the windshield wipers, smearing the gore back and forth with an eerie screech.

Leon tried to shift the car into drive, but his bloody hand slipped on the gear, and when he stomped on the gas, we shot backward, plowing into the truck parked behind us. My seat belt pinned me back hard, but Leon's skinny body pitched forward, slamming his face into the windshield.

"Oh shit, that really hurtssss…" His body shuddered and collapsed, draped over the steering wheel, blood gushing from his wrecked face.

"Momma?" called a little girl from the porch.

"Go back inside, Jasmine. Mama's busy cleaning house. This nasty piece of trash ain't gonna hurt you no more, baby."

The child, maybe five or six, dressed only in a stained yellow T-shirt, underpants, and sandals, ran down the steps to her gun-toting mama and flung her skinny arms around the woman's ample thighs. Crowley eased the gun out of the sobbing mother's hands, and she sank to her knees, clutching her daughter as sirens wailed in the distance.

The sergeant emptied the shotgun, then came round to Leon and opened the door. "You're one lucky hombre it was just bird-shot, or we'd be scraping you off the sidewalk."

Leon didn't budge. Crowley felt for a pulse and then glanced at me. "Well, if that don't beat all. Dumb son of a bitch is dead. He say anything to you?"

I will never, ever forget his last words. "He said, 'Oh shit, that really hurts.'"

I tried to unlatch my seat belt, but my brain had disconnected from my quivering body, and my fingers couldn't comprehend my extreme need to vacate the car of horrors. Crowley came around, reached in, and released me. "You look a little wobbly. Take my arm."

He practically had to lift me out and carry me to the porch steps. A little while later, an EMT checked my blood pressure and gave me water, which I dribbled all over my blood-spattered blouse.

Leon remained in the car for the next few hours as the crime scene investigators collected evidence. A motley crowd gathered on the street, and the local news crews descended.

Eventually child protective services pried little Jasmine from her mother's arms, and Tanya was cuffed and hauled away, crying for her baby. It broke my heart. If I had a kid and someone hurt her, I would want to kill them, too. No doubt about it.

———

When I was finally allowed to leave the crime scene, an officer returned me to my car at the police station. Once I was behind the wheel, I must have shifted into autopilot, because the next thing I knew I was parked in my driveway.

All I wanted to do was get inside, bolt the door, set the alarm, and take a long, hot shower. Daisy, my yellow Lab, greeted me, and when she got a snoot full of blood, sweat, and tears, she slid into Mommy mode, trying to comfort me. Tabitha, my gray tabby cat, had preferred to keep a safe distance, staring at me bug-eyed in that freaky way that cats do when they are about to lose it.

I sloshed a hefty helping of Pinot Grigio into a plastic tumbler, leaving a puddle on the counter. After a few shaky gulps, I stripped to my skivvies and tossed everything into the garbage can, then headed for the shower where I let the hot water sterilize my body.

Feeling a little more human, I climbed into my favorite cookie-print flannels, grabbed the comforter from my bed, refilled my cup, and then curled up on the couch with my two furballs.

I always keep old movies recorded for when I need comforting. *Now, Voyager* with Bette Davis was exactly what I needed. A plain-Jane spinster who blossoms and finds impossible romance. The next thing I knew, sun was shining in my eyes through the french doors.

Available on Amazon
Better Dead Than Wed